Autumn Reflections

The Northern Light Series Book 2

Katie Mettner

Copyright © 2014 Katie Mettner

Copyright 2014 Katie Mettner

No generative AI was used to create this book or the cover. Any unauthorized use of this publication to train generative artificial intelligence (AI) technologies is prohibited.

All rights reserved for this book and its content including the cover by Forward Authority Designs. Except as permitted under the U.S. Copyright Act of 1976, no part of this publication may be reproduced, distributed, or transmitted in any form or by any means, or stored in a database or retrieval system, without prior permission of the publisher. The characters and events in this book are fictitious. Names, characters, and plots are a product of the author's imagination. Any similarity to real persons, living or dead, is coincidental and not intended by the author.

ISBN: 9781495493157

To every man and woman who has ever loved a child, whether for a little or a long time, whether born of you or chosen for you, you change the world every day. You're a shining light in this world, because love never fails.

Chapter 1

Ask any group of kids what their favorite comfort food is and you'll get a confounding amount of answers. Ask my son what his favorite comfort food is and you'll only get one. Peanut butter and jelly on white bread. I hummed to myself as I spread the Jif on the bread and topped it with fresh, homemade strawberry jam. I licked the knife off and asked myself when the world began to worry about how much we were damaging our kids with white bread and refined sugar. It had gotten me this far. Granted, at forty, I might not be triathlon material but I could hold my own on the treadmill.

Now, ask me what my favorite food is and I'll tell you Southern Comfort on the rocks. As much as I hate to admit it, I, Autumn Hanson, am a piping hot mess of stress.

I zipped the bag closed and tucked it into Grayson's Marvel Heroes lunchbox. We had looked long and hard for that lunchbox, but no one around here had it. We finally had to take a day trip to The Mall of America to find it. Some parents would say that's excessive and spoiling, but most of those parents don't have a son like Grayson. He was sweet, loving, kind, and smart. He wished he had superhero powers, so he could fly away from the reality of his physical challenges, though.

Glancing at the clock on the wall above the stove I blew out a breath. Wolverine told me it was seven o'clock. I had better get a move on it if I wanted to get Grayson to school in the next hour. Getting ready in the morning could be a battle sometimes, so I put on my best excited face and pushed the handle down on the door to his room. He was still snuggled up with his favorite blanket and his stuffed Spiderman half under him, half hanging off the bed. The smell of sweet, freshly bathed little boy filled the room and I sighed a little. He was growing up and today was the first day of second grade. I could only pray it went better than first grade. I pulled the curtains back and twisted my wrist, opening the Venetian blind to let the sun stream in across the foot of his bed. His little toes weren't covered and I sang to him as I approached the bed. "If you don't hide those piggy toes, I'm going to snap, snap, snap them off."

He giggled, and I pounced on him and tickled his belly.

"Momma, uncle, uncle!" he yelled. His little arms circled my neck, and I stood up, wrapping his legs around my waist.

"Good morning my little beaner. Did you sleep well?" I moved around the end of his bed and out into the hallway to the bathroom a few feet away. He stretched his little arms up and yawned, his golden blond hair falling over his face and his three missing teeth leaving empty black holes in his gums. "I slept good. Did you sleep good, Momma?" he asked, rubbing his little finger under my eyes where the black smudges screamed the truth. I hated that even at the tender age of seven he knew I hadn't. I also hated that I was about to lie to him.

"I slept like a rock, but now we're running late and we need to get you ready for the first day of school!"

I cheered and roared while I flew him into the bathroom like a superhero, all the while praying my battered nerves would settle.

I climbed into the car and dropped my head back on the seat. My son was officially a second grader. Yes, he was a year younger than all the other kids, but I wasn't one to tell him he couldn't do something when he clearly could. He attended kindergarten for less than a week before he had been moved into the first grade. His teacher told me he was *beyond what I can teach him*. That was exciting to hear as a mother, but also a little intimidating. When the issues began with the bully a few months later, I spent the next six months just trying to get him through first grade. I eyed the front of the school and waited to see if he would beg me to come back and get him. I had a feeling he wouldn't. He didn't want me to take him to class and insisted I leave him at the office. He said he's *got this* and waved, before thinking better of it and taking one hand off his walker long enough to point to his cheek for a kiss.

I started the car and put it in gear. He'd be okay. The teachers here were great and knew how to take care of him. I just had to trust this year would be better than last. Without checking the clock, I knew it was nearly eight and I should be getting to my clinic. When I opened Fall Reflections three months ago, I had no idea I would be this busy this quickly. I made sure that today I only had morning appointments, so I could be back here to pick him up by three. I would be dying to hear about his first day and all the exciting things second grade had to offer. I caught my reflection in the mirror and cringed. The first place I'd better stop was the coffee shop or I would scare my first patient.

It turned out being hopped up on caffeine while attempting to cut a cast off a nervous ten-year-old might not be the best thing either. I rested my chin in my hand and stared out my open office door. It was past lunch, which I hadn't eaten, and nearly time to go pick up Grayson. We would go home and I would feed him supper while we talked about his day. Then I'd put him to bed. If I was lucky, I might even catch a few winks myself.

Since we moved to Cloquet in June and I started my own practice, life had been stressful. It was worth it, though. There were no more on-call days, and I had the flexibility to schedule my own patients and surgery. I still had to count on my sitter,

Tina, to pick Grayson up from school, and stay with him until I was done with surgery some days. Knowing I'd be able to tuck him into bed every night and take him to school every morning made such a small concession easy. I lucked out when I advertised for a mother's helper and found the best one ever. Tina was one of Grayson's favorite people and they go together like peanut butter and jelly. Sometimes Tina even brings him to my office, so he can read quietly while I finish my paperwork.

A year ago, that wouldn't have happened, but that all changed when he met Grant Harris, one of St. Mary's physical therapists, who is now the department chair. You couldn't even say the word hospital, much less bring him to one, or his anxiety would shoot through the roof. Hours of tears, screaming, and hyperventilating would ensue and I would feel like a horrible mother. After he hurt his hamstring this past winter, and started working with Grant on therapy at home, that anxiety slowly dissipated. Grant and I brought him to the physical therapy room back at the start of the New Year and he never cried, screamed, or hyperventilated. It was a red-letter day. Grant keeps trying to chalk it up to Grayson getting older, but I know the truth. Grant was just that good at his job. He cares about his patients, and not just the one issue they're seeing him about, but the whole patient.

We went to visit Grant just a few weeks ago and I had to come clean with him. I'd lied about what really happened to Gray, and I felt bad about it, especially now that we're friends. At the time I didn't want anyone I worked with to know the truth. Grayson hadn't hurt his leg playing basketball. He'd hurt his leg trying to run away from someone twice his size. *Run* might not be the best word. He can't run, but he was scared and when he attempted to get away from the bully, he fell and twisted his leg. I'm lucky he hadn't hurt himself worse than that, but it got my momma bear hackles up. I needed a solution to Grayson's school issues, and our life in general. Something needed to change for the better or I was going to pack Gray up and go live on a deserted island. Cloquet was my solution. Calum wouldn't be a problem this year, but I knew there was always another bully waiting around the corner. It took all I had not to call the school and check on Gray as I sat at my desk, but I resisted.

I shrugged out of my white coat and hung it on the back of my tall black chair. I think those two objects are supposed to make doctors feel important. The white coat, with its ability to cause blood pressures to rise at the sight of it whooshing through the hall and the pockets holding instruments of torture. The black chair, with its comfortable fine leather and its stately posture just waiting to hold the pompous backside of the *man behind the desk*, or in this case, woman. Some feel like medical geniuses sitting in that chair, but I would rather be sitting in a rocking chair with a baby. Geez, where did that come from? I glanced around the room for onlookers. I'm not sure why since I hadn't said it aloud but the thought took me by surprise.

"I'm losing my mind. That's all there is to it. I don't sleep, barely eat, watch sappy movies all night, and talk to myself."

I picked up my purse and slung it over my shoulder, the buttery pink leather falling against my hip. I turned to see my nurse, Nick, standing in the doorway.

"Everything all right, Doc?" he asked casually, and I laughed.

"Everything's fine, Nick. I was just pondering if I was having a nervous breakdown. I'm leaning toward yes right now. If I buy a convertible, promise me you'll have me committed?" I begged with my hands held in front of me like the old nuns from my childhood nightmares.

He looped his arm around my shoulders and walked me past the registration desk to the door. "You're not having a nervous breakdown. You're a mother and you're worried about your child. Phoenix and I will close everything up here. Go pick him up from school and you'll see he had a great day. Then all will be well."

I gave him a dubious look. "And you know this how?" I asked, my hand planted firmly on my hip.

"I have eyes everywhere …" he whispered eerily, his hands doing a cross between jazz hands and Twilight Zone.

I laughed and pushed the door open with my butt. "If you say so, oh great wizard. I'll see you tomorrow." I waved at Phoenix at the desk and he stuck his arm into the door, holding it open.

"Before you pick up Gray, get some lunch, would you? And then tonight make sure you eat supper, stay away from the booze, and get some sleep."

I rolled my tired, purple shadow covered eyes. "What are you, my father?"

"No, I'm your friend, and a lot of us are worried about you," he admitted, his eyes boring into me with concern.

"I'll be okay. I promise. Food, Gray, food, and bed. Nothing else."

I crossed my heart, and he caught the door as I let it go closed with a slow whoosh, but not before I saw the look on his face that said *I don't believe you.*

I rolled over and flipped the bedside lamp off, snuggling into the blanket. It was only September, but it was already getting cold at night. Of course, when you live in Minnesota you sleep with the window open a crack all year round, so that might be why I was chilly. The little brick oven sleeping next to me would keep me warm, though. He had been enthusiastic when I suggested a sleepover in Momma's room tonight. How pathetic is it when a forty-year-old woman needs a seven-year-old boy to sleep in the same room, just so she can actually fall asleep? Yeah, that's what I thought. Pretty pathetic.

When we moved here, Grayson had started sleeping in his own room. Before that he slept in a crib next to my bed. At barely three feet, he was much closer to the size of a three-year-old than his true age, and the modified crib kept him safe and close. Close enough for me to help him in the night if he needed, but as he got older, he never did. Thanks to Grant's help he was stronger and walked with his walker. He was able to do those things on his own instead of relying on me to do the simple tasks for him. It wasn't an easy thing to admit, and took me even longer to accept, but it was time. He was blossoming and that was what mattered in the whole scenario.

Moving to a new town and a new house told me it was the perfect time to transition him into his own room. We shopped for days for the perfect bed, curtains, posters, bedding, and furniture. Nothing made him happier than the Spiderman toddler bed he slept in every night, but tonight he must have decided I needed him more.

He'd had a great day at school, and was even happier to report everyone was nice. His teacher, Ms. Roberts, talked with all the kids about the importance of treating him just like any other friend unless he *asked* for help. I thought that was a pretty cool way to give Grayson the power. He had buddied up with one of his friends from our neighborhood for the day and he was ready to go back tomorrow. I thanked the good Lord when he told me that. I couldn't risk him getting hurt again, maybe even worse this time. He didn't deserve more pain in his life. He'd been through too much already.

I'd never admit it to him, but I hadn't done what Nick asked. I skipped lunch and went straight to the school to pick Gray up. When he told me what a great day he had, I asked him to be my date for dinner. We went to Sammy's Pizza and stuffed ourselves with pizza then topped it off with a Gordy's shake for dessert. I hadn't been that full in a long time, but laughing and being silly with Gray was definitely what I needed. I needed to laugh and be happy again.

I rolled over on my back and shivered at the coolness of the sheets on my shoulders.

Am I depressed? I'm a doctor. I should know these things. No, I'm not depressed. I'm lonely.

Shhhhh, no you aren't. You gave up the companionship of a man for a life with Gray. You're definitely having a midlife crisis. That's the problem. How about if you buy a convertible? Those miles flying by with the wind blowing through your hair are certain to bring back your usual calm, cool, and collected self.

Calm, cool, and collected probably wouldn't happen even with a convertible. I'd still be alone. I fisted both hands in my hair and screamed silently, flopping over to my side.

The last thing you need in your life is a man. Repeat it after me, Autumn. The last thing you need is a man.

I repeated it countless times until I finally fell into an exhausted sleep.

Chapter 2

The first two weeks of school passed in a blur. Grayson came home every night exhausted from his full day at school. He spent most nights reading his favorite books while tucked in bed. His days were so busy now, and without the fear of a bully hanging over his head he was blossoming socially. That said, he was working harder physically than he had to over the summer. He was wearing out quicker and wanted to rest more frequently. That meant it was time to start physical therapy again. I was looking into the new services available at the Cloquet Hospital. Their rehab services were becoming second to none for kids, and I knew Gray would benefit from the therapy. He would miss less class and I would miss less work if he could do it at the hospital. It was a win-win for us. I would give him a few more weeks to acclimate to school and then ask for a consultation.

Maybe his fatigue was nothing more than his new social schedule. He had more friends than he ever did in Duluth and the last two weekends had birthday party invitations piling up. It did a mother's heart good to see him happy and smiling again with friends gathered around him. He spent most of last year hiding, fighting about going to school, or having anxiety attacks in the car on the way there. I convinced myself that the move to Cloquet was for Grayson, but I know it was for me, too. When I turned forty, I couldn't face the idea of losing any more time with my son. The long hours of being on-call and away from him was becoming too hard on both of us.

I let my eyes drift to the clock at the corner of my laptop. I just finished with my morning patients and had ninety minutes before my first afternoon patient arrived. I leaned back in the chair and tossed my Dansko clad feet up on my desk. About six months ago, when I seriously began looking for a building to open my private practice in, I was a nervous wreck. About six months later this community welcomed me with open arms and proved my worrying fruitless. They kept my appointments booked, and word of mouth flowed into the surrounding communities. When I took a chance on Cloquet, I didn't know just how much they would appreciate having a pediatric orthopedic surgeon so close to home.

I'm lucky to have Phoenix running the front desk, taking appointments, and doing the billing. She was a blessing in disguise. She was excellent with everything from answering phones to calming the most terrified little patient. She had a special rapport with everyone who walked in the door and that was something I wasn't used to as a physician. Phoenix grew up here and has ties throughout the community. When we met at the coffee shop for an interview it turned into a friendship in an instant, and I hired her on the spot. I had no doubt in my mind that hiring her was the best decision I'd made in this whole gamble.

Nick came with me when I left St. Mary's Hospital. He was looking for a change in his life, so it was perfect timing for him. With a new baby at home he wanted a more flexible schedule the same way I did. I expected it to be just the three of us for a year or so, but I immediately had to hire a casting specialist. She's been with us only a few months, but I like Ruby a lot. She's good at her job, able to keep the most anxious kid calm, and had way too much fun creating new patterns for casts. The other day I walked in and she was putting a Marvel colored cast on Grayson's Spiderman. I couldn't do anything but laugh at the two of them, and be thankful for the wonderful people I was blessed with here.

It was obvious that Gray settling into school and me settling into the new clinic had a positive effect on me. I was sleeping every night again while Grayson snoozed in his own bed. I no longer kept Southern Comfort in the house, and I threw out every copy of Dirty Dancing, The Notebook, and Sixteen Candles I had. I replaced them with X-Men and Iron Man. Grayson was thrilled and last weekend we had an Iron Man marathon. Grayson predictably covered his eyes, saying *eww, eww, eww* every time Pepper and Tony Stark kissed. He kept me laughing even when I wanted to cry.

When we moved here, I forced myself to find a church home. When we lived in Duluth, we never had time to go to church. I was either working, had just finished working, or needed to rest from working. I wanted my son to experience church and all the wonderful people he would meet there. If you found the right place, they would be your home away from home. A second community that had your back at the worst times and celebrated the good times. The church we found had been welcoming and understanding of our family. Gray attended his first Sunday School last Sunday and he had a ball.

The best part about all of these *firsts* was that Gray hadn't had a full-fledged panic attack before or during any of them. I was starting to think Grant might be right. Gray was maturing and growing out of that part of his disability. I had fought the doctors for years about anti-anxiety drugs. I didn't want my three-year-old drugged out on anxiety medication when he already needed several others every day to keep him walking. Instead, I willingly made lifestyle changes to deal with the anxiety. I won't lie, it was hard a lot of the time. Most days I wanted to call up his specialist and beg for some Ativan to make things easier for him, and me. Then I'd look into his eyes and know he didn't need drugs, he just needed new ways to cope. The doctors told me that wouldn't work. That his brain was too damaged and couldn't be trained, but I refused to listen. Now, I'm glad I followed my instincts and gave him time to find the coping mechanisms that worked for him. It might sound cruel to some, but the fact remains he will need those coping mechanisms all his life, and now he knows they work.

Shaking my head to clear my thoughts, I picked up the phone on my desk and punched zero for the front desk.

"Yes, Dr. Hanson, do you need something?" Phoenix asked immediately.

"I'm just wondering what time that guy said he would be here," I replied, tapping my pencil on the desk.

"That guy?" she asked with laughter in her words.

"Yeah, that reporter guy. What was his name? Kane, Kale?" I stuttered and sighed. I needed to take better notes.

She sighed even louder. "Kade. Kade Franco. He's a reporter with the Pine Journal. He should be here any minute. Has something come up?"

"No, but I don't want to be late for my afternoon patients." The actual reason I asked was in hopes he had canceled. I would do anything to get out of this interview.

"You won't be late. He's always punctual. You need this, Autumn. It's time for the community to officially meet Dr. Hanson. He's extremely professional and the story will be second to none, I can promise you. I've known him forever."

"Forever? Is he ninety?" I joked and she whistled a cat call.

"Oh no, he's far from ninety. Did you look him up on the website?"

"Nope. Haven't you ever heard the old saying, *curiosity killed the cat*?" I asked and there was silence on the line.

"Have you ever heard the old saying, *that is one fine looking man*?" she retorted.

I couldn't stop laughing. "No, I hadn't heard that saying but consider me warned. Send him back when he gets here, I'll just be doing paperwork."

She assured me she would and I set the phone back into the cradle. That is one fine looking man, huh? My hand hovered over the new tab I had opened on my computer. To peek or not to peek? I clicked the x on the tab and shut the computer. Not to peek. I'm not interested in fine looking men anyway. Besides, he's probably twenty-two with pimples and a much too eager need to please. I closed my eyes, running through the morning patients in my mind. One in particular was going to be a tough case.

Molly, a fourteen-year-old girl from the middle school, had blown out her left knee ACL and her right rotator cuff in a bizarre collision in a volleyball game. Her injuries were severe and surgery was required for both. Tonight, I would sit down and lay out a plan to get her healed and back to school. I sent them off to find her an electric wheelchair to use for the next six months, and promised to be in touch regarding the finalization of her surgery.

Molly size cases gave me a feeling of satisfaction that's been missing for the last seven years. Starting out my career as an orthopedic trauma physician and then moving into general orthopedics was like starting out as a beat cop and changing to a desk job. I was doing it for what I thought were the right reasons, but it turned out I gave up a lot for nothing. Why I stayed at St. Mary's for so long I'd never know. Maybe it was safe there and I was tired of taking chances and losing.

There was a knock on my door and I glanced up to see Phoenix in the hallway with a man close behind her. "Dr. Hanson, Kade Franco is here to see you."

She stepped aside and I stood up, my eyes locking with the deep chocolate brown ones of one Kade Franco. "Thank you, Phoenix." She left and I stuck my hand out across the desk. "Nice to meet you, Mr. Franco."

He shook my hand firmly. Not too hard, but no wimpy jello-hand either. "Just call me Kade, Dr. Hanson. Thank you for meeting with me this afternoon."

I smiled against my will. This man certainly wasn't twenty-two, pimply faced, or eager. He was lumberjack tall, trim, and had legs that went on forever. His barely-there wire rims did nothing to conceal his long black lashes, and his neatly trimmed scruff surrounded his *melt me into a puddle* smile. A tuft of curly brown hair topped off the man. My mind was stuck on the thought of how I would like to wrap my fingers in it.

Whoa, sister, back up the boat and stop staring like an idiot.

"Please, call me Autumn. Thank you for offering to do a story about my clinic," I gushed.

Good God woman, take it down a notch. You come face-to-face with a good-looking guy and you can't rub two brain cells together. Sit. He's sitting already. Sit your butt down in the chair.

I sat, not even checking to see where the chair was, and was glad my butt made contact with it. Falling onto the floor in front of him would not be professional.

He pulled an iPad from his bag and set it down on my desk, arranging it just so, then pulled out a notebook and pen. "We like to spotlight new businesses that are making an impact on our city. I've heard nothing but great things about you in the community, and I'll admit I've been rather curious myself."

I sat forward and folded my hands on my desk. "Curious? About me?"

"Yup, about you, and your practice, of course." He motioned around my office and I hoped my cheeks weren't as red as they felt.

"Of course," I said, forcing a professional tone back into my voice. "Please, feel free to ask me anything. I'll only answer the ones I like."

He threw his head back and laughed. The sound was a low timbre of sexiness that was doing nothing to keep my thoughts from drifting to whether there was a six-pack under that white t-shirt. It was covered with a green chamois shirt, the sleeves rolled to his forearms, and I wondered what it would look like balled up on the floor of my bedroom.

No, no, no, no, no. Stop this woman. You know how those thoughts will end up. You'll be brokenhearted and watching chick flicks while drinking Southern Comfort. You're.Not.Doing.That.Again.

"If I was a different kind of reporter that statement might put me off, but I'm not," he retorted and my inner thoughts left me with a smirk, until I stared directly into his deep, dark chocolatey goodness eyes.

I set my jaw and nodded toward the iPad. "What's that for?"

"I like to record my interviews, if you don't mind. Saves my carpal tunnel from getting worse, and my mind isn't as good as it was in my glory days." He winked one of those lens covered sets of lashes at me and I flexed my jaw to keep from swooning.

"Your glory days? You mean last week? You can't be more than three decades old," I smarted back and he clicked his pen a couple times.

"Three decades old. That makes thirty sound absolutely ancient. Is that a doctor thing?"

"Is that a question for the interview?" I sparred, and he shook his head.

"Nah, that's just me being me."

"Well, then that was just an Autumn thing. I could have said thirty but then you wouldn't have had to think about it. I may have been hasty. You might be closer to three and a half decades old."

He shook his pen at me. "You're getting closer. I'm closer to four decades old, but this conversation is making me feel like I should ask you for a prescription for a cane and a bedpan. I do believe this next question will start the interview." His hand hovered over the red button on the iPad, and I nodded my agreement.

"Interview with Dr. Autumn Hanson, September fifteenth. Please state and spell your name," Kade instructed.

"What part of Autumn and Hanson are confusing?" I asked pointedly. He didn't answer. He just stared me down for a long minute.

"Alright, okay, if that's how you want to play this, I brought my A-game today."

I leaned back, far back, as far back as I could without tipping over, and feigned relaxation. "Bring it."

∞∞∞

Oh, he brought it. He brought out all his guns but I held my own against them. Never was I happier, or sadder, to see someone leave my office. Kade Franco was frustratingly smart and surprisingly sassy.

I set our plates of spaghetti and meatballs on the table and grabbed the milk from the fridge. "Eat up Gray, you look hungry tonight. Did you have a busy day at Nicky's?" I asked, helping him with his *shaky cheese* and garlic bread. I guess when you can't remember the word parmesan, shaky cheese gets the point across.

"We did so much stuff today I'd never done before, Momma!" He was teeming with excitement when I picked him up from school and had gone straight to his room when we got home. I checked on him several times and he was at his desk deeply involved with markers. I noticed his braces lying on his bed and when he takes those off, I know he doesn't plan to move for a few hours. I'd left him alone and busied myself with dinner to give him some time.

"Will you tell me about it? I peeked in on you earlier, but you were busy." I pouted like he always does when I'm dictating reports or finishing paperwork.

He laid his fork on his plate and rubbed my arm. "I'm never too busy for you, pumpkin."

My heart melted and I tousled his blond hair. "Good, now tell me."

He reached into the bag on his walker and pulled out a piece of paper. "It was so cool, Momma, he has a whole zoo."

I stopped with my fork halfway to my mouth. "A whole zoo? Like lions and tigers and bears, oh my?"

"Silly Momma, no, those things can't live in Minnesota. Well bears can, but everything else would freeze. There were goats and llamas and umm, you know those animals that look like llamas, but are aww." He stopped for a moment and closed his eyes. It was a trick one of his therapists taught him when he was much younger and learning to work around his speech issues from his brain injury. Finally, his eyes popped open again. "Alpaca."

I had a huge smile on my face but I didn't make a big deal

out of it. When he was younger I used to, but I had learned as he had gotten older he wanted to save the big deals for when it was really a big deal.

"Oh, I love my alpaca sweater. Their hair is so soft." I nodded while I took a bite of spaghetti.

He clapped his hands, his own dinner forgotten. "I told Nicky you have a sweater made from their hair."

"You did, huh? What did Nicky say?"

"He said to thank you for supporting his farm," Gray parroted and I almost snorted my milk up my nose as I drank.

"So, what's that piece of paper?" I asked, pushing my plate away so I could look at it.

"We learned about families on the farm, and how some animals are more closely related than we know. Our assignment was to make our family tree," he explained.

He held the paper out to me, his chest puffed out. The tree only had two branches thickly coated with orange, yellow, and red leaves. Hanging from each branch was a swing, with a stick person on each one. *Grayson Hanson*, it said under one and *Autumn Hanson* under the other. That was it. Just two of us in the whole family tree. The smile faltered on my face.

"You're such a good artist, baby," I said, still staring at the paper. It disappeared before my eyes and I lowered my hand to the table while he slipped it back into the bag on the walker.

"Thank you. I'm sorry I made you sad," he apologized. He stared at his plate and twirled his fork through the spaghetti noodles.

"You didn't make me sad. I loved your drawing," I assured him.

He let his fork fall to the plate, wiggled down off his chair, took hold of the walker, and left the kitchen. I heard the door to his room close with a soft click and I laid my cheek on my hand. That went horribly wrong. Well, not the picture, that was amazing for a second grader. The detail was exquisite, and the colors vibrant and strong. Just like him. It was me that was lifeless and weak.

Why did he think he had upset me? I asked myself, taking my plate to the sink. I stared at my reflection in the door of the microwave and into the eyes of a much younger girl. A girl with hazel eyes that never could hide her true feelings. I pulled the clasp from the clip holding my hair up and let it fall free around my shoulders. The honey brown curls bounced free and curled around my ears, instantly erasing ten years from my face. I resolved to start wearing my hair down more when I wasn't at work. It was a small step toward my ultimate goal, which was being more Autumn and less Dr. Hanson. I turned toward the table and saw his plate hardly touched with two meatballs sitting side-by-side.

First, I had to be Momma and find out why my son was upset. I took his plate and popped it in the microwave to heat while I found a tray. I filled the tray with his Superman cup, napkin, plate, and a piece of bread. I stared at the reflection in the microwave until the woman I was seven years ago showed her face again. I was strong then and determined to show that little boy how important he was to me. I could do that again. I carried the tray down the hallway and knocked once on the door.

"Who is it?" he asked begrudgingly.

"Doctor Doom!" I answered in my best supervillain voice.

"Come in, Momma," he answered, and my shoulders sank a little. If he wasn't playing superheroes he really was upset.

I pushed the handle down with my elbow and held the door with my toe. Once I cleared the tray through the door I stopped at the end of his bed. As I expected, he was propped up with his Spiderman TV pillow reading the latest Big Nate book.

"You forgot to eat your dinner, Batman," I reminded him, setting the tray on his lap and his book on the nightstand.

He picked up his fork and poked at the meatballs, one rolling to the side of the bowl and leaving an indentation in the noodles. I noticed his markers were still sprawled across his desk and went around the end of the bed to clean them up. I picked up the paper that lay under them and sighed. Gray kept his eyes averted but the fork had stopped.

The paper in my hand was a photocopied picture of a big limb filled tree with boxes for leaves. The title said, *MY FAMILY TREE*. This sheet had two boxes filled in and he had colored the tree in many different shades of green, making the empty boxes yellow, red and orange. I let the paper fall back to the desk and pulled his beanbag chair up next to his bed.

"You did a nice job coloring that tree, Gray, but I liked the first one better."

"Thank you," he answered, quickly jamming a meatball into his mouth and chewing.

"Why didn't you want to show me that one?"

He swallowed and took a drink of his milk. "I didn't like all the empty boxes. Boxes are stupid. I like swings."

"I like swings, too. I like swinging with you in the park when the wind is blowing and our feet are pointing up to the sky like nothing can stop us. That's the best feeling." I smiled and he smiled back at me.

"I didn't want to make you sad, so I drew the one with swings to make you happy."

"You make me happy every day, honey." I tickled his toes a little bit.

"You were happy when you picked me up from school. You smiled the whole way home. I liked seeing you smile. You sang while you made s'getti and I like the way you sing. I wanted my picture to make you smile like that, but instead it made you frown. I like your smile more than your frown," he said sadly. My eyes got big and he started to stutter. "I mean I love you all the time and you're still pretty when you frown but ..."

"But when I smile that makes you feel happier?" I asked and he shrugged a little.

"I guess. I like how much happier you've been the last few weeks. Your smile today was nice. What made you smile like that?"

"I met a nice person today who asked me questions no one had ever asked me before. Kind of like when you get to be the one on the *About Me* board at school. It makes you feel special."

"You are special, Momma," he answered immediately and I patted his knee, lifting the tray off his lap and kneeling next to the bed, so I could hug him.

"I love you Grayson Hanson."

"I love you too, Momma Hanson, and I love your meatballs."

I wiped some stray spaghetti sauce off his face and gave him the biggest smile I had in me, praying it went all the way to my eyes.

∞∞∞

Kade

"I can't believe you missed that basket, man. It was like right there," Joe moaned, his hands held up to the heavens but grasping air.

I took a long drink of my Sam Adams. "It wasn't right there. It was right there if you were seven feet tall with no defenders in front of you."

"Franco, you're so full of crap." Joe laughed, slapping the table so hard my beer bottle jumped. "Where the hell was your head anyway?"

They were seriously getting on my nerves. I missed a basket. Who cares? At forty-two they're damn lucky I can still play stand-in guard for another old man who was getting a new knee. Okay, so he wasn't that old, he was forty-five, but all the same.

"His head was probably still lost in the beautiful eyes of one Dr. Hanson," Sal shouted and I groaned.

"Geez Sal, why don't you yell that a little bit louder? I'm sure they didn't hear you in Esko," I yelled back and he just laughed in my face.

"But you aren't denying it. So, are the rumors true? Is she as gorgeous as everyone says? Did you get a kiss?" He came at me making smoochy lips and I pushed him off the barstool, earning me a roar from the rest of the bar.

"Have some respect. She might have to fix you or your kid someday," I spat out and he smirked.

Okay, so he had me. She was gorgeous, and she had beautiful hazel eyes I hadn't stopped thinking about, but there was no way in hell I was going to play that game. I lifted my beer to my lips and drained the rest of it, letting it come down hard on the table. I stood. "Goodnight to you all. Enjoy the rest of your evening but I have a real job to go to in the morning."

They all laughed and leered, being their usual high school selves until I closed the door of the old Northeastern Bar. The bar had been a staple on Dunlap Island since the lumberjack days when the island was known as the place to go when you needed a woman and a good time. Thankfully, the island now had some respectable businesses, including my employer. The park by the river was also a place I found myself more often as I got older

I crossed the street and sauntered toward the river. It was getting late in the season and the geese, which usually hung out under the bridge, had long since ditched us for places like Florida and Mexico. Without the fear of being attacked by a surprised bird, I walked along the shore for a bit. It was a nice cool night, with a soft breeze that smelled of autumn. I picked up a rock and tossed it into the lazy river. Autumn. She was more beautiful than any idyllic autumn scene ever painted. If her eyes didn't capture you, her honey brown hair tied at the nape in a bun, would. Sitting there today, trying to be a professional reporter, I had to fight the urge to pull it from its trappings and watch as she shook her head, the locks flying everywhere. It didn't happen, but I knew I would be awake tonight wishing it had.

She was absolutely stunning and it had been a long time since I'd been that distracted in an interview. I knew I was a goner when I broke my staunch professional code and asked personal questions. The reporter's creed of get in, get the story, and get out wasn't working this afternoon. Pretending I was a high school kid playing basketball tonight didn't work, either. I did have my head wrapped up in the manly desires of

Autumn Hanson, and could have cared less about winning a game. I found myself back at the steps to the bridge, but didn't remember how I got there. Oh brother, I was going to be in deep trouble if I ever saw her again.

I headed up the hill toward home and stuck my hands in my pockets when the wind blew hard across the bridge. When I left her office today all I knew was she had a son, but there was no Mr. Autumn Hanson. As far as I was concerned, that was all the information I needed.

The moment I met her today the shock of knowing that one day I would be Mr. Autumn Hanson hit me straight in the solar plexus. The only thing I had left to figure out was how to convince her. The look in her eyes told me that wasn't going to be a walk in the park.

Chapter 3

I sat in my car hiding behind a cup of large coffee while I stared dubiously at my picture on the front page of the paper. I was leaning on the reception desk in a casual conversational pose. My white coat covered my green hospital scrubs and I held a computer while I laughed at something Phoenix had said. I hadn't been aware he was taking pictures at the time, but even I had to admit it was a halfway decent picture of me. I took a long pull on the hot liquid and averted my eyes from the rest of it. Against my will, however, my eyes kept drifting back to the title. *Fall Reflections Brings Colorful Change to our City*. It was a well-written, eye-catching kind of title. So was the byline name, *Kade Franco*. My mind's eye kept drifting to his chocolate brown ones ringed with his spectacles that made him look studious, with a side of scary sexy.

Like when he quirked one eye at me and asked for my personal information. I went on the defense and he assured me he just wanted the readers to feel connected to me. To know I was invested in their community. I tried the simple answer that I reside in Scanlon with my son, Grayson, and our beta fish Magneto, but that didn't appease him.

Is there a Mr. Autumn Hanson, too? he had asked.

It took all I had not to snort and roll my eyes. I answered with a simple, but concise, *no*. What he said as he took his final note was what played like a broken recording all week. *Yet.*

I wanted to yell *ever*, but restrained myself long enough for him to exit the clinic and climb in his Paul Bunyan sized Ram truck. Then I'd dropped my head to my desk, and banged it a few times.

Okay, deep breath, that was then and this is now. Now you're the consummate professional again. You don't have to look into those eyes ever again unless there happens to be a community event. If that situation were to arise, you could avert your eyes and move along. Yes. That was exactly what was going to happen. Avert eyes. Move along.

Alright, that's sorted. Now it's time to start my afternoon patients and forget about Mr. Puddlemaker. I snickered, grabbed my briefcase and bumped the car door closed with my ample backside. *Mr. Puddlemaker*. That was funny on so many levels even if it was true.

"The world needs to see more of that smile," a voice said from my left. I jumped sideways, nearly toppling what was left of my Cloquet Lumberjacks mug onto my brown clogs. The person who stood with a grin on his face was none other than Mr. Puddlemaker himself. I tried to lie to myself and say my pulse was still racing from the scare. It totally wasn't from the scare.

"That's a great line," I said, giving him a finger gun. "You must just rake in the ladies."

His smile offered no answer, but he took my briefcase from my hand and pushed the handicapped button on the door. "Ladies first." He motioned and then followed behind me.

"Why are you carrying my briefcase?" I stopped suddenly to ask the question and he was a hairbreadth from my neck.

"Because I'm being a gentleman," he answered logically and I groaned.

Phoenix was finger waving from the front desk. I hurried to her desk and rested my arm on it. I had to put a safe distance between me and Mr. Puddlemaker. "Any messages for me, Phoenix?" I asked desperately, praying there was a sudden emergency at the hospital.

"Yes, the school called and they need you to come in for a meeting next week. I sent the specifics to your email, and your one o'clock had to move their appointment to next week."

I glanced at the note from Washington School and saw it was

for an IEP meeting. I thought we had finished those, but stuffed it in my pocket in case he could read it from where he stood, rocking on his black loafer-clad feet. "So, no patients until one thirty then?" I asked and she nodded but she wore a ridiculously large grin.

"It's only noon, did you get lunch yet?" Phoenix asked like a mother.

"Not yet. Just got done with surgery and was going to dictate." I smiled, my eyes making weird swirly movements at the man behind me, so she would catch my drift and hold her tongue.

Phoenix's eyes drifted to Kade still standing there, his one hand in his pocket, his other still holding my briefcase. "Did you have an appointment, Kade?"

He gave her his barely-there smile. "Nope, just ran into Autumn in the parking lot, and here we are."

Here we are indeed. He looked like he was enjoying this. "Why are you here?" I finally asked and that's when I got that full on *melt me* smile.

"Glad you asked. I always deliver a paper to my front-page neighbors for the week." He held my briefcase out and I took it from him, carefully, so our hands wouldn't touch.

"That's very nice of you, Kade, but ah, where is it?" I asked and he held up a finger, backed out of the door, and jogged toward his lumberjack truck.

"Is he always this odd?" I asked without looking at Phoenix.

"He's a nice guy. You should give him a chance," she scolded me. "He's single, gorgeous, and not gay. If he wasn't forty-two, I'd be all over him."

My brows went up in complete surprise. "He's forty-two?"

"Yeppers, or thereabout. What has he got?" She quickly pulled back and came around the desk to punch the handicapped door opener again. The doors opened just as he walked in, carrying a flat box in both hands.

"One newspaper would have been enough," I joked, pushing the magazines off the table and pulling it over for him to lay the box on.

"I only brought one," he insisted, motioning to the box.

I pulled the packing tape off and lifted the flaps. Inside was a glass covered frame. I pulled it out carefully while he held the box. Today's article had been matted with a picture of me to the right, and framed in rich honey oak. "Kade, this is, wow. This is beautiful." I heard the genuine tone of my voice and surprised even myself. "I don't know what to say other than thank you. This means so much. Do you do this for every business?"

"Every business, yes," he answered, nodding as though he was hoping I would believe it. I didn't, but I wouldn't insult him either.

"I haven't even been able to read the article yet," I admitted. "I picked one up on my way here, though." I motioned to the briefcase and his lips tilted a little.

"You did approve the rough copy Friday, so I guess you get the gist of it." He took the frame and walked around the office with it. He held it up to different walls and searched for just the right place to hang it.

Phoenix took it from him and set it against the wall. "But she really should get more than just the gist of it, and she needs lunch. So why don't you two skedaddle and get a sandwich, since you have an extra half an hour today."

Oh, if I didn't love that girl, I would fire her right now for this little trick. I waved my hand. "Oh, I'm sure Kade has work to do. New stories to write, that kind of thing," I stammered and he rocked back on those heels again. I noticed today he had on a pair of khaki pants and a V-neck sweater with the sleeves pushed to the elbows. His forearms were strong, and tan. I stopped myself before I could go any further with those thoughts.

"It's true. I do have stories to write and work to do," he parroted, holding out his hands. I almost did a fist pump before I remembered he was standing there.

"See, just like I said." I gave her the palms and grinned like an idiot.

"But," he held up a finger, "they don't mind if I eat lunch, which I haven't yet, by the way."

"I do. Have work that is. Those reports aren't going to dictate themselves," I apologized.

"As a matter of fact, I just sent your surgery reports to the transcriptionist. You must have done them and forgot all about it," Phoenix mused, tapping her temple. "That means you have at least an hour for lunch. Scoot." She started shooing us toward the door like barn animals. "Nick and I will hang your picture while you're gone. Have fun you two."

We found ourselves standing in the parking lot staring at each other. "I'm sorry, she's kind of pushy. We can ignore her."

He laughed and I liked the sound, a lot. "She always has been pushy, ever since she was a little nip. I went to school with her mother and I know exactly who she takes after."

Of course, he knew her. I was the one at a definite disadvantage here. "Forgive me. I'm the newbie around here. I love her, but she's bossy." I shook my head, and he did that laugh again. The laugh that made parts of me tingle that hadn't tingled in a long, long, long time.

"So, lunch. Whatcha hungry for?" he asked, his eyes dancing while he awaited my response.

∞∞∞

"You were right," I finally admitted, "the chicken and wild rice soup is the best."

He smiled at me with his spoon halfway to his mouth and then slipped the spoon through his perfect lips. The sensuality of that simple motion made me question whether or not I was forty or fourteen. I had nervously agreed on Gordy's Warming House for soup and a sandwich. It was just across the street from the clinic, and I had the added bonus of getting a coffee on the way out. The short drive over, in separate cars, gave me a few moments to catch my breath and stiffen my resolve. Being friends was safe. Anything else was not. Especially anything that involved those lips. Those perfect, pink, *bet he's a great kisser*, lips.

"Is everything okay at your son's school?" he asked, sipping a Diet Coke.

My head came up too fast and I'm sure my eyes were a little crazy. "Yes, why wouldn't it be?"

He laid his hand on mine. "Hey, I'm sorry. It was an innocent question. Phoenix said they called for a meeting."

I abruptly pulled my hand out from under his large, warm one. "No, I'm sorry. I didn't mean to be defensive. He's new to the district, so we have to adjust things here and there as they test him. We're working hard to make sure he's in the right classes."

"IEP?" he asked, one brow going up just slightly.

I lost my appetite and lowered my sandwich. It wasn't a secret, but for some reason I didn't want to tell him about Grayson. Maybe knowing he knew what we deal with every day would make it harder to keep him at a distance. I barely nodded and looked anywhere but at him.

"If you ever need any help, please let me know." He had his hand back on mine and I fought against the urge to snatch it away. "I'm on the board, so if I can help facilitate ..."

"You're on the school board?" I asked surprised. "Do you have kids in the district?"

"I do have kids in the district. Lots of them, some I'm even related to, but none that are actually mine." He lifted his hand and took a bite of his turkey sandwich with green and white sprouts poking out from every direction.

"But you ran for school board even without kids in the district? That's noble." I took a bite of my sandwich to avoid talking about Grayson.

"Noble isn't really the word I would use. I used to cover the meetings as a reporter all the time. A seat came open halfway through a term, so I filled it. Not sure that I'll run when my term expires next year, but it does give me a new appreciation for a lot of things."

"Like what?" I asked, happy to keep the topic off me and on him.

"Like the things school districts have to do just to keep the doors open. How the community loves their schools, but the taxpayers don't always want to pay for them."

I nodded. "I hear ya. Sometimes it's painful when the property tax bill comes, but someone paid for me to go to school, so I write the check. I want educated and diverse graduates to come out of our schools and help change the landscape of the workforce. It has to happen."

He smiled at me again and I rubbed my hands on the legs of my scrubs to keep myself grounded in reality. This was lunch with a friend. Nothing more.

"I couldn't agree more. My point was, if I can help with anything for Grayson, don't hesitate to ask."

I wanted to thank him, but the words stuck in my throat. I didn't want to share Grayson with him because then ... I don't know. Then, what? "Thank you," I answered, without gazing into his eyes.

"Do you have a picture of Mr. Grayson? I love to meet the kids in the district. They remind me why I'm sitting on that board." He set his sandwich down, chewed slowly, and then swallowed, his Adam's apple bobbing. Suddenly, his eyes rounded in recognition. "I'm sorry, that sounded creepy. Forgive me. Sometimes my brain doesn't work at full speed when I'm sitting next to a beautiful woman." He gave me an apologetic smile and I couldn't stop the laugh that escaped my lips. I shook my head and kept giggling, so much so he started, too. Pretty soon we were both laughing so hard we had to stop and take a drink of soda, just to get ourselves back under control.

"I'm not even sure what was so funny there, but I just love the way you laugh," he confessed. His soda glass was in his hand and his leg was stretched out across the floor, almost touching mine.

"You said you were sitting across from a beautiful woman." I rolled my eyes a little and rested my cheek on my palm.

"How is that funny?" he asked, his brows going up above the wire rims.

"Well, I'm not beautiful, but thank you for the compliment. For the record, I didn't think you were being creepy. I just have a hard time sharing Grayson with people I don't know well."

"For the record, you're more than beautiful, you're gorgeous. You remind me of Rebecca Romijn. That said, I understand about Grayson. It's my fault for asking."

"Rebecca Romijn? You mean Mystique, from the X-Men?" I asked shocked, and he nodded.

"Yes, but when she's herself, not when she's blue." His eye came down into a wink that left me unglued. He so wasn't going to be able to wink like that or my resolve was going to shatter in a matter of one lunch. "You're a little mysterious like Mystique. You make me want to know more about you. You've really never eaten here before?" He changed the subject abruptly and the look in his eyes said he knew I was uncomfortable.

He thinks I'm gorgeous sitting here in my hospital scrubs, no makeup, and my hair held at the top of my head in a bun holder. Against my will, my hand went to my head and pulled the stick out, letting it fall to my shoulders. I shook it a little and reached down to tuck the holder in my briefcase. I'm sure I heard him groan, but I tried to pretend I didn't. Why did I do that? My hair was just fine tucked up neat and tidy in that bun, now it hung around my shoulders and was already beginning to curl. When I glanced back up, he had one cheek in his palm while he stared at me. "Stunning, absolutely stunning."

Answer his question you fool.

"I really haven't eaten here before. I've had their coffee and the ice cream, but nothing else. That changes now. We don't eat out much, but I'll be stopping by for lunch this winter."

"You don't eat out much?" He shifted in his chair a bit with a look of pleasured pain on his face.

I tried to focus on his question and nothing else. "Not really. Grayson has his favorite places and new places can be, can, uh, cause some …" I moved my hand around like an idiot, and he took it, lowering it to the table.

"Anxiety?" he asked, and I nodded.

"Yes. He's getting much better though, and loves to come here for ice cream. Maybe we'll venture out for breakfast this weekend. The muffins and scones look mouthwatering." I glanced away from the bakery case and straight into his eyes.

"They are. Maybe someday you'd let me buy you and Grayson breakfast. Maybe even show you around our fair city, since you're new to town and everything," he added just as his phone beeped. He checked it quickly and his shoulders sank a bit.

"I'm sorry, breaking story it looks like, and they want me to go cover it." He stood, and I did, too.

"No problem, I have to be getting back to the clinic for patients, but thank you for the well-written article, beautiful gift, soup, and the company. It was nice."

He reached down and picked up my briefcase, handed it to me, and then held the door while I walked down the ramp to my car. I laid the briefcase on the backseat and then opened the driver's side, unhappy with the disappointment in the pit of my stomach. He stood on the running board of his truck and stared over the roof of my Equinox, and straight into my eyes. "If you decide to come over for breakfast, give me a ring. I'll meet you here."

"I don't have your number," I answered, giving him the palms.

"You do, actually. You just have to know where to look."

I gave a quick nod and then held one hand up as a gesture of goodbye before I sat down hard in my car. I just had to know where to look?

The vision of him carrying the frame into the office filled my head and I crooked a brow. Part of me hoped Phoenix hadn't hung it up yet and part of me hoped she had.

Chapter 4

"Momma, do you hear that?" Grayson sat on the couch in my office while I finished notes on the patient I had just seen. I looked up at the Spiderman clock on the wall. It was nearly seven-thirty. Who would be knocking? I stood up from behind the desk and went to the office door.

"Stay here, Grayson. Let me see who it is," I instructed him and he nodded, before going back to his book.

The lights were on in the reception area and I could clearly see the nighttime knocker. I fought against the smile that wanted to take over my face when I saw him. I unlocked the door and let him in before locking it again. Did I just lock myself in with this man? Best not to think about that.

"Kade, is everything all right?" I asked, looking him up and down for an injury.

"I was about to ask you the same thing. I was on my way to the football game and noticed the lights were on. I was concerned." He took hold of my left shoulder and the heat from his hand burned through the light fabric of my white coat. "It's kind of late for you to be here. Is Grayson okay?"

I nodded. "Yes, sorry to worry you. I met a patient and his mother here. His cast was so loose it was almost falling off. We're trying to avoid surgery on the wrist. Coming in to change it myself was easier than having them do it in the ER and having to take report Monday. I was just finishing up the paperwork before heading home."

He dropped his hand and slid it into his pocket. "You're a devoted doctor. Most would have sent them to the ER and stayed home."

I shrugged. "Kids are tricky, and as I said, this is a special case. He's only two, and I think getting it to heal with proper casting and setting technique is better than putting him through surgery."

"It just worries me you being here alone." He glanced around the office and I followed his eyes.

"Why? The doors are locked, and I'm not letting just anyone in," I said pointedly.

"The parking lot isn't that well lit and there are always drug seekers out there. This is a doctor's office," he pointed right back.

"It is, but alas I don't keep any drugs here, other than smelling salts and a bit of Novocain. As for the parking lot, that's why I have my car parked right there." My eyes drifted to the front door where my Equinox sat under the overhang for patient drop-off. He threw his hands up, just as I heard a little voice.

"Momma, who is it?" I turned on my heel slowly and stared at my towheaded son. He was braced on his walker and eyeing Kade curiously.

Before I could answer, Kade walked over and bent at the waist, offering his hand, which Grayson took. "Kade Franco, nice to meet you, Grayson Hanson."

My son shook his hand for a moment before gripping his walker again. His legs were shaking and it took everything he had to remain upright. "Kade Franco. You're the reporter who wrote the article about my momma. That made her smile. I like it when she smiles."

Kade had a smile on his face that was a cross between pure happiness and pure satisfaction. "I like it when she smiles, too. She's so pretty, and she gets these little lines right here." He pointed to the corner of his eyes. "You know when you see those little lines that a woman is truly happy."

"I didn't know that, but I'm only seven. I don't really like girls," Grayson shared and I clapped my hand over my mouth.

"That's okay, girls can be kind of a pain at seven, but later on you'll find you can't stay away from them. Then you'll be looking for those little laugh lines, I promise." Kade was kneeling now on one knee and Grayson was almost sunken to the ground, only upright by putting the weight of his body on his arms.

I was about to pick him up when I saw Kade motion toward his leg braces. "Now those are some kind of cool. Would it be okay if I set you in that chair over there so I can check them out?"

Grayson looked relieved when Kade picked him up gently under his arms and swung him into one of the cloth reception chairs. He propped Gray's feet up on his thigh and checked out the braces that went from inside his shoes to his thigh, hinged at the knee for flexion. "Dude, these are the most awesomest things I've ever seen. Do you have every superhero on them?"

Grayson beamed from his spot in the chair, and tears pricked at the back of my eyes. "No silly, there are thousands of superheroes!" Grayson exclaimed laughing. "But I have all the major players."

Kade nodded, looking them over, turning them every which way. "You sure do. Hulk, Spiderman, Superman, Wolverine, Silver Surfer, and Iron Man. I wish I had cool apparatus like this."

"You do?" Grayson asked surprised. "Mostly, I don't like having to wear them."

Kade let Gray's feet drop back to a natural position. "I suppose they get hot sometimes, but not too many kids get to walk around sporting their favorite superheroes every day. I say, *if you got it, flaunt it.*" He winked and Grayson grinned, his missing teeth making him look like the jack o' lantern that would adorn our front stoop next month.

Kade stood and nonchalantly lifted the small walker and set it next to Grayson. "So, are you done here?" he asked and I nodded.

"Yup, just need to shut down the lights and grab our coats. Time to be getting home for bed," I answered breezily, trying to ignore the groan from the chair in the corner.

"But Momma, it's Friday night," Grayson whined from the chair, and Kade turned on me.

"Yeah, Momma, it's Friday night." He jutted his lip out like Grayson and I couldn't keep from laughing at the two of them ganging up on me.

"Why don't you and Grayson come to the game with me? We've already missed the first half, but that's okay. I'm sure the Lumberjacks are going to play just as well in the second."

Grayson looked at me excitedly and then his face fell when he caught sight of the walker. Football bleachers were hard to maneuver, and he was getting hard for me to carry through throngs of people.

I rubbed my hand over my face. "Kade, could you help me with a stuck drawer in my office?" I asked, and he looked perplexed, but nodded.

"Be right back, Grayson. I'll grab our coats while I'm in there."

Gray nodded mutely, and Kade followed me back to my office and stood by the door while I got our coats. "You don't have a stuck drawer."

I shook my head. "No, I don't."

"And you don't want to go to the game because it's too hard for Grayson to manage the bleachers, and you don't want to embarrass him," he finished, leaning one arm on the doorframe. He was wearing a purple Cloquet Lumberjacks sweatshirt and try as I might, I couldn't convince myself he didn't look sexy in purple.

"He had a busy day at school and as you saw, his legs are tired. He won't be able to stand much longer. He'll just be done."

"And?" he asked.

"And it's a crowd of people yelling and cheering. He can get anxious sometimes if things get too loud, or something takes him by surprise."

He pushed off the door and stood in front of me. The only thing separating us were the coats wrapped over my arm in front of me. He reached out and rubbed my shoulder for a moment as if it would give me the strength I didn't feel. "You're his mother and I respect your decision, but as a member of the press I get special seating. No steps and no bleachers. I'm happy to carry him on and off the field if you want to go. There's only half a game left, so it won't be more than an hour. I would love the company."

I stared into his eyes and saw the sincerity of what he was saying. I weighed the intelligence of agreeing to do anything with this man. It was too easy to be comfortable with him, and comfortable was too easy to like. "Let's ask Grayson?" I heard myself say and he patted my shoulder as he turned on his heel then motioned for me to go first. I shut the lights off at the door, and we entered the waiting room where Grayson sat with his eyes focused on his feet.

Kade went and sat in a chair next to him. I liked that he always got down on his level. Most people didn't think he deserved that little bit of respect. "Do you like football?" he asked my son who nodded his head without looking up. Kade pulled something from his pocket and handed one to Gray. "What's that say?"

Grayson read it aloud. "It says press pass."

Kade nodded. "It sure does. Around here that means I get special treatment." He gave Gray an exaggerated wink and then continued, "I don't have to sit in the bleachers. I get a bench right up front where the players are. I get to take pictures of them all mashing at each other as they tackle the quarterback, or run the ball past me on the way to the goal line." He was mashing his hands around and throwing his arms up in the air making fake cheering noises.

Grayson sat up a little straighter. "That sounds cool!"

"It is cool. Sometimes the water boy even sneaks me a glass of Gatorade from the cooler." Kade nodded along like he was telling secrets he shouldn't be, and he had sucked Gray in with his storytelling. Kade checked his watch. "It's almost halftime, so I have to go over there and take pictures of the band, and then watch the second half. It's my job you know."

"You have an awesome job!" My son was bouncing in his chair and I was trying not to roll my eyes, but his smile was infectious.

Kade blew on his fingers and rubbed them on his shirt. "Want to be my assistant tonight? You and your mom can sit on the bench with me. I'll even give you a piggyback ride in and out of the stadium."

I could almost see Kade holding his breath as he waited for Gray to answer. When the resounding *yes* came, I let the laughter spill out.

"All right, I'm in, too," I laughed, helping Gray on with his coat. I lifted his walker up to carry it out, since he was already piggybacking it to the car on the back of a purple-clad man of steel.

∞∞∞

"Oh, my word, that was so much fun," I said in awe as I walked into the living room where Kade sat in one of my chairs and sipped his Gordy's shake.

He was still smiling and I couldn't wipe the one off my face, either. We had arrived at the game in time to see the band performing Katy Perry's *Firework* and then watched as a full display of lights lit up the sky. Kade had done as he had promised and piggybacked Gray onto the field and sat him not on a bench, but on a chair he had asked me to carry. Without being told, he somehow knew Gray wouldn't be able to keep his back straight and hold himself up, so he gave up his huge sling back chair to my son, who tucked himself inside and watched the action. Kade also slipped him a pair of ear mufflers, exactly like the ones he was wearing, explaining everyone on the field wore them for safety. Only a boy as excited as Gray was wouldn't notice they were the only two wearing them.

"I haven't had that much fun at a Friday night home game in … I don't know when," he whispered and set his cup down on the coffee table.

"No need to whisper, he never moved the entire time I stripped off his braces. He's out," I assured him. "I can't wait to see the pictures, especially the ones from the end of the game."

I sat down on the couch and tucked my leg under me, the image of Grayson on the quarterback's shoulders still leaving me speechless.

"I'll download them as soon as I get home. I'll send the good ones by email, and get a signed release for you from the players," he promised, rubbing his hands on his jeans. "I wasn't expecting that. Sorry if it worried you."

I waved my hand a little at him and took my time swallowing my shake. To be truthful, it had done more than worry me. It had petrified me. I had stood rooted in place as our Lumberjacks won the game with a last-second touchdown. They had all piled onto each other in a mosh pit of players. Kade was out on the field taking pictures from every angle, nearly getting tackled a few times as he moved in close for the right shot. Grayson had wiggled down from the chair and crawled close to the line to see what he was missing. The quarterback saw him and scooped him up, another player put a helmet over his head, and they carried him around the field. Gray held onto the quarterback's head while the helmet bobbed around on his own. Kade ran after them, taking pictures and keeping a protective hand on his back. After a trip around the field, the quarterback set him back in my arms.

"I was petrified for the first few moments, but he's a little boy, and that was like a dream come true. He'll never play football, heck he'll never play any sport, so that was pretty darn cool for him." I smiled, patting the edge of the couch.

Apparently, it was a tradition that after the homecoming game everyone in the city goes to Gordy's High Hat for a celebratory shake. You couldn't even get near the place to park, so when we finally got in line, every player stepped behind us until we were at the front of the line. Kade, and my son riding on his back, were the local celebrities of the night. Gray was sporting a new Lumberjack sweatshirt over his coat, a mile too big, since it was the linebacker's, but it was filled with signatures from the players of both teams. Those players had changed into their street clothes and lined the parking lot to celebrate with their girlfriends and parents while they ate onion rings and drank shakes. I enjoyed one of the last warm evenings of the fall, and everyone made me feel like a welcomed member of the community.

"He's a rock star and every one of those players meant it when they invited him to the dance tomorrow night, if you think he can handle it," Kade stressed.

"After seeing that, I can't imagine he couldn't handle it. Thank you, he really needed that boost of confidence. The last year hasn't been easy." I snapped my jaw closed and refused to say more. I was thankful when he didn't push it.

Kade stood and stretched, but it was just a way to get closer to me. He sat down on the couch, picked up the remote, and clicked on the local news channel, then let his other hand fall over mine. "We better see if we made the news. I saw a couple buddies of mine out there."

We watched in silence for the first fifteen minutes of the news and weather. We sipped our shakes and he rubbed the top of my hand with his thumb. It was a feeling of familiarity that I liked, even though I shouldn't. The natural aura he gave off was of familiarity, and being your best friend. Maybe it was a reporter thing, but right now it felt very much like a man thing and I liked it far too much.

After the weather, the anchorwoman turned to the sports reporter. "Some big games were played tonight. Who was your choice for the biggest winner?" she asked. This particular channel always picked the biggest winner of the week, even if they lost. It was more about showing team spirit and sportsmanlike conduct.

"It was a hard call out there tonight. So many good games were played, but my choice this week was a tie. The Cloquet Lumberjacks and the Hermantown Hawks fought it out tonight down to the last few seconds of the game."

The TV flashed to the stadium where the players were lined up at the end of the field. "It was Cloquet's homecoming game and Quarterback John Nelson, of the Lumberjacks, takes the ball over the line to win the game twenty-seven to twenty-one at the buzzer. What happened next is the reason they're my biggest winners of the week."

Kade squeezed my hand as the screen filled with all the players, Gray on Nelson's back as they passed through the hand slapping *good game* line at the end. All of the Hawks players were also high fiving Gray, and I felt the tears of a mother's joy on my face. You could see Kade in the background, his camera in his hand and an eye on Gray.

He gave me a little shoulder bump. "See I told you, rock star."

He didn't acknowledge my tears, and I was grateful to him for that small amount of dignity. You don't mother a special needs child and ever dream of seeing him on a football field surrounded by players high fiving him. You just don't. To be sitting here watching this, and knowing I almost missed out on it, was causing the tears as much as anything. If he hadn't insisted we go to the game, I would have lost out on this memory, but more importantly, Gray would have.

The clip ended and the camera shifted back to the three anchors, all wearing bright smiles. "Who was that adorable kid?" the anchorwoman asked, and I puffed my chest out, wiping my tears on my shirt sleeve.

"Grayson Hanson, a second grader at Washington Elementary. He was there for his very first Lumberjacks game. What a memory that will be for him."

"For sure, for sure. That was the best play of the week in my opinion." The anchorman went on and Kade clicked the remote at the screen. The room was bathed in silence again.

He stood up and set the remote on the coffee table. "Well, I should be going. I'm sure you're ready for bed. I'm glad we went to the game together. I really enjoyed myself."

I stood and he took my hand, squeezing it between both of his. It was a gesture I'd experienced before, but never on this level. His hands were soft and warm and I liked how mine fit between his, almost as if it was meant to be there.

"Thank you, again. You made his whole year. I can't wait

to show him that on the computer tomorrow. He won't quit smiling all day." I trailed off, my eyes looking past his shoulder to the room where Gray was sleeping in peaceful bliss of everything going on around him.

"So, I'll see you tomorrow morning then?" He walked toward the door without dropping my hand.

"Yes, again, I'm sorry about that. If he hadn't fallen asleep, I would have gone back to get my car, but transferring the car seat would have woken him and—"

He laid his finger on my lips and I stopped talking. "Don't apologize again, Autumn. I'll be here to pick my rock star and his momma up at eight o'clock sharp. I'll drive you up to the clinic and drop you off. Will you be okay here tonight without a vehicle?" he asked, concern in his eyes.

"Of course. No more emergency calls for me tonight. I've been doing surgery since seven a.m. and I'm worn out. But my first appointment isn't until nine thirty, so nine would be fine," I reminded him.

Last night, two of the players were trying to shake off injuries after the game, but I insisted they come to the clinic at nine-thirty for me to check them over. I wasn't in the business of being open on Saturdays, but I also wasn't in the business of letting injuries go unattended.

He nodded. "Okay, if you need anything, you have my number. I'll be here at eight o'clock sharp. We need to start the day with a good breakfast. It was my aunt's number one rule."

I smirked. "So now I'm cooking breakfast?"

He pulled the door open and stepped out onto the front steps. "Nope, I'm buying breakfast. I promised Grayson I would introduce him to the best lumberjack pancakes in town."

"Is that so? How can I say no to pancakes?" I asked, giving him the palms up, and he gave a fist pump, not even trying to hide it.

"You can't, so that's why I'll be here at eight."

I leaned against the open door and rested my head on the narrow strip of wood. "We'll be ready."

He jogged down the two steps and waved from the bottom. "It's a date."

"I don't date," I informed him in my no-nonsense doctor voice.

He stopped and turned. His eyebrow was high and he rested his foot on the step. "You don't date?"

I shook my head. "Nope. It's against my religion."

He chuckled and took the steps in one leap of his long legs. He was in front of me then and I tried to act cool.

"You should change religions then. Dating is kind of fun." He smirked, his smile only quirking half of his face.

"In my world, dating leads to one thing, heartache. I've had all I can handle in my life," I whispered, not sure why I was telling him this, or what it had to do with my religion. One thing was clear. I was going to have to throw every defense I had at him if I didn't want this to become something more than friends.

He rubbed my shoulder and stared into my eyes but I noticed his looked hurt. I felt bad for even starting this conversation, but I guess at some point it would have come up.

"I'm sorry for whatever happened in the past, Autumn. Whoever it was, he was crazy not to treat you like the most extraordinary woman you are. If all we can be is friends, then I want to be your friend."

I held my breath as he spoke with his face dangerously close to mine. His forehead was resting on mine as the word friend came out. My eyes darted to his lips and then back to his eyes. He held my gaze and I was mesmerized by the flecks of gold that reflected when the light hit them just right. He laid his lips on mine in a gentle kiss. One that if a neighbor saw, it would be nothing more than a friendly goodnight kiss, but it brought to life something I hadn't felt in a long time. He stepped back and took the steps two at a time again.

"See you at eight?" he asked a little nervously, and I nodded.

He waved and then disappeared into the night. I closed the door and leaned against it. It's a date.

Kade

 I set my laptop on my bed and picked up my pen and the list I'd been making. Spending the night with Autumn and Grayson had been torture, but in the best way. Grayson is such a sweet boy. I saw where he got his fighting spirit from, his momma. The way he calls her momma, and the adoration in his eyes for her, made me smile just because I knew them. A few times she even got caught up in the game enough she had let her guard down. That was when I felt like I really got the chance to see the real Autumn Hanson. Her hair had been down, and when the wind blew, it tossed it around her shoulders and face. Every so often Gray would reach up and tuck it back behind her ear, and she would kiss him on his head. She was scared to death as she watched him being up so high and carried around a field full of football players, but she played it cool, at least until she watched it again from the couch. The tears she cried made me want to pull her to me and kiss them away, but I didn't. That was her moment, and whatever she was feeling was hers alone.

 I didn't ask what Gray's challenges were. I could see his outward ones, and she had explained some of his hidden ones. The scar on his forehead told me there was more to the story, but tonight, watching him have the best time he had ever had, was the only thing that mattered.

 I clicked back through the pictures I had downloaded as soon as I got home. I wasn't going to sleep anyway, so it was something to do. It was also self-torture, because the pictures kept replaying the night in my head. The way she smiled and laughed at Gray and his little boy excitement. The way she set her jaw and her posture changed when she was dealing with high school boys who thought they were invincible. The way she apologized for almost everything, for a reason I had yet to figure out. Tonight, she was so afraid of what I might do to her world that she tried to push me away, only to have it backfire and let me into her world a little bit more.

Dating is against her religion. I had to laugh. It was a nice attempt, but I knew the truth. What she had against dating was every guy who ever broke her heart. What I saw in her eyes when I kissed her was a war being waged, a war between being afraid of love, and wanting to give herself to me. I closed the laptop and smiled. I had every intention of winning the war.

Chapter 5

I sipped a cup of coffee and watched Gray tuck into a stack of pancakes of epic proportions. True to his word, Kade had picked us up in his truck at eight o'clock and brought us to the Family Tradition House just a few blocks from my clinic. There was a long line of people waiting for *the best lumberjack pancakes* in town, and my heart sank when I realized we wouldn't have time to eat before the players got to the clinic. However, after the newscast last night, Grayson had become an overnight celebrity and we were seated immediately at the insistence of everyone else waiting.

"Can I have a bite?" I asked him. He looked up at me with sticky maple syrup running down his chin and grinned.

"I'll always share with you, Momma," he reminded me. I cut a piece off with my fork and held my hand under it as I brought it to my mouth. The syrup and butter dripped off them, and they literally melted upon contact with your tongue.

"Oh. That's good." I eyed his plate some more and he pulled it back a little.

"You didn't want pancakes," he said very grown up. "You wanted eggs."

I set my cup back down in my saucer and noticed Kade smirking. "You did. You said you wanted eggs."

"You're taking his side in this? Men," I harrumphed and crossed my arms over my chest. Our food was on its way, but apparently the cook also heard the rock star was in the house and sent his right out. My plate was set before me with eggs and, surprisingly, a heavenly pile of flapjacks. "A Mrs. Lumberjack for you, and a full Mr. Lumberjack breakfast for you, Franco." The waitress ruffled Grayson's hair and then left us to eat.

I glanced up and Kade was smirking. "What? I can't help what they call things."

"Mrs. Lumberjack," I muttered. I took the jar of syrup from him and our hands touched just long enough to remind me that could never happen.

∞∞∞

"I'm glad your ankle is feeling better, but remember, don't overdo it. I'll be at the dance tonight, so I will know," I teased Adam as he hobbled out to the waiting room.

Adam stopped and smiled. "Are you bringing Grayson to the dance?"

I nodded. "I really can't say no. He's too excited to see all his friends again." I put friends in air quotes, and Adam grinned.

"I can't wait to see him there. We have some fun surprises planned, but don't worry, we know we can't actually surprise him or anything. Just fun little things for him to look at and do," he explained quickly.

I raised my brow a little. "Oh, you know about Gray's challenges?" I asked, and he glanced nervously at his mother who was biting her lip to keep from smiling.

"Franco mentioned that he gets anxious about new situations. I'm sorry about that last night. We got a little carried away," he apologized sincerely, and I shook my head.

"No, don't apologize. He had a blast last night and I was thrilled to see he didn't get scared or anxious. I do appreciate that you have planned some activities for him tonight. I also appreciate that all of you have taken him under your wing, and care enough to make sure he's not overwhelmed."

"He's super cute and I know we're football players in high school, but Gray's cool, so we're happy to have him." Adam blushed, and I smiled, patting his back.

"You better head home and get some ice on that ankle then. Rest it until tonight and you'll make it through the dance. I want to see you on Thursday before you even think about practicing or playing in next week's game. Got it?" I asked, hit the handicapped door opener, and he hobbled through.

"Yes, ma'am, I got it." He waved and crutched to the car with his mom following behind him.

I closed and locked the door and shook my head. Both the players had come to the clinic as I had instructed, and both had gotten off lucky. They would only be sporting an ankle brace and a knee brace to the dance tonight. I recommended crutches, but something told me they would be discarded by the time they got home.

Gray had watched his favorite Saturday morning cartoons on the TV in my office, with his belly stuffed full of flapjacks. When I walked past the office a few minutes ago, I noticed him sacked out on the couch. I sat down at Phoenix's computer to do my work, just to keep from disturbing him. He still had a lot of rock star action yet today and catching a nap wasn't a bad thing.

Kade had transferred his car seat into the back of my Equinox after breakfast and helped us in the door of the clinic. Then some sneaky boy whispering happened right before he left. I shook my head at the two of them. You would think they had known each other for twelve years, instead of twelve hours. They were constantly whispering or high fiving each other. I was a little nervous letting Gray become such good friends with him, but then I reminded myself we weren't dating, so there was no reason Gray and Kade couldn't be friends.

Phoenix's computer loaded the desktop and her wallpaper made me smile. It was a collage of pictures from the last few years. Pictures of her mom and dad with her at graduation, her and another girl jumping off a rock into a lake, and her cheer group on the field. There was one that caught my eye, and I leaned into the screen a little further to make it out better. In the middle of the collage was a picture of her with another woman, who was stunningly beautiful. She towered over Phoenix, and could easily be a model for any of the plus size clothing companies. She was dressed in a Cloquet Lumberjacks jacket and leaning into Phoenix as they held foam number one fingers.

Feeling like a peeping Tom, I shook my head and opened my inbox. I had been checking my inbox for the photos he promised to send to no avail. He hasn't sent them yet because you've been taking up all of his time.

He probably has a life, I scolded myself.

Something told me with the number of inner conversations I was having with myself, I was definitely having a midlife crisis. That would totally explain why I couldn't sleep last night after he left, and had to take a cold shower at one a.m. just to catch a few winks. The convertible was looking better and better. I wonder if they make them with room for a car seat in the back.

After lunch I took stock of Gray's closet for anything that was even remotely presentable for a dance. I was happy when everything he had was too small. We made a trip to Walmart, the only store in town open on Saturday. It was also the only place that stood a chance of having a dress shirt and slacks small enough for my little man. We lucked out and found a pant set, with a vest to boot, and it fit him perfectly. It was a five toddler. I beamed when I showed him. *I'm growing!* he had exclaimed in the dressing room. I didn't need the new size to tell me he was growing. He needed new leg braces already, and the ones he had were less than a year old. Looking at his face right then though, I would pay for ten thousand sets if it made him that happy. The outfit must have been a straggler from Easter, because at the clearance price of three dollars it was a steal. We picked up a new pair of shiny black shoes, one size bigger, and checked out. Grayson told the checkout lady all about his dance tonight, and she was beaming as big as he was by the time we left.

After supper was eaten and cleaned up, Grayson dressed in his dapper new outfit and called me in to brush his hair and help with his shoes. He jumped down off the bed and grabbed his walker. "Come in your room, Momma. You need a pretty dress for tonight, too."

I followed him into the room shaking my head like I was shooing a fly. "No, I don't. I'm just taking you. I don't need to dress up, only you do."

He turned, his long little boy lashes fluttering against his cheeks. "Please, Momma, for me?"

That was so unfair. He already knew I would do anything for him, so playing me with his cuteness was dirty. I rubbed my forehead and opened my closet door. "I don't think I have anything that fits, Gray."

"That's 'cause you don't eat enough. Even Kade said you didn't eat enough breakfast," he parroted, sounding very grown up.

Kade's lighthearted banter about me eating like a baby bird came back to me. He said I wouldn't make a very good lumberjack wife if I didn't eat at least one whole pancake with my eggs. Gray had given me his lash fluttering then too, so I stuffed myself just to get them off my case.

Gray couldn't see me while I was facing my clothes, so I did an immature mimicking of Kade and then snickered at my own joke. Wow, I might need to get out more. I pushed the clothes around in the closet and Gray was right behind me.

His hand shot out instantly. "That one, Momma! That's a pretty one."

He was pointing at the dress I had bought and never worn. The tags still hung from the arm and the sash was tied loosely at the back. I had bought it for what was going to be a very special night. A night that never happened. The old memory hit me in the gut again and I wondered why I had even moved the dress from our little house in Duluth. I should have donated it then, back when I sat on my bed looking at old pictures and holding the dress in my hands, anger and frustration leaking from my eyes. But I hadn't donated it. I'd brought it here.

"What's the matter? Don't you like it?" Gray asked. His legs were getting tired as he stood watching me.

"I always loved this dress, buddy. I just never had a reason to wear it. Maybe tonight is a good night to put it on." I smiled at him, firm in my resolve that I was taking back this dress, and my life.

"You're going to be so pretty. I can't wait for …" he stopped and smiled a little. "I can't wait to see you in it."

I resisted tousling his newly combed hair and helped him to his chair in the living room to read while he waited for me to get dressed. I stood at the door of the room and addressed the dress. It hung there, mocking me. Daring me to put it on and pretend that all those things that happened in the past didn't make a damn bit of difference in my life anymore. I couldn't do that, but I could put it on and pretend the dress didn't make a damn bit of difference in my life anymore. Most of the past I considered a lesson, and the things that hurt the worst were tucked away where they would never see the light of day again. I didn't know if there was a lesson in those things yet, so it was best not to think about them.

With surgical skill, I sliced the plastic holding the tags on the dress, and threw them in the garbage can.

Tonight, I take back my life.

"Look at him. He's the hit of the dance." Kade smiled, leaned back in his chair, and crossed his legs. When the doorbell rang at seven, I had opened it to a suit-clad lumberjack sans glasses, and his hair freshly cut. He had his camera slung over his shoulder and we had stared at each other for too many seconds.

My sneaky son had invited Kade to be our chauffeur, and that was why I needed to wear a pretty dress. I left my hair down, fighting with all my might against the beautiful bun holders beckoning from the drawer where they waited to do their job, but they lost. No bun tonight. Just fly away hair that curled at the tips and brushed against my bare shoulders. The dress was as pretty as I remembered it to be. The sash was a perfect solution to my weight loss over the last months, too. If I kept eating like this morning though, there might be hope for my wardrobe yet.

We arrived at the dance and took pictures with the football players, the homecoming court, and several Washington School teachers who were at the dance to chaperone. They were all surprised to see Gray at the dance. He was having a ball and was currently dancing the hokey pokey in the middle of a large circle. Even holding onto his walker, he was killing it. Kade jumped up for more pictures, and I leaned forward to get a better look at him taking pictures of my son.

I loved that he had an amazing eye for the human experience and a natural talent for writing stories to go with them. Skills like that aren't taught in any college classroom. Skills like that are nurtured from a young age, encouraged, and supported. It made me wonder about his family and who encouraged and supported him for years.

My eyes strayed to the easel at the side of the punch table. On it sat a collage frame of pictures from last night's game. After Kade dropped us off this morning, he had gone to Duluth and had them printed and framed for tonight's dance. The players had all signed it, and it would come home with us tonight. Those pictures showed my son in a new light. He was part of a team, a team bigger than just me and him. He had this whole team of big kids who would protect him from anyone who tried to mess with him. Gray had a natural trust I didn't get to see often, probably because I protected him a little too much. He was always a fighter and I loved his tenacity for life. He never said *screw you, world* like he would have every right to do. Instead, he took pleasure in all the simple things of his day-to-day world. Things like a new Marvel book, the birds in the backyard, or the joys of bringing cupcakes to school. Maybe I'm doing something right after all. Maybe we're going to be just fine.

"You're captivating as a woman, but even more beautiful as a mom. You know that?" I glanced up into Kade's face and he was smiling at me. It was a genuine tender smile. He wasn't putting on airs or trying out lines. He meant what he said.

"Thank you. It's not always easy, but he's so worth it." I smiled, watching him dance with two of the girls from the court. They had joined hands and he was resting on their arms dancing to a slow song.

Kade set his camera on the table and stretched out his hand. "Come dance with me. We'll move in close enough to make sure he's not putting the moves on those girls."

I laughed and shook my head while I gazed up to the ceiling. *What the hell?* It's just one dance. I stood slowly and smoothed my dress before taking his hand. It had been a long time since I had done this, and he seemed to sense it. He walked me to the edge of the floor and pulled me into a slow dance embrace. The lights were low and the music was easy to fall into a soft sway. He kept his hand resting lightly on my back, his other holding mine against my shoulder. He was focused on my face and his eyes, not hidden by his glasses, drew me in. I traced my finger down the laugh lines by his eyes.

"I like being able to see your eyes," I shared and he rewarded me with that puddlemaker smile.

"I don't like contacts for everyday wear, but I didn't want anything between us tonight."

I stumbled at his words, but he held me, acting as though I hadn't just tripped on my own feet. Jason Mraz sang that he wouldn't give up and I lowered my head to his chest to avoid those eyes. He pulled me in closer and his arms held me protectively across my back in an X. He smelled of Old Spice and I inhaled deeply.

"I love you in this dress," he whispered, feeling the fabric in his hands. "It makes me wish I knew you in high school."

I laughed against his chest. "It must be a real miracle worker."

"I'll tell you a secret, it's not the dress. It's the woman wearing it."

"It's new," I blurted out, then rolled my eyes, glad he couldn't see me. "I mean it's the first time I've worn it. Gray found it in the back of the closet."

His breathing was even as he spun me slowly toward the middle of the room where Gray was now dancing with two other girls. My son finger-waved at me and I waved back, not lifting my head.

"Remind me to thank him for his keen eye, but why was a dress as beautiful as this hanging in the back of your closet?" he asked. He spun me back toward the corner of the room that was dark and deserted.

"I bought it for a special night that never happened," I told him. I purposely kept my answer short. That was a lot easier than giving him the long version.

He was quiet and we danced to the last few bars of the song until it ended. He leaned his head over my shoulder, holding me tight to him. "It just happened."

I sucked in a breath, but fought against looking up at him. I didn't want him to see how hard taking back my life really was.

Chapter 6

Kade

"This is an incredible piece of reporting, Kade." My editor lowered the paper to her desk. I was sitting across from her and waiting for the go-ahead to make it the front-page sports story. "I really think this is front page material."

I shook my head with determination. "I would like it to stay in sports for a couple of reasons. In my opinion, the story is about the boys and what they did that night, nothing else. The sports section is where it belongs."

She eyed me over the top of her glasses, and I knew she had the power to put it wherever she wanted. I could only pray she heard and understood my reasons. Finally, her head nodded once. "Alright, sports, but it gets a full two pages. I'll be putting a picture on the front page to make sure it catches people's eye, or they may miss it and not read the sports section. I can't control if News Tribune or someone else picks it up. Fair warning." She took her glasses off and set them on the desk then leaned over it to stare me down.

"I understand. I appreciate that you get this is more about the kids than selling papers." I stood and walked to the door ready to escape her scrutiny.

"You like her, don't you?" she asked with a lilt in her voice, and I stopped long enough to give her a long look.

"I have every intention of marrying her. It's all about how long it takes her to come around to the idea," I stated matter of fact.

She sat back in her chair and kicked her legs up on the desk. "Well, well, Kade Franco has met his match. I'm on your team.

Let me know if I can help." She smirked, and I laughed, waving goodbye as I shut the door.

Team Franco. That sounded like some teeny-bopper movie thing, but I was all for anyone who was rooting for me. I had spent Sunday putting together the story for this week's edition between repeatedly picking up my phone to call her. I never did get up the nerve to actually dial, and instead went to the gym and took out my frustrations on the elliptical machine.

My frustration was stemming from how beautiful she was despite the fragile look in her eye. Being a student of human nature, I'd spent the better part of my life reading how people actually feel by looking in their eyes. Last night she flat out refused to let me look into hers, and that told me she was afraid of what I would see. On a purely physical level, I couldn't quit thinking about how that dress had hugged her every curve, and how the front lay across her chest giving me far too much of a view for my lower half. Keeping myself under control while we danced had been nothing less than exhausting.

I slid into my desk chair and opened my laptop. The picture of Gray wearing the king's crown, while the whole court surrounded him, was still open on my screen. He had been so happy he didn't want to leave, but when he finally fell asleep on Autumn's lap, I carried him to the truck and took them home. I clicked the image closed, but it was too late. My mind had already wandered to the kiss I had snuck on my way out the door, and the feel of her hand on my chest.

I opened my inbox to check for my next story. I had been racking my brain for a reason to see her again, but I couldn't find one. Then my email pinged, and a smile grew on my face. Oh, now this is interesting. I think this will do just fine.

Autumn

"Good afternoon, Phoenix. What's on tap for the rest of the day?" I asked the now black-haired receptionist. She'd had her hair dyed over the weekend in what I suspected was the color to complement her Halloween costume.

"Hi, Autumn." She looked around me and I waited, wondering why she was so secretive. "I need a favor," she whispered, and I leaned across the desk.

"Of course. What's going on?" I asked. I realized she was scared and I touched her shoulder to comfort her.

"My friend is in the backroom. She's hurt and won't go to the ER. I brought her here. I think she's hurt badly this time," Phoenix said frantically and I was already following her down the hall.

Phoenix pushed open the door to room two and a woman lay on the table. She was bleeding from her lip and looked like she had been in a war.

Phoenix closed the door behind me and approached the woman. "Winter, Dr. Hanson is here."

The girl on the table was visibly shaking. "Hi, Winter. I'm Autumn." I tried to joke a little, but I took one look at her face and my heart sped up. "Oh, my goodness, sweetheart."

She grimaced and tried to wave, but one arm was at an unusually funny angle. "I'm okay, just had a car accident."

"Did the car run over you?" I asked shocked

She tried to smile, but her face was too swollen. "No, but the airbag had a bad attitude." She grimaced again and I took a quick assessment of her injuries. The left side of her face was swollen to the size of a grapefruit. Her lip was going to require stitches as it was sliced down almost all the way through.

"When did this happen?" I asked, worried she had a concussion.

"Last night, but I'm okay. It looks way worse than it is." She couldn't smile, and her words were somewhat slurred from the swelling.

"Did you go to the ER?" I asked, and she tried to shake her head, but thought better of it.

"Nah, just hit a deer going fifty-five and set the airbag off. Knocked me a little silly, but no harm no foul."

"Winter, look at your face. Yes, harm." Her face was deformed and I was pretty sure she had fractured her cheekbone. What I really didn't like was how glassy-eyed she was and how scared she looked. "I think we need to get you to the emergency room for x-rays."

She shook her head, but grabbed at it in pain. "No, no, I'm using ice. Phoenix just freaked out and said I had to see someone. She didn't give me a choice."

I glanced at Phoenix who was rubbing Winter's leg and the look that passed between us told me Phoenix saw through Winter's story.

I checked Winter's face and examined her wrist carefully, so I didn't cause her more pain. The swelling around her eye made her face like mush. I really wasn't comfortable with what I was seeing. "Winter, I really, really think you need a hospital."

I wasn't into treating critically injured patients in my clinic, regardless of how scared they were. Something niggled in the back of my mind as I stared at the battered woman on my table.

"You're the woman from the computer," I said shocked, and Phoenix nodded.

"She is. She's been my bestie since I was old enough to push my way onto the seat on the bus." She put her hand on her hip and pierced the woman with a hard stare. "Winter Cheyne is her name and stubborn princess is her game."

I laughed and shook my head. "Okay, this is what's going to happen. We'll go back to the x-ray room now. I'll take a couple of pictures and make sure there isn't an unstable fracture of your face or arm. Then I need to stitch that lip or it won't heal, and personally, I like your pretty face. Depending on what I see on the x-rays will determine if you go to the hospital after that."

Nick was getting the rooms ready when we made our way

back to the triage area. I gave him a look, and he went to man the front desk while I set Winter up on the table and took x-rays of her face from several different angles. Her wrist was swelling more and more by the minute, but I managed to get some x-rays of it as well. The pictures came up on the screen and my fear was confirmed. Her cheek had a fracture. The rest of her face was solid though, and the fracture was hairline. I didn't need to call in a facial surgeon, at least. Her wrist, well, that was going to require a cast.

I helped her sit up and gave her a moment in case she got dizzy. "The bad news is you have a fracture of your cheek. The good news is it won't need surgery. The other bad news is your wrist is broken. I'm going to have to splint it today, and you'll have to come back for a cast in a few days when the swelling goes down."

She gave me the thumbs up. "See, I was right. I'm fine."

I pinned her with my best doctor glare. "No, you're not *fine*, but you will be if you do what I tell you to."

I led her into the exam room where Nick had set up the suture tray after my text from the x-ray room. My lips were set in a thin line as I sutured. I may not be a plastic surgeon, but something told me if I didn't suture this, she wouldn't go to the hospital and have it done either. At least it was in an area that wouldn't leave a terrible scar, but my skills for suturing to minimize scars were coming in handy.

Winter didn't make eye contact the whole time and kept her eyes trained on the ceiling. She was lying to me, we both knew it, but I couldn't prove it. "Winter, is it safe for you to go home?" I asked. To her credit, she barely reacted, but the way her eyes closed slowly told me it wasn't. I pulled my hand back, so she could talk and she muttered something I couldn't understand.

When I finished her lip, I splinted her arm and checked the reaction time of her pupils. It was obvious she had a concussion. I couldn't send her home alone, or to whatever was waiting for her there. I called the front desk and asked Phoenix to join us. She jogged in the door and went right to Winter, putting a protective arm around her.

"She has a concussion and I can't send her home if she's alone." I stared pointedly at Phoenix who nodded with understanding in her eyes. "So, can she stay with you until Thursday? I need her to come back in and get her cast on Thursday morning. Just take the next few days off. Nick and I will handle it."

Phoenix glanced to Winter then back to me and nodded. No argument was made, and none was needed. This would be a paid vacation until I decided if I had to report this to the authorities.

∞∞∞

The week passed quickly between surgery, patients, and picking up the slack from Phoenix being gone. When Winter came back on Thursday, I was relieved to see she looked much closer to the picture I had seen on the computer screen. Her bruises were turning a sickly yellow, but the swelling was gone, and she said her face didn't hurt anymore. While casting her arm I talked with her, trying to find out more about how the accident really happened, but she was sticking to the deer story. I didn't believe it for a minute. When she told me she was living at home again, I nearly bit through my lip trying to stay quiet. I didn't believe for a second her injuries were from a car accident. I knew they were from a fist hitting her face. What I couldn't prove was who did it.

Grayson's school meeting went well and he was moved to third-grade reading and writing. We adjusted his individual education plan to allow for use of the private bathroom in the special education room, and got permission to use a special chair at his desk in the regular classroom. His weekly sessions at therapy were really improving his core strength, and he was able to stand longer every day. His confidence was at an all-time high and every kid in the school wanted to be his friend. Every one of them made an extra effort to help him when he asked, and he was getting better about asking as his confidence improved. He even wakes up before me every morning ready to go to school, which has been refreshing. He was blossoming here and that made the stress and worry worth it.

I fingered the leaf that hung over the vase of flowers on my coffee table. I wondered if the sender of said flowers had anything to do with the cooperation from the district regarding all the changes. Most likely not, after all he was only on the board, but it seemed like they were bending over backward to help us. I hadn't seen him since last Saturday night when he drove us home, me in the front seat and Gray in the back of the truck with his eyes closed after the long dance. Kade held my hand the whole way home, and the silence that filled the truck was comfortable. I didn't feel the need to fill it with needless chatter and instead watched the stars pass in the black of night. He carried Gray inside, helped me get his braces off, and tucked him under the covers. When I offered him a nightcap he declined, but left me with a gentle kiss.

When the Cloquet Greenhouse brought this vase of dwarf sunflowers on Wednesday, I knew they were from him. My house is filled with sunflowers. Some might say I have an obsession, but I've tried to keep it classy and not gaudy. When he asked me about them on Saturday night I laughed and told him sunflowers are my sunshine on a rainy day. When I read the card attached to the vase it said, *A little sunshine for a rainy day*. Down at the bottom it said *I won't give up*.

He didn't sign it. He didn't need to. I had no doubt they were from him. I started and deleted three texts, but couldn't screw up the courage to send it, so I sent him a quick thank you email instead. He had responded with nothing more than a smiley face. I found his response heart calming and refreshing that he had no hidden agenda other than to make me smile.

I had tucked the card in my pocket and left the sunshine on the reception desk for the rest of the week. Now they sat on my coffee table and his words filled my head like the leaves that filled the bouquet, spilling over the sides into my heart. Gray asked me whom they were from and I was honest with him. His response was a simple pat on my shoulder, and then he went back to his book with a little smirk on his face.

I was too busy to read the paper this week, but now that Gray was in bed and my Friday night was over, I picked it up off the coffee table. I flipped through the first section and didn't see a byline by him. He was their lead reporter and I assumed he ran the first-page article nearly every week. I flipped back to the front page again to double check, and the picture at the bottom caught my eye. My eyes darted to the dark maple frame that hung above the TV. It was a centerpiece in our home now and in ten years when I looked at it, I would still remember my feelings from that night. Pride and happiness in a way I'd never experienced before, and that would always make me think of Kade Franco. If I hadn't met him, I would have missed out on that.

The picture down at the bottom of the paper was one from that same collage. I found the sports section and the first thing that caught my eye was the title *Autumn Reflections* by Kade Franco. My eyes scanned the pictures in the article that extended into page two and three. The photos of the band, the fireworks, and the quarterback making the final touchdown were all there on the first page. The second page held pictures of my son, going through the game line, his head tossed back in boyish laughter at Gordy's, and then dancing with the homecoming king and queen at the dance.

My heart filled with so much love for my little boy. For his perseverance and fight to stay alive, so he could be there that night. When my eyes cleared from the blur of tears, I read the article slowly, not wanting to miss a word of the story he wove. It was a story about football, two communities, and a little boy. A little boy who was really every boy. It was about how little boys look at these football players as giants, and how the giants' actions that night, on and off the field, should be revered. The youth of today are often accused of being self-centered and self-absorbed, but that night, on a football field in the middle of autumn's splendor, they showed sportsmanship that made both teams winners.

He had quotes from the team captains, coaches, and superintendents. The captains had both complimented each other's team for playing a hard-fought game that in the end wasn't about the game at all. It was about two communities who put aside the rivalry to display the love of the game from a child's eyes. *Cloquet's Superintendent summed up Friday's night game well when he said 'As educators and parents we don't always get to see the lessons we teach come to fruition, but when empathy is shown, empathy is learned. I couldn't be prouder, not only of my students, but also of the students of Hermantown, for coming together for the love of the game.'*

The final paragraph Kade used to share his own thoughts. He opened it by stating his articles were always written from a neutral point of view, but having experienced the event through the lens of his camera, he had this to say. "*I've lived in Cloquet most of my life and I've been a newspaper reporter for fifteen years. As a member of the Cloquet school board, I've ridden the rollercoaster that is education these days. I often wonder if we're making the right decisions for the families in our district. Last Friday night, as I watched the events unfold through my lens, I saw the answer. Over the years, I've been part of some pretty great stories, but Friday night I was never prouder to be called a Cloquet Lumberjack.*"

I dropped the article to my lap and glanced at the clock. It was nearly ten, and I felt bad for having not taken the time to read the article sooner. I picked up my phone, toying with the phone app, and wiping the tears off my face. He was probably at a game or something. I bit my lip and opened my email, but closed that, too. Before I could rethink it, I sent him a text asking if he was busy.

My phone beeped and the text said, *No, just sitting here downloading pictures from tonight's game, while thinking about last week's.*

I tapped the phone on the arm of the chair, letting it slide up and down through my fingers. The right thing to do was call him and acknowledge the article, but that also meant being in contact with him again. The words on the card were screaming at me, mocking me, from where it stared back at me from the coffee table. *I won't give up.*

Maybe he was just referencing the song from Saturday night, I told myself logically.

The song you slow danced to with your face buried in his shirt, you mean?

It wasn't buried in his shirt! Ergh, talking to yourself is the first sign of psychotic behavior. I hit the call button and listened to it ring in my ear, still debating the intelligence of this.

"Hello, Autumn," he answered in a timbre that was relaxed and comfortable.

"Hi, Kade. I hope you don't mind that I called so late," I stammered.

"Autumn, I told you to call anytime, and I meant it," he scolded. "Did you have a nice week?"

His words settled my stomach a little bit. "It was really busy, actually. That's why I'm just calling now. I wanted to thank you again for the flowers. They're beautiful. I also wanted to apologize. I was so busy I just now had the chance to read the paper. Your article was moving, from the title to the final sentence."

"Thank you for that. I tried to keep the focus on the players and not Grayson. I didn't want you to feel like I was invading your privacy or exploiting him," he explained in his soft, casual, easy-going way.

Listening to him, I was already curled up in the chair, relaxed, and waited for him to say more. The silence that crossed the airwaves left me peaceful until I realized he was waiting for me to say something.

"Sorry, I was picturing Grayson's face that night," I jumped in and he chuckled a little.

"That's okay. I was too, and also thinking of your face

Saturday night. It's all I've been able to picture all week."

I cleared my throat and tried to steer the conversation back to where I wanted it. "Right, well you succeeded, with your story I mean. The story was definitely about the players and their conduct at the game. And I appreciate that you didn't make it all about Gray. I did get a lot of great referrals and new patients this week, so I'm grateful for that."

"This community has always believed in the underdog, Autumn," he answered, and I wondered just what he meant by that. Did he mean me or Gray? Did he mean I'm an underdog and need someone to lift me up so I succeed? My blood pressure went up a little and then his voice carried across the line from wherever he sat in the city tonight.

"Don't over think this, Autumn," he whispered gently. "You're here now, and everyone in this city will make sure you and Gray are taken care of. It's just what we do."

"I don't have a lot of experience with people taking care of me. That's kind of my job. I'm the caretaker of everyone in the city," I tried to explain.

"You're most definitely a caretaker. You take great care to do your job and fix people. In return for that, we take care of you. Every relationship is give and take. We can't take and not give. That wouldn't be fair."

"It wouldn't? I guess I'm just always in mom or doctor mode." I rolled my eyes at my fantastic, brilliant surgeon brain doing its thing.

"Sorry, but the buck stops here. Speaking of taking care of each other, I was wondering if you and Grayson had plans tomorrow." His voice suddenly sounded a little nervous and hesitant.

"I have big plans," I answered, forcing my voice to sound sad and disappointed.

"You do? Darn," he sighed and I tried to hold in the snicker.

"Yeah, that laundry has been calling my name all week. The gall of it, wanting to be washed and put away all the time." I smirked, even though he couldn't see me.

There was silence for a minute and then he laughed. I pictured his head leaning back and his Adam's apple bobbing like it does. "You almost had me for a minute there. You might have a second career as an actress."

"Wow, one of my worst performances and I still pulled it off." I made some fake cheering noises and then fell silent. "Truthfully, I don't have any plans that can't wait."

Why was I telling him this? He didn't need to know this stuff. I called to tell him I thought he did a nice job with the article and to thank him for the flowers. Did I thank him for the flowers?

"Did I thank you for the flowers?" I stuttered, not sure if I said it aloud or not.

"You did, several times. I'm sure they're beautiful, but not nearly as beautiful as you are. I might just send you flowers every week if it means you'll call me every Friday."

"You don't have to send me flowers every week, but I could still call you every Friday if that would make you happy." I rubbed my forehead and glanced at the clock. It was the fatigue. That was it. The exhaustion had turned my brain to mush.

"That would make me happy. Do you know what else would make me happy? A breakfast friend date with Mrs. Lumberjack and her son, tomorrow morning."

"I don't know, Kade," I said lamely, wishing for an earthquake or tornado to suck me out of my current state of idiotic tendencies. Not likely either would happen in October in Minnesota.

"If it matters, I could also use Grayson's help with a story I have tomorrow in Esko."

I could see he wasn't going to give in easily. "He doesn't like big crowds. Well, I mean he did okay last time you know, but I have to give him the option and if he refuses then I can't make him do anything he doesn't want to do. I would feel terrible if you had a story all lined up, and then he wouldn't cooperate …"

"Autumn."

"Yes," I answered and snapped my mouth shut. I knew I sounded like a lunatic and I had no explanation.

"I know Grayson doesn't like crowds, and I wouldn't ask him to do something he wasn't comfortable doing just for a story. This story is simple. All he has to do is play with dogs. Does he like dogs?"

I shrugged my shoulder a little, afraid to utter my next sentence. "Yes, he loves dogs," I answered and bit my tongue to keep the rest from spilling out.

"Okay then. I'll pick you up at nine-thirty and we'll stop for breakfast wherever Gray decides he would like to eat. That is if you want to." He waited and I traced my finger over the floral pattern on the arm of the chair. The chair he had sat in just a week ago and filled the room with masculinity of which it, nor I, had ever experienced.

We're talking puppies here, Autumn. No harm in letting your son play with some puppies.

"Nine-thirty would be great, but expect him to choose McDonald's," I answered and I swear I heard him whisper *yes.*

Chapter 7

When Gray woke me up this morning, I brought him to my bed for Saturday morning cartoons while I snoozed a little longer. We spent some time telling secrets, and mine was that we were having breakfast with Kade and that he needed Gray's help with a story. His little blue eyes lit up like the Fourth of July as he clapped his hands excitedly. He threw so many questions out that I couldn't answer any of them. While we got ready for our lumberjack to arrive I answered as many as he could ask, one at a time.

The first question that needed to be answered was, where's breakfast? I gave him the choice and he studied me closely, tapping his finger on his cheek. *I think we should go somewhere grown up. You like coffee for breakfast, so who has good coffee?* He'd asked me and I smiled. That was my boy, always worried about his momma and what she liked. I told him his favorite ice cream place had coffee, along with some really yummy-looking chocolate chip muffins that were just waiting to be tasted. When Kade arrived, he informed him very grownup-like to drive us to The Warming House. It was the opposite side of town, but Kade assured me we had plenty of time, so off we went for coffee and muffins. I insisted we take my Equinox this time, so we didn't have to transfer his car seat in and out.

At seven, most kids aren't in a car seat anymore, but Gray doesn't weigh enough to be in a booster with a seat belt, so I had little choice. I want him safe, and he doesn't have the body strength most kids his age do. I had acquiesced and gotten a new toddler car seat that had a Batman cape, full Batman figure on the seat and Bat hands that were cup holders. When it arrived by

UPS, Gray had refused to get out of it and insisted it stay in the house so he could watch Batman with Batman.

"You were right, the scones were delicious," I admitted on our way up Highway 61 to Esko.

"They must have been. You ate the whole thing." Kade glanced at me from his spot in the driver's seat. I had agreed to let him drive since I wasn't familiar with where his appointment was.

I patted my tummy. "I won't need lunch, that's for sure. How about you Gray?" I turned to the backseat, and he was reading The 39 Clues. He glanced up and smiled at me.

"I'll need lunch. Can we go back and get another smoothie?"

I blew him a kiss. "No, but nice try."

He giggled and then went back to his book. I turned back to the front. "He loves smoothies."

"I noticed." Kade smirked as he drove. "I thought you were kidding when you said he would drink the whole thing, but you weren't."

"Nope, that's my boy. As long as you give it a unique superhero name, or tell him it will give him superhero powers, he's all in," I whispered.

"You bribe him to eat healthy by telling him it's what Batman does?" Kade asked, his mouth hanging open, but the sparkle in his eye gave him away. He was just messing with me.

"I'm sure Batman does eat healthily. I mean, good heavens look at him. He's got more muscles than, than, than." I gave the palms up. "Anyone I know."

His left brow and right cheek went up. "How do you know? Maybe I have muscles. Do you want to check?"

My eyes went wide. "That's a trick question and either answer is wrong." I dropped my head into my hands and shook it a little.

His hand started rubbing my back patiently. "It wasn't a trick question. I was just joking around. I'm sorry for making you uncomfortable." He removed his hand from my back, and I sat up. I looked out the window, so he wouldn't see my reddened cheeks.

"Batman has a lot of muscles, Momma, but Hulk has more," came a voice from the backseat.

"Thank you, Gray," I managed past the dryness in my throat and pulled my thermal take-out cup from the cup holder. I sipped my coffee slowly, mostly to keep my mouth busy from saying something stupid again.

"It's so weird riding in the passenger seat," I said offhand and he glanced over at me for a split second then back to the road. "This is the first time now that I think of it."

"Sit back and enjoy it. We're almost there, only a few more miles." He turned right by the high school, and wound through the homes.

"Where are we going anyway? What is the story about?" I asked for the third time this morning and again he didn't answer. The car came to a stop in front of a brownstone home, with a neatly clipped yard raked of leaves. The few that had fluttered down from the trees lay here and there helter-skelter. The front steps were surrounded by wrought iron railings and the windows were framed in white.

"We're going here," he answered finally, unbuckling his belt and turning to Gray. "Stay there, buddy. I'll get your walker."

Gray unbuckled his harness and I climbed out of the car and pulled the back door open to help him scoot out. He waited at the edge until Kade handed me his walker, then I lifted him down and stood him in it. Kade led the way to the front door and we waited at the bottom of the stairs while he rang the bell.

The door was opened by an older woman, her golden-brown hair spotted with grey, and her hands gnarled with arthritis. "Hello, Kade, so nice of you to come today." She noticed us standing at the bottom of the stairs. "And you brought friends."

Kade smiled sheepishly. "I hope you don't mind, I thought Gray might like to play with the pups while we talk."

"Kade Franco, you know I never mind. The pups will be happy to have someone to play with." She glanced at Kade and then back to us.

I took the two steps quickly and stuck my hand out. "I'm Autumn Hanson, and this is my son Gray." I smiled and Kade snapped to attention.

"I'm sorry, yes of course, I should introduce you. Autumn this is Kat Franco. Autumn is an orthopedic surgeon in Cloquet," he explained.

Kat smiled and shook her head at him. "He's always been a knucklehead this boy. I'm his Great Aunt Kat, though you wouldn't know it with my youthful glow."

Kade laughed at her as she patted her page-boy cut and then motioned to the ramp. "He can use the ramp."

I stepped down the stairs. "I'll just lift him." I was about to pick him up when Kade grabbed my arm. "Here, let me get him."

He handed me his camera bag and Gray wrapped his arms around his neck. I didn't like how natural it looked, and how easily he swung him up into his arms. His biceps barely bulged with the added weight as he held Gray close to him, protecting him as they went up the stairs. I hated it and loved it all at the same time. He carried him into the house and I brought up the rear, folding his walker so it would go through the opening. I tried not to feel uncomfortable, but it was building inside me. We were going into his aunt's home and I was definitely the underdog here.

I closed the door behind me and took my shoes off on the mat, just like Kade did. "I'm sorry if you weren't expecting company," I began and she patted my hand.

"No, I love company. Especially your kind of company." Her eyes moved to Gray, who was on the floor with two puppies already crawling over him, his giggles ripe in the air. I noticed his shoes and cringed.

"I'm sorry, I can't take his shoes off, they hold his braces on." I was agitated that Kade hadn't told me where we were going so I could prepare. I didn't like being in someone else's home and not being able to respect their rules.

"Kade Franco, you haven't told her, have you?" Kat scolded him and he flashed his Mr. Puddlemaker smile. She shook her finger at him. "That smile doesn't work with me. It might work with her, but it doesn't work with me."

"It doesn't work with me either," I sang, even if it was a lie.

Kat raised a brow at Kade, but addressed me. "Don't worry about the boy's shoes, Autumn. They're probably cleaner than the paws on even one of those pups. Please sit, if you don't mind dog hair." She motioned to a couch.

"A little dog hair will never hurt anyone," I assured her, sitting on the small loveseat, so the couch was open for Kade and Kat. A small red pup ran over and pounced on my feet, before tumbling off and doing a somersault toward Gray.

His giggles floated through the room as the pup rolled into his arms. "Momma, did you see that? He was like an acrobat!" he squealed and I couldn't keep from smiling at him as he let the pups kiss his face.

"What kind of pups are they?" I asked Kat, distracted by a golden one running at me full force.

"They're golden retrievers, the last two of my last litter. I'm hanging up my vest and will live out my days with just a few dogs of my own now," she answered as her eyes strayed to the corner where a larger dog was laying, its eyes following the pups, but not joining in.

"Hanging up your vest?" I asked, wondering what she meant. The bigger dog caught Gray's attention and he frog crawled over to where it was on the bed. With its large head resting on its paws it looked asleep, but its red hairy brows moved up and down, giving away its attention to what was going on. "Gray, I don't think you should pet him," I said urgently, and he turned to look at us.

"It's okay, you can pet him. He loves little boys," Kat said. "He would never hurt you."

That was enough of an answer for Gray and he patted the dog on the head, running his hand down each side and over his ears. I could hear him introduce himself to the dog and the dog's ears perked up as he spoke. The dog's coat was beautiful and glistened in the morning sunshine streaming in the patio door.

"Is he the pups' dad?" I asked, the logical answer being yes, but Kat shook her head no.

"No, he's about four years old, but not their dad." She pointed to the backyard where another dog was resting in the sunshine on the grass. "That's their mother. I pay for stud service when I want a litter."

"I see, well they're all beautiful dogs. I'll stop asking questions. Please do your story, Kade. I'll just keep an eye on Gray."

Kade already had his camera out, snapping photos of the dogs and Gray. I looked back and Gray was talking to the big dog again who had rolled over to its side for a belly rub. Gray was singing about him being a good dog, asking if he liked his belly scratched. Pretty soon the dog was all the way over on his back, feet in the air, listening to Gray laugh as his feet moved with every belly rub. My son wrapped his arms around the dog's neck and got a big, wet tongue lick up the side of his face. Kade was in front of me now, kneeling down snapping pictures of the dog as he stood up and gave a big shake. Gray squealed as the hair flew every which way. I couldn't help but laugh at his joy in the simple things like a dog wanting to play.

Gray was still frog sprawled on the floor and scooted around to look at us. "What's his name, Ms. Kat?"

Kat smiled. I couldn't be sure, but it looked like she was trying not to cry. "Just call me Aunt Kat, sweetheart, and his name is Ace." The way her voice cracked on his name told me I was right.

Gray clapped his hands. "Momma, Batman and Robin's dog was named Ace! Ace the Bat Dog, remember?"

I nodded in agreement, but stood and sat next to Kat. She was sad suddenly and I wanted to offer her comfort. "I do remember, Gray. Why don't you tell Ace all about Bat Dog?" I encouraged him, settling an arm around Kat's shoulders. She patted my knee gently and her hand shook a little with the motion. Gray spun back around to Ace and started chattering away. Ace watched him closely, turning his head one way and then the other. Kade was still snapping pictures, having gone to the patio door to shoot from that angle.

"Are you okay, Kat? If you don't want him to play with Ace it's okay, I'll distract him with the puppies," I assured her. I tried to stand, but she kept her hand on my knee.

"I'm fine dear, and don't even think about taking him away from Ace. This is the first time in two months that dog has done anything but stare out the patio door."

I turned back to Gray just as Ace grabbed the back of his shirt. I reached out and tried to jump up, but she held me there and put her finger to her lips. My eyes were locked on my son, the dog's jaw gripping the back of his Spiderman sweatshirt. Gray's eyes were laughing and I knew he wasn't scared. The dog stood slowly, until Gray was standing on his feet and then he let him go, stepping in front of him so Gray could hold onto his big neck. They walked toward Kade, Ace moving at a speed Gray could keep up with, until they reached the patio door. Kade slid the door open and I moved to object, but Kat's look hushed me.

"But there are stairs!" I realized and jumped up. I ran to the door where Kade caught my arm.

"Watch," he said in his gentle voice and I stopped mid-step. They were on the deck at the stairs and Ace nudged Gray. When Gray didn't move, he nudged him some more in his belly and his leg with his long nose. Pretty soon Gray didn't have a choice but to throw his leg over the dogs back. He instinctively held onto the dog's neck and they went down the stairs one, two, three. In the yard he walked around, Gray still on his back, and I could hear Gray pretending to be Robin, riding the back of Ace the Bat Dog to save Gotham City. I looked to Kade, and he had that smile back on his face with his camera to his eye.

Ace finally stopped his walk around the yard and lay down. Gray slid off his back and lay next to him. The mom of the pups watched over the two of them as Gray talked and Ace kept licking Gray's face every so often.

"Autumn, they'll be fine out there. Ace will take care of him and the yard is fenced. Come sit. You too, Kade," Kat said from the couch. Kade reluctantly lowered his camera and put a warm hand on the small of my back. It went against the mother in me to leave him out there, but I could see them from the loveseat where I sat. Kade settled in next to me, and the warmth of his leg through the denim strangely comforted me and scared me at the same time.

"You lied to me," I started, but Kade shook his head.

"No, I didn't lie to you. I came to do a story for the *Our Neighbors* section of the paper about my aunt. When she says she's hanging up her vest, she means she's going to retire from training service dogs after what, Aunt Kat, thirty years?"

She nodded. "Thirty-three years. I started out training guide dogs, but found as I got older there was a greater and greater need for service dogs for the disabled. It came naturally to me. The dogs and I have a special bond." She held up her gnarled hands and scooped up the red puppy from the box at her feet. "This one is Spike," she pointed to the other pup in the box chewing on a small toy, "and that one is Suzie. I'm keeping both of them. I'll train them to be comfort dogs and go out to the nursing homes, hospitals, and schools in the area. The big girl out there, she's my service dog. I trained her when she was no bigger than this guy here," she explained, rubbing Spike's belly until he fell asleep in her arms, upside down like a baby.

"I understand now," I said, "You wanted pictures of Gray playing with the puppies for the story."

Kade nodded. "I did. There aren't any little kids in the family anymore and since it's a human-interest story, a boy and his dog are always a good combination."

"But that's not his dog." I stood and looked out the patio door. They had found an old tennis ball that was probably once yellow. Gray would throw it and tell Ace to get the Batarang and bring it to Batman. Ace was romping with the ball in his mouth and Gray was laughing his little boy head off.

I sat back down and Kat laid the puppy back in the box. "Ace is a service dog I trained a few years back. He went to live with a family who had a little boy with cerebral palsy. They were a good match and Ace did everything for that little boy. A few months ago, Collin, that was the boy's name, got sick with pneumonia and died. The family couldn't keep Ace because it was too hard on them with Collin gone. They called me and I agreed to take him back until I could find a new home for him, but I haven't found one. He barely eats and lays in front of the patio door most of the day."

I didn't even know the mother, but I felt her pain. Losing a child is like losing part of yourself, and my hands shook on my lap as tears filled my eyes. Kade laid his hand over mine and rubbed my back with the other.

"Are you okay?" he asked concerned.

I took a deep breath and nodded. "I'm sorry to be emotional, but even as a doctor sometimes I can't stomach some of the things that happen in this world."

Kade had his hand on my back, and I focused on the warm spot it left. His hand was so big it went from ribcage to ribcage. I leaned back against the loveseat and trapped his hand there. He didn't make a move to pull it out.

Kat's eyes were focused on the patio doors and a small smile played at her lips. I could hear Gray gleefully encouraging Ace to get the ball. "Ace has a purpose again."

"Excuse me?" I asked, not sure what she meant.

"Service dogs are trained to be the eyes, ears, hands, and feet of their handler. When they don't have their job to do anymore, they're lost. Ace has been lost, but look at him now." She smiled and all the sadness was gone from her voice.

I stood then and went to the patio doors, leaning against the wood frame to watch them. Ace nudged Gray to push the braces underneath him as he stood, and knew the exact speed to walk, so Gray could get to the other side of the yard. Ace had a purpose again, but my son wouldn't be his boy. "What's going to happen to him after we leave?" I asked, my eyes still focused on the scene in the backyard.

There was silence from both of them. I heard rustling and then Kat's hands were on my shoulders. She stood with me, seeing the same thing I was, and then she opened the patio doors. "Ace, bring Gray inside. He needs to rest."

Immediately Ace's ears perked and he turned his body while Gray held onto his coat. He walked Gray back to the bottom of the stairs and repeated the nudging, but this time Gray hopped right on and he went up the stairs and across the threshold of the door. Gray finger-waved as they went by. The dog lay down and my son slipped off his back, then Ace sat at attention. He was regal with his coat hanging down between his front paws, his face turned toward Kat.

"Ace, Gray needs a drink. Get him a drink," Kat instructed and Ace headed toward the kitchen. Not knowing what was going on, I looked around the corner of the door to see the dog pawing open the refrigerator and pulling out a small kid's cup by the handle. He closed the door and carried it back into the room. Gray looked at me, and I nodded for him to take the cup. He pulled the blue handled cup from the dog's loose jaw and patted Ace on the head.

"Thank you, Ace. You're a good boy," my son cooed and tipped the cup to his mouth. Ace laid down right next to Gray, and looked to Kat expectantly.

"Rest time," she said, and he laid his head on his paws, but his eyes never stopped roving the room.

"That's pretty darn impressive." I admitted. I joined Kade on the couch again. "You're an amazing trainer. He knows exactly what to do."

"Momma, I have to use the bathroom," Gray said, his eyes wide from where he sat on the floor.

I looked at Kat expectantly.

"Can he use the bathroom on his own?" she asked.

I nodded. "But I have to get his walker, unless it's upstairs, then I'll carry him." I stood, and she took my hand and pulled me over next to the dog.

"Tell Ace to take Gray to the bathroom," she instructed and I raised a brow at her. "Tell him."

She went back to the couch, and I stared at the dog, who was now sitting at attention.

"Ace, take Gray to the bathroom." It felt awkward addressing a dog like this. The dog nudged my hand with his wet nose, and then crawled next to Gray. My son glanced up at me unsure. "Go with Ace. Send him out if you need help." I didn't know what to say, but that felt like the right answer.

Gray wrapped his arms around the dog's neck and the dog stood, going through the same routine with his braces until he was walking him through the kitchen into a hallway. I noticed Gray walked more naturally with Ace than he did with his walker. His movements were less jarring and his braces didn't knock together like they did with his walker. Ace led him through a doorway on the left and I saw the door swing close, but not latch, with the push of a paw.

"You're sure he'll be okay?" I asked Kat.

"I am now. I was very worried about that dog. I didn't think he was going to come out of his funk. I was certain I was going to lose him from a broken heart." Her eyes shone as she spoke.

"I meant Gray."

"Gray will be fine, too," she answered.

"Autumn, come sit down." Kade motioned and my eyes focused on the bathroom door. "He's okay in there. Ace will tell you if he's not."

I walked back to the loveseat and sat again. I glanced at Kade and then his aunt. They had the same eyes, deep chocolate brown framed by long lashes. "What did you just say? About the dog, I mean. A broken heart?"

She nodded. "It's true. When Collin died, Ace lost his purpose. He's a working dog, and suddenly he didn't have anyone to take care of. You know how good it feels to help someone when you fix their ankle and they can walk again?"

I nodded. "Of course, that's the best feeling. Watching people get back to their life."

"It's kind of the same for Ace. He has to take care of someone because that's what he was trained to do," she explained.

Kade rubbed my knee and it felt good, even if it was a little too natural for my taste. "Have you ever thought about getting Gray a service dog?"

I leaned back against the couch and rubbed my forehead. It was a habit I had picked up in medical school when I had to talk to a patient or family about an uncomfortable situation. "I looked into it once, but I felt like with as much money as is invested in these animals, someone else should benefit from one. I can take care of Gray, so I decided against it. I wouldn't want to take a dog from an adult who really needed one."

"You're right. These dogs can be very expensive. For me, I only have the cost of vet bills, their service dog vests and backpacks as they grow, plus the cost of socializing them. Most of my expenses the last few years have been minimal, as I've collected enough vests and backpacks that I no longer have to buy them. To offset the vet bills and food costs, I breed and sell them to others to train. My pups are sought after for their intelligence. This will be the last litter because Kipper has had three and that's enough. She needs to retire, too," Her eyes drifted to the big dog coming up the stairs. She pushed the door open herself and came in, closing it behind her.

"She's gorgeous," I breathed out. "Why is she so much bigger than Ace?"

"Ace was one of her pups, actually. He was the runt of the litter and I kept him. I intended to keep him just as a pet, but his petite size was perfect for a pediatric service dog. He was so smart, and wanted to do what the other dogs were doing. I didn't have the heart to tell him no. He's turned out to be one of the best dogs I've ever trained. He loved his boy. It was such a sad, sad day when I got that call."

I sat next to her then and put my arm around her. "I can only imagine as a mother of a special needs child. It breaks my heart." Ace came galloping through the kitchen door and stopped in front of me, sitting and laying a paw on my leg. He whined and looked toward the kitchen. I turned to Kat, and he whined again.

"What's he saying?" I asked, and she whispered in my ear.

"Ace, does Gray need my help?" I asked and the dog did a

half circle jump and a bark, waiting at the kitchen door. I stood quickly and followed him while he checked every few steps to make sure I was coming. He pushed the door open with his nose and Gray stood bracing himself on the bars built around the toilet.

"Good job, Ace." He grinned at the dog who then plopped down on his butt next to the sink

"What's up, buddy?" I asked and he motioned to his leg.

"Can you help? My pants and the strap of the brace and bag had a fight."

I giggled at his silly explanation, and knelt down to straighten out his clothes then adjusted the Velcro strap attached to the brace. "Better?" I asked and he nodded.

"Thank you. I need to wash my hands," he answered, grabbing the sink from where he stood, and Ace nudged him with this nose the few steps he had to take. "You can go now Momma. Ace will help me back to the living room."

I ruffled his hair and backed out of the room. The hallway was long and spacious with enough room for a wheelchair and a dog to walk side-by-side. I noticed the bedroom with an adjustable hospital bed as I walked by. It became clear her arthritis was the reason she was retiring from training dogs. I stopped in the kitchen and took a breath before stepping back into the room where Kade and Kat sat. She was answering questions and he was writing on a pad of paper.

"Everything okay?" he asked and I nodded.

"Yeppers, he just had a problem with his brace and his pants. They got in a fight, as he said."

Kade laughed. "I love that little boy. He's so funny."

I tried to look anywhere but at him. The word love and my son coming out of his mouth wasn't something I was prepared to hear, ever, from any man. He was my son. I couldn't think beyond that simple statement. I rubbed my forehead again. "He shooed me out and said Ace would take care of him."

"He will," Kat said, "because now he has a boy again."

I waved my hands in front of me. "Oh no, no, Gray isn't Ace's boy. We're just visiting, but I'm sure he wouldn't mind coming back and playing with Ace again if that would help."

She shook her head. "No, that won't help." Her eyes drifted to Kade and she patted his knee. "You were right, she is a stubborn one."

"Excuse me?" I jumped up, planted my hand on my hip, and kicked his New Balanced foot on the floor.

He laughed a wide open *I'm laughing at you* laugh, while flashing his smile. "We were just talking and I mentioned that you might have a stubborn streak."

"I'm not stubborn. I'm take charge. There's a difference," I replied, the words hot on my tongue.

He was still laughing and shaking his head. "Oh, I'm sorry. I didn't learn that in school. Okay, I'm sorry, Aunt Kat. She's not stubborn. She's take charge."

I plunked down on the loveseat and saw Gray coming back down the hall. He stopped at the entrance to the kitchen and grinned. "See I told ya he would bring me back."

I groaned a little. I was being ganged up on from all directions. "You were right," I said chipper as ever, and he gave me the thumbs up.

"Can we go back outside? I want to throw the ball for Ace."

I looked at Kat and she nodded. "Tell Ace what you want him to do, Gray."

Gray looked at me and I shrugged, not even sure of my own name anymore. "Ace, I want to go outside and play."

Ace promptly pushed the door open with his paw and repeated the steps like earlier until they were on the grass rolling around.

"See, I told you. He just needed a boy again," Kat said smirking. I motioned my finger back and forth between the two of them.

"You guys set me up. Tell me what's going on," I demanded.

Kade set his paper aside and turned to me. "We didn't set you up, but I will admit I knew about Ace. I was here the last few Sundays, and he wouldn't even go for a run with me. That said, I agree with Kat. Look at the difference in the dog since we walked in the door an hour ago. He went from forlorn to frolicking in the grass. How can you deny what you've seen with your own eyes?" Kade asked. I extracted my hand from his and went back to my forehead rubbing.

"I can't deny it. Ace is a fantastic dog, but he's Kat's, not Gray's. Now I feel terrible for coming and making the dog happy, only to leave again."

Kat sighed an exasperated sigh and I looked to her. "He's not my dog. He hasn't been my dog for over two years. Don't get me wrong, I love him. That's why he's here, but I have a dog." She called Kipper who came and lay by the puppies in the box. "Kipper is my service dog and a handler can only have one. If I can't find Ace a home, I don't know what will happen to him."

"Why don't you just give him to a family full of boys? He'll be in heaven."

"It doesn't work that way. He was born with an intrinsic need to help. His whole personality is based around doing what comes naturally to him. Putting him in a house of boys wouldn't work. He must focus on one, and he must have a job to do for that one. I'm sorry to say, but he just might not make it."

"What do you mean might not make it?" I asked, watching the dog romp around the yard. "Look at him. He's full of life running around out there."

"I've had a desperate plea out for someone to take him, but haven't gotten a response. He's too small for most adults and he's already four. It doesn't help that service dogs are hard to place after they've already had one handler. Too many more months of this and he'll slip away." Her words were steely, but her eyes told me how worried she was.

"You want me to take Ace?" I asked the light finally coming on in my mind. Kade started clapping and I gave him a death glare.

"It took you long enough." He grinned and I jutted my hip out again.

"I don't know the first thing about dogs, especially service dogs," I sputtered, throwing my hands up in the air.

Kat sat me down at the table near the patio door. I know she did it so I was forced to watch Gray romping around with the dog as if they had been best friends forever. She took several files out of a file cabinet and joined me at the table.

"Taking care of Ace is simple. Learning to be a handler takes a little bit more time, but you're a smart woman and you're lucky, because Ace is already used to a woman commanding him when his boy isn't. You saw how he came right to you when Gray sent him?"

I nodded. "Yes, now that you mention it, he didn't come to you."

"Because I'm not his handler, you are. Well, rather Gray is, but Ace was trained to connect the relationships. He knows who takes care of his handler, who is okay to be around him, and who isn't."

"How does he know that?"

Kade came and sat down by us with his camera, laying it on the table. "He's a smart dog and my aunt trained him. That's how."

I leaned into his shoulder a little bit and smiled. The idea of taking Ace home was exciting, and scary. I had been thinking about getting Gray a dog for a while now. I just couldn't figure out how to deal with a dog at home all day by itself while he was at school and I was at work.

"I can't leave Ace home all day alone. That's not fair. That's why I haven't gotten Gray a dog," I explained. "Sometimes I work long hours or surgery goes later than expected, then Tina has to get Gray."

Kade stared at me funny and I noticed Kat had the same look on her face. "What?"

"Autumn, Ace would go to school with Gray. As long as you introduce Tina to him and she spends some time with Gray while you're there, he'll adjust to that. He won't be home alone all day. He'll be working." Kade pushed his glasses up on his nose as he spoke. I found it to be distracting and difficult to follow his words when all I wanted to do was stare into those eyes.

I cleared my throat and winced. "Of course, he's a service dog. I'm an idiot." I rubbed my forehead and he reached up and took my hand down again, not letting go.

"You're not an idiot," Kat insisted. "We're throwing a lot of things at you right now. I second what Kade said. All of the important things you need to know as a handler are in this packet." She slid a stapled pack of papers my way, and I flipped it open to read it.

I looked at Kade. "Will school allow him to be there with Gray?"

He nodded. "The district supports service animals that are registered and current on vaccinations."

"Is Ace registered?" I asked Kat, and she held up another sheet.

"He's still registered. If you decide he's right for your family, we'll fill out this form and I'll file it with the proper administration. He'll then be registered to Gray and they'll send you the paperwork he will require. In the meantime, you'll have temporary paperwork from me with his registration as a service dog, just not the previous handler's name."

Kade was rubbing my back again and I focused out the door at my son, now resting his head on Ace's back as he gazed up at the sky. I picked through the packet of papers and read the information on the basic understanding of how a service dog is obtained, trained, and adopted. It explained in detail the importance of developing a bond and went through basic commands. The back was a list of the important equipment the dog must have, as well as a list of numbers to contact for help.

"This is pretty intense. It'll take me a while to learn all this. It says here you're supposed to have multiple training visits and test runs in public before you know if they're a good match." I read from the paper and Kade had his camera to his face again. He adjusted the lens and then handed it to me.

"Look out there." He motioned and I took the camera.

He had set the zoom on the lens so I could see my son's face.

He was burrowed into the dog's coat lying on his big front paw. Ace had the other paw over his stomach and Gray scratched his ears. I lowered the camera to the table and looked to Kat. "You have to tell me how to proceed. I can learn this packet fast, but will it be enough?"

"From what I've seen in the last hour, it won't be a problem. Ace knows his job. He just needed someone to take care of again. I think if you three spend the weekend together with Kade, by Monday morning everyone will be comfortable."

"What? Kade? Why Kade?" I stuttered. No way was I spending the whole weekend with Kade. It was already dangerous territory every time we were together. This was likely to put me right over the edge into his arms, and then I wouldn't want to leave.

"Kade has trained dogs with me his whole life. He knows the ins and outs of what the dog will need as far as supplies, and he can teach you the commands quickly. If you decide to take Ace, I'll come to the school Monday morning and introduce Ace to the class. I'll need to explain to them the importance of not petting him while he's working and that kind of thing."

"Really?" I was surprised she would do that. I hadn't even gotten that far. I hadn't gotten past spending the weekend with Kade.

"I do it all the time. I expect you have his teacher's contact information and can let her know about this development?"

I nodded my answer and tapped my finger on the table. I had so many questions I didn't know where to start. Kade went back to rubbing my back, as I stared hard at the backyard. At my son who was laughing, and at the dog who was kissing his sweet face.

"It's a lot to think about. Take your time," Kade said.

"I'm sorry. You had a story to do." I groaned, realizing we had been here almost two hours and so far, he hadn't asked a single question.

"I've got most of what I need. I mainly came to take pictures and get a few of the important details about exact years training and how many dogs, that kind of thing. I just have to write the story now and send it to Aunt Kat for approval," he assured me.

I squirmed in my chair. I still couldn't decide if I had been set up, but if I had been, could I be angry? Could I be angry that these two people loved my son enough to offer such a special gift to him? To us? Ace would be as much for me as for Gray. He would be a safety net I didn't have right now. A protector when I couldn't be there. Maybe it would give me more peace to drop him off at school knowing he had someone to take care of him all the time. That was the hardest part of being a mother of a physically challenged child, worrying about him falling, or getting hurt, and no one finding him quickly. Worrying that he was scared and alone and I wasn't there to help him. Kade's warm hand fell away as I stood up and went to the door of the patio and pulled it open slowly.

Ace's ears perked immediately and I called out to him. "Ace, bring Gray inside. He needs to rest." The dog jumped into action and soon was carrying Gray through the door. He deposited him on the floor in the living room again and sat, looking to me.

"Ace, bring Gray a towel to wash his hands," I commanded. I wanted to see just how much the dog could really do. Ace walked by me and into the kitchen, tugged the towel off the stove handle, and brought it back. He left again and bounded to the bathroom and when he came back, he had a wet washcloth in his mouth and dropped that into Gray's waiting hands.

"Thank you, Ace," Gray giggled at the dog being a show-off. Gray made a show himself of washing his face and hands then dried them. He held both towels out to the dog. Ace proudly took them and carried them back to the kitchen. He pushed down on a foot pedal, the hamper lid opened and he dropped in the towels. He came back and sat next to Gray immediately.

I laughed then. At the dog, at the boy, and at the crazy situation I had found myself in today. "Rest time," I said through my laughter and Ace bounded into the kitchen where I heard him slurping water from a bowl and then crunching. I heard crunching, loud and clear.

"He's eating!" Kat cheered. Gray excitedly crawled to the kitchen to watch him, far enough away not to disturb him.

Kade picked him up and carried him over to the couch, settling him down onto the cushion and then motioned for me to sit by him. "I think you two have some stuff to talk about." He winked his black lashes at me and I wiped my hands on my jeans.

I sat on the edge of the couch and patted my son's leg. "Did you have fun today?" I asked and he nodded enthusiastically.

"I've had so much fun, Momma! Ace is the coolest dog ever. Did you see all the stuff he can do?" He gazed up at Kat who was smiling wide. "The puppies are cute too, and so is Kipper," he added, using his polite voice. Kat clapped her hands in front of her mouth. "Thank you for bringing us here today, Kade. And thank you, Aunt Kat, for letting me play with your dogs."

My mother's heart swelled with pride at how polite he was being. Kat had her hand over her heart shaking her head. "No, Gray, thank you for playing with Ace. He really needed a little boy to play with."

Ace came through the door and looked at her. She flicked her eyes and he walked over and sat by us. His ears were wet from his water bowl and Gray reached a hand out and absently stroked them. I reached my hand out and stroked his head, too. His coat was so soft it was like velvet. Soon I found myself on my knees, rubbing his neck and under his chin. His eyes were soulful, but bright and quick. They darted around the room, and he took a quick assessment of everything near Gray.

"Did you like riding on Ace's back?" I asked Gray and he nodded. "Was it helpful to have Ace with you in the restroom?"

He bobbed his little head. "Yes, Momma. I know you like to help, but it was nice not to need a grown-up with me. It was pretty cool that he could come get you, too."

I chuckled a little and nodded. "It was pretty cool. Even I have to admit that. While you were outside Aunt Kat said that Ace needs a new home because he's lonely living here. He needs a little boy to take care of."

Gray looked to me and then to Kat several times, his eyes

excited but hesitant. "I'm a little boy still," he murmured. "He could take care of me."

I shrugged my shoulder nonchalantly. "Well, you are a little boy, and you do need someone to take care of you when I'm at work."

He was squirming on the couch, his little butt barely able to contain his excitement. "Can we be Ace's new home?"

I raised a brow and nodded my head toward Kat. "I guess you would have to ask Aunt Kat."

Gray looked up at Kade who gave him the palms up. I noticed Kade was smiling so big his one crooked tooth was peeking out.

Gray wiggled down off the couch and Ace stood up immediately. Gray threw his arms around him and walked toward Kat. He stood in front of her, his arms across the back of the dog and stared up at her. "Aunt Kat, can we be Ace's new family?"

She laid a hand on Ace's head and the other on Gray's hand. "I would love for you to be Ace's new boy."

Gray gripped the dog's neck and cried little happy tears, and he wasn't the only one.

Chapter 8

It was after one by the time we pulled away from Kat's house. To celebrate Ace finding a new home she had ordered Eskomo Pizza and had it delivered, while we went over all the information I needed to know about the dog. Kade was indeed incredibly knowledgeable about training dogs, and I was secretly glad he was driving us to the store. Gray was in his car seat with Ace next to him. He kept his head on the arm of the car seat so Gray could pet him. By the time we got onto the highway they were both asleep.

"He's so happy right now," I sighed, watching them in the mirror I use to keep my eye on him when I drive.

"I think Ace is pretty happy. They make a great pair." He smiled at me, and I nodded.

"I'm not going to get mad, but did you set me up? Did you know about Ace?" I asked, and he stared at me from under his eyebrow.

"As I said, I knew about Ace, and I knew he wasn't doing well. I honestly just wanted some cute pictures of a kid and puppies. I'll admit though, when you were in the bathroom with Gray, I conspired with Aunt Kat to make sure he left the house with us."

He kept his eyes pointed forward at the road as we started down the hill toward Duluth.

"Thank you," I said, and that got me a fast head snap.

"Thank you?" he parroted and I nodded.

"Surprising, right?" I joked. "But I mean it. Thank you. I needed a push, but I think Ace is just what Gray needs to keep him moving toward getting stronger. The truth is, I could never afford a service dog."

He looked at me again and hit the brake a little. "Autumn, you don't pay for service dogs. Did someone try to get you to buy a service dog from them?"

He was agitated, and I laid my hand on his shoulder. His biceps bulged under my hand, and I pulled it away quickly, not sure what had gotten into me. "No, but I was reading a website that said they cost about forty-two thousand dollars. I don't have that kind of money to spend. I mean I make a living, but his braces and equipment are expensive, and the insurance doesn't pay much for them. I couldn't justify that kind of expense."

The lines of his face relaxed a little. "The average service dog can run as much as that to buy, feed, train and such, but they don't sell them. Once they're placed with a handler, there is no charge beyond your everyday costs."

"I probably missed that part. To be honest, I was selling a house, opening a new clinic, and my life was in an upheaval. I probably just used it as a reason not to deal with it then."

He took his hand off the shifter and laid it on my knee. "It sounds like it's been a tough year. I'm really happy Ace was there today. Maybe he'll make you smile more, since I can't."

I glanced at his hand on my knee and up to him. I didn't like that statement. I put my hand over his, fighting against the heat and the way our hands looked together. "You make me smile, Kade. I really appreciate everything you've done for Gray over the last week."

"Gray," he said, frowning a little.

"And me. God, I'm bad at this." I leaned my elbow on the door handle and settled my head into my hand.

He pulled his hand out from under mine and put it on the wheel, pulling us down into the Fitger's parking ramp, and into the handicapped space by the door. He pushed the gear shift into park and turned to me, swiping a hair behind my ear. "You aren't bad at anything, Autumn. I think you're an amazing mom, and from what I've heard, a fantastic doctor. I think you're stressed out and tired, which is clouding your otherwise sharp mind. You have your son's best interest at heart and I commend you for that."

Ace whined in the back seat and I sat up. "Thank you for that, too. I am a little stressed out and tired, but you've helped. Up until last week, Gray and I hadn't done anything fun in a long time. You've taken us under your wing and shown us around the city. Now you've given us Ace. I owe you, big time."

He rubbed one thumb ever so gently down the side of my face to my chin, cupping it with his hand. "No, you don't owe me anything. I told you. We take care of each other here."

"Right, the underdog," I whispered, the feel of his hand on my chin warming every part of me.

"Can I hug you?" he asked and my eyes went wide.

He dropped his hand and sat back in his seat, straightening his hat. "Right, okay, so what's the plan here?" he asked quickly, changing the subject.

I reached over and took the key from the ignition and turned to Ace. "Ace, stay with Gray while I get his stroller," I instructed. Ace nudged his hand until Gray lifted it in his sleep.

I motioned for Kade to join me at the back of the car, and he unfolded his long legs and stood, closing the door behind him. Today he was dressed in a golf polo with the small Pine Journal emblem on the right breast. His windbreaker was half zipped over it, and a Minnesota Twins hat sat perched on his head. I took a step forward and slid my hands under the zipper of the coat until I was against his chest and his arms were around me. He leaned against the tailgate and rubbed my back in wide circles.

"I didn't want the gear shifter between us," I said as explanation. He laughed softly, my head bouncing with the movement. He didn't pull back and he didn't say anything. He just hugged me. It was warm and it felt good to have contact with someone who had no intentions but to offer comfort. I slowly pulled back and looked up at him a little shyly. "I guess that was an inappropriate amount of time for a hug."

He shook his head. "Nope, I have no time limits on my hugs. That one felt so good I could have done it all day."

His words made me feel good, scared, and anxious all at once. I can't get involved with another man. My mind knew it, and my heart had sure as heck better know it, but it wasn't listening. I pulled the hatch open on the back of the car and looked into a little face. "You woke up," I said, and Gray nodded, swiping at his eyes.

"Where are we?" he asked.

"We're at Fitger's, buddy," Kade said, taking the stroller from me and opening it by the back door. "There's this really cool place here that sells everything Ace will need to be your service dog."

Kade had mentioned a new pet shop had opened, and since I didn't own one thing I would need for a dog, I told him we had better go right away. Cloquet wasn't likely to have all the items on that list.

Gray eyed the stroller dubiously. "I don't want to ride in the stroller. It makes me look like a baby."

"But it's Batman," I said a little frustrated.

"It's a really long walk to this store though, Gray," Kade explained.

Gray crossed his arms in front of him and shook his head. "No, I'm not riding in the stroller."

I ran my hands through my hair and sighed. "Can you do it just this once, and then I promise we'll shop online tonight for something better? Please don't be difficult," I begged him, and he bit his lip a little as his resolve wavered about the stroller.

Kade was busy hooking Ace up to the leash and collar Kat had lent us. He looked in on Gray who hadn't left his seat. "I'll show you a trick Ace can do if you get in the stroller."

Gray eyed him to decide if it was a trick. God, I was a terrible mother. He was too old for a stroller, but he wasn't too big for it. Buying him a small wheelchair would be the next step, but I didn't want to buy one until he was a little bigger and had outgrown the stroller. It made sense to me, but he was a kid who was tired of the indignities he dealt with in life.

I went around the back of the car again and took a deep breath, so I didn't get upset with him. It wasn't his fault. During the deep breath I resolved to find a wheelchair for him as soon as possible.

Gray started laughing and when I got around the car again, he was in the stroller and had Ace's leash gripped tightly in his little hand. Ace was pulling him through the door while Kade steadied the stroller over the bumps. I hit the lock button and jogged to catch up. They were waiting at the elevator when I came in the door and I mouthed *thank you* to Kade. He smiled and took my hand, leaving them hanging at our sides. The ride up to the next floor left us with plenty of ramps to use, so we followed the brick hallway through the maze, past the Brewery store until Gray reined Ace to a halt at the bookstore. "Look, Momma, they have the new Origami Yoda book."

They indeed had the new book of his favorite series and I bent down next to the stroller. "Because you're being a good sport about the stroller, when we're done at the dog shop we'll stop back here. Let's get Ace a good harness so he can go in the store like a true service dog. Okay?"

"Okay!" he exclaimed and then remembered what Kat had told him. "Ace, walk forward."

Ace pulled the leash taut again, and we went up the ramp to the store called *A Place for Fido*. I glanced at Kade. "Guess we're in the right spot."

He put his hand on the small of my back, as Ace pulled Gray in the doors, stopping in front of the counter. The pretty blonde behind it smiled at my son. "Welcome to A Place for Fido. Can I help you find anything today?"

She came around the counter and looked at Ace and Gray, then back to me. "Service dog?"

I nodded. "How did you know?" I asked. He wasn't wearing anything but a collar and a leash.

"It's the way they sit when they're working. He's protecting him from me. He hasn't been told I'm not a threat to his handler," she answered, taking a step back to show she wasn't a threat to Gray.

Kade jumped in. "Of course, I'm sorry. It's the first day with the dog," he explained. He knelt next to Gray and whispered to him.

Gray dropped the leash on the floor. "Ace, rest time."

Ace immediately went to the water bowl for a drink and then looked up eagerly at the clerk. She laughed. "Can he have a treat? We have all-natural treats with no wheat."

I realized very quickly I was out of my element here. I didn't even know what that meant. "Sure. That would be fine." I smiled and she handed it to Gray to give to the dog. He chomped it happily and Gray grinned.

"We just picked Ace up from Kat and we need some gear and some food," I explained.

She was petting Ace's head and glanced up. "Oh, this is one of Kat Franco's dogs?"

I nodded, and Kade stuck his hand out. "Yes, I'm Kade Franco, her nephew."

"And that's Ace!" Gray exclaimed, his voice so full of excitement he was wiggling again.

The clerk got down on one knee next to the stroller. "Ace, hmm, did you know Batman had a dog named Ace?"

Gray's eyes widened to the size of saucers. "How did you know that?"

"I have a little boy who loves Batman, too. He's four," she explained.

"Do you have any Batman gear?" Gray asked.

She tapped her finger on her lip and walked to a shelf where leashes and collars hung. She pulled down a leash and brought it over. It was black with a string of yellow running down the middle.

"Does this fit the bill?" she asked, and Gray nodded excitedly.

"What else do ya got?" he asked, and I knew this was going to be a long and expensive visit. I didn't care if it emptied my bank account. Spending the afternoon with my son and Kade Franco was worth every dime I had.

Chapter 9

I sat on the deck in the beautiful night air and listened to the crickets chirping. October was here and the nights cooled quickly. I pulled my Sherpa jacket up around me a little bit more to fend off the chill. We had left Fitger's hours ago and filled the back of the Equinox with all of Ace's supplies. I'm pretty sure A Place for Fido had a good day today, but then again, so did I. A surprising and completely unexpected day, but a good one all the same.

I never expected when I got up this morning to come back with a dog, an ecstatic little boy, and a sexy man that had me out of my element. Grayson ate his favorite chicken nuggets while Ace slept in his new bed, covered in Gray's little Batman blanket that was too small for him now. He insisted Ace needed it so he wouldn't get cold. I had to admit it was pretty cute, and we certainly didn't want Ace to get cold. After supper, I had given Gray a bath while Kade walked Ace. Then we spent the next hour going through commands and learning the important things about having a service dog. We didn't buy a typical guide dog harness, since Gray is so small. The bulky handle wasn't going to work, so we bought a harness, yellow and black being the only acceptable one, of course. This would allow him to hold onto the straps instead of Ace's coat. Adding the backpack and the service dog patches had rounded out the ensemble.

As promised, Gray got to try out the new harness and walked into the bookstore with Ace, all the way to the kid section to get his book. He was so happy, excited, and independent that I even let him get a miniature stuffed Spiderman on the way out. After our learning hour, Gray had politely asked Kade to read to him from the new book. He only lasted a few pages before he drifted off to sleep with Ace sprawled out next to his bed. When I checked on them a few minutes ago they were snoring in harmony.

That left me to deal with the sexy man part of the equation. He was currently in my kitchen making dinner. He moved about so easily in my home I had to leave the kitchen while he cooked. It was too comfortable having him in my space. He was wearing my oven mitts, drinking from my glasses, and reading bedtime stories to my son. I liked him too much already and his way of ingratiating himself into my life raised my hackles. I shook my head and leaned back, tossing my feet up on the chair opposite me.

Who are you kidding? Your hackles aren't raised. You're just scared to death you're going to start trusting him, and he's going to ditch you like every other man you've ever known, from your father to William.

I sighed at the voice of reason in my head. It wasn't as if I hadn't learned my lesson. Maybe not the first or the second time, but the third time was the charm. My life had turned out to be something I never expected when I was eighteen, or twenty-four, or thirty-six. At forty I'm a physician, a single mother, and everybody's friend. I thought about it for a few moments, and realized I actually didn't have many friends. I had Tina, Phoenix, Nick, Grant, Carla, and that man in the kitchen. I was pathetic, that's what I was. I'm sure there was some psychological name for this. What do they call it? Attachment disorder or something? I don't know. I call it being burned too many times.

I stared at his silhouette through the kitchen window. We could be friends, I told myself. I could enjoy his smile and his hugs. He could take us to breakfast and football games as a friend. He was just being nice this weekend when his aunt dropped this in his lap, I told myself. I would send him home after church tomorrow, so he could write his article and go back to his life. I wouldn't monopolize the whole weekend, but I did want him to help me take Ace to church for the first time. My confidence level was still somewhat low when we were in public with the dog.

The part I was skipping over was the part about him spending the night. I have a guest bedroom, but don't even have a bed in it since I have no guests. Pathetic, I know. Church is early though, so it would make sense for him to stay here. Oh, but he doesn't have any clothes here. Perfect. He needs to go home, and then he can come back early tomorrow morning. That's the perfect solution. So why did I feel disappointed instead of relieved?

Probably because you're having a nervous breakdown. You're every psychiatrist's dream right now.

He opened the patio door before I could tell my inner voice to shut up. "Dinner is ready. Are you hungry?"

I stood and stepped through the door. I tried to brush past him, but he snagged my arm. He pulled my jacket off, hung it on the handle of the patio door, and pulled it closed. His hand brushed my back, and he used it as a hook to pull me to him. His other arm came around me, and I laid one hand on his chest. The muscles underneath told me what I already suspected. He worked out and he could hold his own against Batman.

"You smell so good all the time," he whispered.

"So do you," I admitted.

"I'll tell you mine if you tell me yours," he promised against my temple.

"Yours is Old Spice. The real kind. The one in the bottle with the little metal tip."

"How did you know?" He kissed my temple, and my heart skipped a beat. Maybe it wasn't from the kiss, maybe I was having a heart attack. That was it. I was having a heart attack.

"My grandfather always wore it to church on Sunday."

He blew out a breath. "Are you saying I'm old?"

I laughed and patted his chest. "No, I'm saying you smell good. I looked forward to church every Sunday, so I could sit by grandpa. Mine is called Forever Sunshine."

"I've never heard of that, but I really like it."

"It's just a simple body spray. As a doctor, I can't go around smelling like a French whore. Some people have strong allergies."

"A French whore? You make me laugh, Autumn." He was laughing, and I liked how it felt against my cheek.

I glanced up at the same time he looked down. I reached up and took his glasses off. I don't know why, but I wanted to see his eyes. I wanted to see the truth in them. I wanted to see if this was all just in my imagination. His eyes closed and his long lashes brushed his cheeks as he lowered his mouth to mine. Against my will my eyes drifted closed and I held my breath until his lips met mine. They were soft and warm, just like his hands around my back. I stretched up on my tiptoes, my breasts pressed against his chest, and his warmth making them tingle. I ran my hands up until they were tangled in his hair, the way I had wanted to do since the first day I met him in my office. He angled his head and deepened the kiss, holding the back of my neck tenderly. He pulled back and I heard myself whimper when his lips left mine. I left my hands in his hair and rested my forehead on his chest.

"You're beautiful," he whispered against my hair. I slowly unwound my fingers, reaching up and slipping his glasses back on his face.

"You're a great kisser," I whispered back. He pulled me into him, holding me so tightly I had to hold my breath. Finally, he released me with a reluctant sigh.

"I'm sorry if I overstepped. Your lips have just been taunting me all week, all day, every minute." He ran his finger across my lips when my tongue slipped out to wet them.

"It's your eyes in my dreams all week that have tortured me." I smiled timidly and he pinned me with the puddlemaker smile.

"I'm glad it's not just me then." He slung his arm around my shoulders and walked me to the kitchen. "We better eat before the food gets cold."

I sat down at the table and put my napkin on my lap. He turned to get our plates and my hand went to my lips, still warm from his kiss.

I brought the glass of wine to my lips. The chardonnay was crisp and left your palate coupled with apples and pears. It was a nice way to end the meal of fettuccini alfredo, which he had made from things I didn't even know I had.

"That was wonderful. Thank you for cooking tonight. I'm awfully tired."

He turned from the sink and laid the towel on the handle to dry. He picked up his glass and the bottle of wine then motioned for me to follow him. I carried my glass with me to the living room where we sat on the couch.

He picked up the wine bottle after I settled in and topped off my glass. The wine glistened through the cut glass, and I raised a brow at him but didn't object. The wine was relaxing and I was tired of being wound up tighter than a grandfather clock. The woman in me was so exhausted it took the doctor in me to keep her going. Keeping up this pace with no downtime was becoming a problem, and I planned to address it this week. It was time to adjust my schedule so I could rest, and I wasn't talking about my clinic schedule. I sipped the wine and he rubbed a slow pattern over my calf.

"Can I ask you a question?"

I nodded, twirling the wine glass by the stem. "As long as I don't have to promise to answer it."

He smiled the same smile he did in my office that first day. "Fair enough. I want you to know I'm only asking because I care. I don't understand, but I want to." I nodded my agreement, and he set his glass down on the table. "Grayson."

I'd been expecting it. Since he met him last week, he hadn't asked. He was astute, and quickly figured out what needed to be done to help Gray without me telling him. Now I know why. He had worked with the disabled for all the years he helped

Kat raise dogs, and those experiences gave him confidence most people don't have. I would tell him, but how much was yet to be determined. I raised my gaze to his and he had gone back to rubbing my exposed calf.

"He's smart as a whip," he started and I nodded.

"He's seven and reads at a third-grade level. His IEP the other day?" I asked, and he nodded, taking another sip of his wine.

"They tested him and discovered he needed to be moved to third grade for reading and writing. They also felt he needed a more supportive chair at his desk, so they've provided that for him. They've been incredibly easy to work with, and have bent over backward to accommodate him. Did you have something to do with that?" I asked, the wine freeing my tongue a little.

He held his hands up in front of him. "No. I don't get involved in any of that unless a parent comes to the board. No."

"Okay, I had to ask, sorry. I guess I'm just not used to getting things done when problems arise." I rubbed my forehead and blew out a breath, setting the glass down. Enough wine. If I drank any more wine I'd be telling him things I shouldn't.

"Okay, we've established he's smart. I would really like to know more," he prodded. I nodded my head for a full minute, my eyes focused on the grain of the wood in the table. He patted his thighs and stood. "Maybe I should go. I'm going to check on Ace first, but I'll be back in the morning to take you to church. Thanks for taking Ace for my Aunt Kat. I know she'll sleep better knowing he's happy again." He went to step around me, but I stopped him with my hand.

"He's not my son, not by birth. I adopted him when he was just a few months old," I blurted out. He stopped and laid his hand on my shoulder. "You have to understand I don't talk about this. Even Grayson doesn't know."

"I'm not going to tell anyone." He sat back down on the couch and took my hand. "But the story is clearly painful, and I don't want to cause you pain."

"Only one person really knows the whole story. Ugh." I rubbed my forehead. Honestly, I couldn't suck at this more if I tried.

"Tell me about Gray's challenges. That's all I'm really asking, love. I just want to know, so I don't say or do something that would hurt him."

I smiled at him gratefully. "Of course, I'm sorry. I'm new at this."

"Stop apologizing. You have so much on your plate and you do such a wonderful job as a mom. I just want to know how I can help." He smiled encouragingly and my resolve weakened.

"Well, as you can see, he wears braces. When he was a baby, he had very little lower body movement. They told me he would be in a wheelchair for the rest of his life, but as a pediatric trauma surgeon I wouldn't accept that. I took him to therapy, worked with him at home, and slowly he was able to sit up, and then frog-crawl like he was today." I glanced at him and he nodded his understanding. "Eventually the doctors agreed with me that we should let him try to walk. We got custom made braces and a gait trainer. As you can see, he took to it like a fish to water."

"He's a little rock star, like I said," he agreed, and I smiled. He was my rock star and I would do anything to protect him, anything. "And is that it? Just wearing braces and difficulty with getting around?"

I shook my head no. "I mentioned he gets anxious. He used to get terrible anxiety and panic attacks. I refused drugs for him, and instead used lifestyle to manage them. He was little and not in school, so it wasn't as hard to do then. As he's matured, he's gotten better with his anxiety. Now he rarely has any problems, unless he's really scared or hurt. Up until this January, I couldn't even bring him to a clinic without a full-blown meltdown, even if he wasn't seeing the doctor."

He shook his head. "I guess that was probably pretty hard as a physician."

"Like you don't know. Last December he hurt his hamstring when a kid at school was bullying him and he fell trying to get away from him. I couldn't bring him to the hospital, but thankfully one of the therapists was willing to come to the house to see him. Grant worked with him over the last months and now he feels comfortable in the clinic. I think he's finally old enough to understand just because he's in a hospital or a doctor's office that doesn't mean he'll be hurt. He's gone through a lot of hurt in his life."

His lips were thin set. He took my hand and rubbed his thumb over my knuckles. "A kid was bullying him at school? Is that the reason you moved here?"

I gave him the so-so hand. "It was a big factor. All last year he had panic attacks and cried every day before school. He ended up spending the last half of the year in the special education room, just so he felt safe. He wouldn't go on the playground or eat lunch in the cafeteria. That bully hurt more than his hamstring and I wanted a fresh start. Also, I wanted to get out of the hospital environment and the constant on-call requirements. It was time to make a change and Cloquet was in need of a stand-alone clinic, at least in my opinion."

"I think most of us here would agree you've filled a void, especially for kids," he agreed.

"I hope so. That's why I'm here. I wanted to give Gray a fresh start. It was the right choice. He's become a different kid in the few short months we've been here."

"He's such a happy boy. I love seeing him. He makes me happy, too." He smiled as his fingers continued to rub my knuckles.

"I'm always smiling when I'm around him. He has so many challenges, but he never quits trying."

"That's for sure. Did you see the way he was determined to walk all the way to the back to get that book today, even when they had a display up front?" He shook his head a little and I smiled. "Can I ask one more question? Why is he so small?"

"We really don't know why he's small. We don't know anything about his uterine development or his mother's nutrition. We only know he was six pounds at birth. With the damage to his brain, I'm sure it's a constellation of reasons. He's healthy though, so we don't worry too much about it. He'll either catch up or he won't, but either way it's just what it is."

"I guess I can understand that. As long as he's healthy, not that I'm worried that you aren't on top of it." He rubbed his hand on his thigh. "I'm kind of bad at this, aren't I? I just care about the little guy ..."

I tried not to make eye contact with him because I was afraid to see how much he cared. "You care about him, so I don't mind that you ask questions."

"I do care about him, and I also care about you, Autumn," he said softly.

I raised my eyes to his, even though I suspected it was a bad idea. "I know. The fact we're having this conversation should tell you just how much I believe that to be true."

He rubbed a thumb down my face for a moment and then dropped his hand to my waist. "Gray is really smart and reads voraciously. I guess the brain injury didn't hamper his learning?"

I tried to drag my mind away from the heat at my waist and back to his questions. "In the beginning it did, but the brain is such an amazing organ. It can recover its function over many years. We started out having to teach something as simple as using a bottle, and as he got older the parts of his brain that controlled learning healed. However, the motor cortex was damaged beyond full repair. The fact that he's walking at all is pretty spectacular, considering what his brain looks like on MRI. Sometimes he'll still take a long time to search for a word that he knows, but can't say. They call it dyspraxia, but he struggles less and less with it."

"So that's all I need to know then?" he asked, holding my hand.

Oh, there was so much more. I had barely dulled the tip of the pencil that would tell Gray's story, but deciding just how many chapters I wanted him to know was hard to do. How much of the story would satisfy him, and how much would have me watching his worn-out Wranglers walking out my door?

"I've been here all day, and I noticed he only used the bathroom at Kat's and then before bed."

"You're observant," I chuckled.

"I'm a reporter. I'm paid to be observant."

I sighed. "He has a neurogenic bladder, which means his brain doesn't tell his bladder to work right, and the muscles don't contract."

"I'm confused."

"He takes medication to help his bladder relax. He used to have a traditional catheter, but he got so many infections I finally found a pediatric urologist in Duluth who would do a suprapubic tube catheter."

"Tell me what that means."

"It's a catheter that goes into his bladder from his abdomen and attaches to a bag. He only has to empty the bag when it's full. We can cap the catheter to give him a chance to try to go naturally. He's doing better, and I'm hoping in the next few years we can get rid of the catheter all together." I picked up my glass from the table and tossed back the warm wine.

"Thank you for telling me. I wouldn't want to be surprised about something he asked me to help him with. You know, if I ever have to help him."

The wine went straight to my head, and I blurted out more. "He also has a shunt in his brain that drains into his belly. They had to put it in when he was a baby to relieve the pressure on his brain and stop the seizures."

"He has seizures, too?" he asked surprised.

"Not anymore. The shunt is still in place, but it doesn't function. I could have it removed, but I haven't seen the need. It's not hurting anything, and I figured there was no sense putting him through surgery if it wasn't necessary."

He was quiet and stared into his glass. I could tell the reporter in him wanted to know the rest of the answers. Maybe it was the wine, or maybe it was just that telling him now was better than telling him in a month, or a year, when he found out the truth and left. The last few weeks had been great, but now it was time to accept that this could go no further.

"His official diagnosis in the beginning was Shaken Baby Syndrome. I worked at Children's Hospital in Minneapolis, and when they brought him in, he was in bad shape. He had a broken skull, swelling of the brain, and facial contusions. We didn't know his name or anything about him, other than he was about two weeks old. The story came out that his mother was killed by his father, and we had assumed it was because she found him shaking the baby. The truth was he killed her in a fit of rage, and then turned his attention to Grayson. He would have killed him if someone hadn't heard the altercation and called the cops." I watched him set his wine glass down and stand up.

He walked past me, his hand falling to my shoulder for a moment before it fell to his side and he walked out the front door. I heard it latch and I blew out a breath. Exactly what I expected would happen. He was the one who asked and now he was doing exactly what I expected him to do. Walk away.

I sighed and patted my thighs. The story always left me exhausted. Reliving those moments when that little six-pound baby lay in front of me, destroyed by someone who should have been his protector, made me want to vomit. It was the defining moment in my career. It was the first time I left the room and cried in the bathroom until the next patient came through the doors.

I stood up and stumbled over my own feet to the hallway. Damn the wine, and damn him for not listening a week ago when I told him we couldn't be anything more than friends. The need to see Gray burned in my chest and I opened the door quietly and snuck inside. He was on his side, practically falling out of bed so he could keep his hand on Ace's head. Ace looked up at me with his bushy red brows.

I patted my leg quietly. "Come on Ace, outside."

He stood up, and Gray's hand sensed the movement. "Momma?" He struggled to sit up and I patted his shoulder.

"It's okay, bud. He has to go potty. He'll be right back," I whispered and pulled the blanket up over his shoulder. He drifted back to sleep, and I led Ace down the hall to the patio doors to let him out. I leaned against the railing as he disappeared into the dark and hung my head. When I adopted Gray, I accepted I would never get involved with anyone again. No one willingly walked into this kind of life if they had a choice. I knew it then, and I knew it now. I thought I had accepted it, but sitting on that couch watching his face just now, I realized I hadn't. There was still a small corner of my heart that said I could be a mother to Gray and a lover to a man. That small corner of my heart had no choice but to accept the truth now. I would be a mother to Gray, but the woman in me would remain alone.

Ace climbed the stairs and nudged his nose under my hand. I rubbed his head and opened the patio door. "Ace, Gray is sleeping. Rest time," I whispered to the dog. He padded down the hall to Gray's room and flopped back down on his new bed. His tongue stretched out and kissed Gray's hand that still hung over the bed.

It was time for me to rest, too. We had church tomorrow and now that Kade was gone I would have to figure out how to do it all myself. Nothing new there, I guess. I'd been figuring things out for myself since I was ten. I didn't need a man to take a boy and a dog to church.

I shut the lights off outside and returned to the couch to clean up the wine, in case Gray got up before me. I jolted back in surprise when he was on the couch. His glasses were off and his eyes were soft. He motioned to me and I walked to the couch, my breath held in my chest. He held his hand out and I reluctantly reached for it. His usual warm hand was chilled and I instinctively held it between both of mine until it was warm again.

"It's cold outside," he started to say, and I dropped his hand.

"Yes, it is. Listen, Kade. It's okay. Don't feel like you have to say anything. I get it. I accepted it when I adopted Gray," I started to explain, but he shook his head.

"No, I have a lot of things to say. I'm sorry for leaving, but

I didn't want to look like I couldn't handle my alcohol. I don't know if your bushes will ever be the same again, though," he joked, all while looking pained.

"Are you sick?" I jumped up and went to the kitchen. I filled a glass with ice water and brought it back to him. He accepted it gratefully and took a long drink, but he didn't make eye contact. He pulled a roll of something from his pocket and popped two in his mouth. The wrapper told me they were antacids.

"We'll be fine here. You should go home. Can you drive or would you like me to call you a cab?"

He shook his head to both. "No, I'm not sick, not like you think. I'm sick of men who think violence is the answer to anything. I'm sick of little babies like Grayson suffering because the people who were supposed to protect them hurt them. I'm sick about what that sweet little boy has had to go through in his life. I'm sorry. I'm just sorry," he finished, setting the glass down on the coffee table and taking my hand again.

"It's why I had to quit working in the emergency room. I couldn't stomach it anymore."

He ran a finger down my cheek. "Tell me how you adopted him."

I leaned back and eyed him. He was still here and he deserved to know the truth. "I couldn't get him off my mind, so I went to check on him when my shift was over. I was surprised to see he was holding his own. All I could do was rub the one spot on his belly that didn't have a tube or a bandage. He was in an incubator and hooked to a ventilator. He needed someone to touch him, hold him, and love him. Every night and on my days off, I would go sit with him. Eventually, I could take him out of the incubator and hold him to me. After his shunt was placed, I made it my mission to teach him to use a bottle, so he could get one more tube out. His father was in jail and his mother was dead. I kept waiting for another family member to come forward. A grandparent or an aunt or uncle, but no one did. He was going to go into the foster system and be a lost child. No one was likely to adopt him. He would be moved from foster home to foster home, and the fighter I knew he was would be lost. No one would ever work with him and teach him to sit, walk, or read. He would just exist. I didn't want him just to exist." My words were clipped and forced, and he wrapped his arm around my back. I rested on his shoulder awkwardly and tried to calm down.

"Somehow you took him home …"

The reporter in him was great at helping a person tell their story, I realized. "Sort of. I petitioned the county to be his foster mother. I wasn't an approved home, but I was a physician. I got emergency approval for him to live with me due to his medical needs. I had already contacted the county about officially adopting him. With that in mind they agreed he would be better off with me than in another foster home. When I had to work there was around the clock nursing care for him. His father was required to sign off on his parental rights by the court, but I still had to wait for any objection from another family member. During those six months I got the adoption papers ready and after the time was up, the adoption went through. He was mine."

"That takes guts," he murmured and rubbed my arm just below where my t-shirt was. It was a secret erotic spot of mine, and the closer he got to the inside of my elbow, the further into his side I leaned. "There's so much more to the story I know."

I took a deep breath. As nice as this was, it didn't matter. In the end it never did.

"But that's enough for tonight. You're exhausted and you need some wind-down time so you can sleep." He ran a finger over the dark circle under my eye.

"You're staying?" I asked sleepily.

"I told you, I'm not giving up," he whispered, his warm breath blowing across my cheek. I smelled peppermint with a hint of wine and I wanted him to kiss me again. I wanted to close my eyes and be kissed into a stupor, even if in the end there was no place for this to go. I let my head fall back against his shoulder, and my eyes drifted closed. The room darkened as his lips came down on mine. His warmth spread from my lips downward, until all I felt were tingles of electric warmth filling me. I sighed against his lips, not deepening the kiss, just loving how he made me feel.

"So beautiful," he whispered, stroking my cheek until I couldn't pull my eyes open.

∞∞∞

Kade

I groaned and turned over on the couch in another desperate attempt to fit my six-foot-three frame onto the cushions comfortably. It wasn't happening. I was too keyed up. I pulled my glasses off my face and closed my eyes, praying for the images to stop reeling through my mind. The images of a tiny baby, barely clinging to life and the woman charged with keeping him alive, mixed with the image of that baby now sleeping in his room clinging to his dog. Nothing angered me more than the thought of a parent harming a child in such a devastating way. Their own child, someone who was part of them, it was beyond anything I could even comprehend.

Watching Gray and Autumn together today I knew they had rescued each other. I didn't have it figured out yet, but there was more to her story. Something happened in the last seven years that left her this jaded.

I let my hand fall from my eyes to my stomach, and thought about the feel of her against me as I carried her to her bed. She let me kiss her again, and when I pulled away, she was half asleep. I rubbed her thigh in wide circles, until she was sleeping deeply. It was the first time since I met her that I didn't see the mask of wonder mom she always wore.

For the first time, I saw the woman she was. She was youthful and beautiful. Her face was devoid of lines in her sleep, and her lips were still slightly puckered from our kiss. I had traced them with my finger, and she didn't move, even as I gave myself the pleasure of running one hand through the curls resting at her shoulder. I wanted nothing more than to lay down with her for the night.

Before I could do that, I had to figure out what she was hiding. Until I knew that I wouldn't stand a chance at winning her heart. Time to revert to being the Man of Steel, and show her even Wonder Woman was no match for me.

Chapter 10

Autumn

It was an unusually warm October day and I needed to feel some sunshine on my back before the cold Minnesota winter set in. I left my car parked in the hospital employee lot and walked the three blocks to the clinic. The air was crisp and you could smell just a hint of Sammy's Pizza floating through the air. The leaves on the sidewalk crunched under my feet as they had started to fall from the cool nights.

One of those cool nights was Saturday and we missed church on Sunday. It was a gloomy day, and we overslept, all tucked up warm in our beds. I remembered Kade carrying me to bed and covering me before he slipped from the room. Ace was the one to wake me when he licked my hand until I followed him to Gray's room. He was waiting for me with a bright smile and lavished praise on his new friend.

I had no idea if Kade had stayed or not, but my stomach did an unusual happy flop when I found him on the couch, half covered with an afghan from the back, and his stocking feet hanging off the end. His glasses hung in his hand, and his long lashes fanned his cheeks. Since it was too late for church, I let him sleep, and got ready for the day. He joined us at the table for breakfast but apologized over and over for oversleeping. Then he did the most unusual thing. He offered to take us to his church.

I stooped and picked up a red maple leaf, remembering how Ace and Gray had gone on a leaf hunt, searching for the perfect ones. Kade drove us to Dunlap Island by the river and we sat at the banks near where the big voyager stood sentry over the city. Kade told me about his early life growing up there with his Aunt

Kat. He joked with me, saying he called it the Church of Aunt Kat. They spent every Sunday there at the river when it was nice out. They picnicked, prayed, and as he put it, he learned how to be a man.

In the winter his church was at nursing homes and hospitals, where they would take one or two dogs in for the residents to pet and love on. He had lived with his Aunt Kat from the time he was about two. His parents decided that raising a child was cramping their *hippy* lifestyle. Apparently, they had intended to leave him only for a month or two, just long enough to protest another injustice, but had never come back. Didn't I know that story all too well? Kade told me Kat tried to find them, but it was as if they had fallen from the planet. He surprised me when he said he still loved them for one simple reason. They gave him a good life when they dumped him on his aunt's doorstep. He would never complain about that. When he graduated high school and left for college, Kat had moved to Esko to have more space for the dogs.

While Ace and Gray played ball, he even got me to open up about my early life. He figured out without being told that it didn't involve picnics at the river and prayer. When my father left my mother, she became an alcoholic and I was left to my own devices. My grandparents had passed on by then, so there was no one to care for me. Instead, I became the caregiver of my mother. I made sure she got to work on time so we could eat, and when I was old enough, I worked every night and weekend so we could pay the rent. Every month I stashed money in a secret account, and the day of my high school graduation, while she was sleeping off a hangover, I left. I took my suitcase and my diploma and boarded a bus to the Twin Cities. I had been accepted as a pre-med student on a full scholarship there. No one had been there to celebrate that accomplishment with me, but I was still proud as hell to board that bus and leave my old life behind.

He had asked me what happened to my mother, and I told him she had managed to hunt me down. She would beg for money every few months and when I didn't send it, I wouldn't hear from her again for another couple months. Then one day I realized a year had passed since I'd heard from her. I searched the internet and found a newspaper archive of her death notice. It was two lines. Those two lines summed up everything she was on this earth. So that was that. I even admitted to him that I don't trust anyone. He asked me why and I gave him the honest answer. I have no reason to. Trust is learned and it wasn't a lesson my mother ever taught me. The pinched look to his lips as he stripped the bark from a tree branch was his only reaction.

When we got home, I had a message from the district administrator. Somehow Kade had used his position on the school board to arrange a meeting for Sunday afternoon to discuss an all-school assembly about Ace. Kat met us later in the afternoon and the smile on her face made spending the weekend in a fully uncomfortable state all worth it. You could see she was so proud of her dog, and relieved that he was happy again.

Yesterday morning, in front of a whole school full of kids, Gray introduced Ace to them while Kat explained the ins and outs of having a working dog in their school. Kade was there, in a professional capacity, taking photos of Kat and Ace to use in his article. He had postponed it a week, so he would have time to write a follow-up about Ace. That was the last time I had seen or heard from him.

I waited at the corner for a car and ambulance before I crossed the street to my clinic. By the time Sunday morning was over, he knew more about me than anyone before him, and he still didn't know it all. I was relieved I hadn't allowed my worst demons to slip out. At least now if I see him in the community I won't have to turn away in embarrassment.

My fingers strayed to my lips as the wind billowed my white coat out behind me. I could still feel the warmth of his lips Saturday when I kissed him and when he had kissed me. He had initiated the contact then, and now he was stepping back. I had to respect that and be thankful he didn't string it out.

I pulled the clinic door open and stopped at the reception

desk. "I'm early," I declared proudly.

Phoenix glanced up and clapped, then handed me a chart. "Good, because you have an emergency patient in room two."

"We have a hospital. Why didn't you send them there?" I asked, following her down the hallway. I dropped my briefcase by my office, and she had her hand on the doorknob when I caught up.

"Because he refused," she answered, pushing the door open.

Kade was half reclining on the exam table holding a dripping ice pack to his arm. He gave me half a crooked smile, but I could tell he was in pain. "You wouldn't return my calls."

I was at the side of the table in two steps and threw the folder on the counter. "You didn't call," I started, and he held up three fingers on his good hand.

My hand slipped inside my coat pocket and pulled out my phone. There were three missed calls and the ringer was off.

"What happened?" I asked, ignoring the implications of the phone.

"Just a stupid accident. A bundle of papers fell on my arm."

"That's not what I heard," Phoenix sang from the door when she pulled it closed.

I turned back to him and raised a brow. "Patient-doctor confidentiality applies here, but if this is going to workman's comp and you lie, then there will be a problem."

I was inspecting his arm as I spoke, there was no doubt it was broken. The injury was traumatic, too. That kind of break told me his story was just that, a lie.

He was embarrassed and glanced away as I lifted his arm and checked the underside. His teeth were clenched, and his face was etched with pain. "It was a freak accident. The door on the back of the paper truck gave way and came crashing down as we were unloading the truck. My editor was throwing bundles, and it would have broken her neck. It came down on my arm when I pushed her into the truck. I think, anyway. It all happened so quickly."

He grimaced when I laid his arm down. For comfort, I put the ice pack back on gently.

"What you're saying is, you're here for a broken arm instead of your editor for a broken neck?" He nodded as an answer. "That's pretty heroic."

He shook his head and closed his eyes on the white paper covered pillow. "Anyone would have done it."

I was concerned I was losing him. He was ready to pass out and I pressed my knuckles to his chest and rubbed roughly. "Kade, stay with me," I said loudly, my heart pounding in my chest.

He jumped, and his eyes flew open. "If you want to cop a feel, just ask. I'll take my shirt off."

I let out a breath, unnerved by how unprofessional I felt at that moment. I gave him a hard stare and he had the good sense to look contrite.

"Do you think it's broken?" he asked, while I typed into the computer.

"No, I know it's broken. Probably both bones, but I'll know more after x-rays." I hit two more points with the stylus, and then slid it back into the holder.

"X-rays sound painful at this moment," he admitted, and I could see the pinched line around his lips. It was a higher degree of the look he had this past Sunday and it helped me understand him a little better. I leaned against the table and laid my hand on his belly. It was far more familiar than I should be with a patient, but I didn't like to see him in pain.

"I think you should go to the hospital. They can offer pain control there. The best I can do here is Tylenol with codeine."

He shook his head firmly. "No hospital."

"Why?" I asked perplexed. With the break he had, I could only imagine the pain he must be in.

"Because they'll call Dr. Goldschmidt and he's not as pretty as you are." He smirked and I was glad to see he still had his sense of humor.

I tried to be professional, but felt my cheeks redden at his words. "First thing we're going to do is give you some medication, then the x-rays. After that, Ruby is going to put a splint on it until I read the x-rays and decide on treatment. You can lie on the couch in my office and ice it while you wait. If I don't like what I see, then you're going to the hospital."

He opened his mouth to object and I held up my hand. "I'll be your attending, but it might need surgery and that requires a hospital."

He grimaced hard and finally agreed to the stipulations.

∞∞∞

I leaned against the door to my office and he waved a little from the couch. "Sorry it took me so long to get back to you." I pushed off the doorframe and moved a little closer to him, but not too close.

"You apologize too much, Autumn. I dropped in on you, and you graciously gave me a comfy place to rest. It's more than I would get at the hospital." He joked around but I could hear his voice was forced and he was hurting. "What's the news, doc?"

"It's not news you're going to like," I told him, and he sat up on the couch, cradling the arm close to his belly.

"Let me have it."

"Both bones are broken, but I think we can avoid surgery." I sat next to him on the couch, and he turned a little.

"How bad is it? Be honest with me."

"I can show you the pictures if you want to see, but to put it in layman's terms, the bones are broken, but not crooked or in pieces. I don't know how you pulled this off. Most adults need surgery when both bones break."

He laughed hard then and it made me feel a little better to hear his voice strong and vibrant. "I bet it was all my muscles protecting the bones." He winked one eye and even as he sat there in pain, I wanted to kiss him.

"I firmly believe you saved someone's life and He cut you

some slack." I pointed to the ceiling, and he laughed a little.

"You might be right. I won't lie though, it hurts like sin. Do we have to cast it?"

I pushed up off the couch. "The bones aren't displaced, so yes, we'll cast it. Even though the arm is still swollen, a cast will hold the bones in place better than a splint. I can't risk them becoming misaligned. We have to be very careful, or you will require surgery."

"I don't want you to do surgery on me." He sighed, and then his eyes went wide when he realized how it sounded.

"I'm more than capable of fixing your arm. It's like you writing an obituary. We can do it in our sleep." I knew it was the pain talking and I didn't hold it against him. I'd been told worse in my career.

He put his head in his hand, and shook it a little. "That sounded horrible. I just meant if you do surgery on me, you'll see parts of me I would much rather show you when we're the only two in the room."

I raised a brow and tried to hide my smile. "I've seen giblets before you know."

"I'm sure you have, but not mine, and not while I'm unconscious."

I lost it then. The giggle snuck out and I slapped my hand over my mouth. He was funny, but part of the laughter was nervous laughter. Just the thought of seeing his giblets when he wasn't unconscious made me freak out.

He stood and got in my face. "Are you laughing at an injured man? That's not very professional, Dr. Hanson."

I held my hand up and tried to catch my breath. "I know, I'm sorry. I'll try harder."

He leaned in a little bit further and his lips touched mine. My hand went to his hair, and when his curls twined in my fingers, I jumped back. "I can't kiss patients," I stammered and he tucked a piece of my hair back behind my ear.

"I'm not just any patient though. Right?"

"No, you aren't. You're a friend and I take care of my friends,"

I answered, nodding my head. I had to try and convince myself of that as much as him.

He hung his head a little and shook it. "How long will it be before you can cast this?"

"Right now. I can do it right now." I walked quickly to the door, mostly to put some space between us.

He moved slowly and kept his arm braced against his belly. "I won't give up, Dr. Hanson."

My steps hesitated long enough for him to know I heard him, even if I pretended I didn't.

Chapter 11

"What are you doing?" I asked, and he turned around, somewhat surprised to see me.

"Buying a book," Kade responded, his smile bright.

"Harry Potter?" I asked, and he nodded. "Two of the same Harry Potter?"

He nodded again. "Yep, two copies of The Sorcerer's Stone."

I was standing in the checkout line at Walmart, and it was late Saturday morning. Gray and Ace were at a friend's house and I was heading over to pick them up. He had spent the night with his friend Chris whose mother was an aide in the special education room. I was extremely comfortable letting him stay there, and it was good for Gray to go out and experience life away from me.

Last night I had been tempted to call Kade, but I didn't. I caught up on housework, sipped wine, and took a long bath. I fell asleep watching The Tonight Show and woke up to Looney Tunes. It was a little like how I felt sometimes. Mature with a side of looney. At the moment my eyes roved over his well-worn pair of Wranglers and thermal Henley, open at the neck and pulled to the elbows, just above the cast on his right arm.

He set the books down on the conveyor belt and I noticed his cast. I set my basket next to the books and motioned for his arm. He held it out and I could get half my hand inside the cast. I glared at him. "I told you if the cast loosened to come in and get it changed," I scolded him.

"Just happened like overnight. It'll be fine until Monday. Hey, where's my buddy?" He glanced around behind me. I was surprised it took him that long to notice I was alone.

"He's at a friend's house for a sleepover. I'm on my way over to pick him up, but first we're going to my clinic for a new cast."

"He's at a friend's house? That's great. I'm happy he's doing so much better here. I'm really proud of him, too. I know he probably doesn't like to be away from you very often."

I knew he was ignoring me about the cast and that was his way of saying Gray's anxiety was improving. "I think Ace has been the biggest help. He's always with him, and if he gets anxious Gray just buries his face in his coat until it passes. Ace is definitely one more thing I owe you for."

He took my hand in his casted one and squeezed it just for a second. "You don't owe me anything. I'm your friend and I like to help."

I pulled his casted hand up. "Right. The underdog." I winked, but wouldn't let go of his arm. "What do you say? You and me and the casting room when we're done here?"

His eyes shuttered and trailed the length of me, in a way that left me feeling beautiful rather than dirty. "I'm in."

∞∞∞

I eyed the Harry Potter books in the bag at his feet. When we left the store, I had herded him to my car, lest he get in his own and drive away without getting his arm fixed. After a quick stop for coffee at Bearaboo, because I'm all about a drive-thru, I called Chris's mom. She was happy to keep Grayson a little bit longer. Kade didn't look overly thrilled when I hung up the phone. He was out of arguments and didn't have a choice but to go with me to the clinic.

"So … Harry? One for every room in the house?" We crossed the bridge over the river and my mind instantly drifted back to last weekend.

He turned in the seat and leaned against the window. "Do you think it's weird that I bought two?"

I tried not to smile. I really, really tried. I knew he was just kidding around, but he managed to make me smile with just about everything. Just about.

"Some might say it's a little odd." I peeked at him from the corner of my eye as I pulled into the clinic lot.

"I'm starting a book club and I needed two copies," he explained rationally. "Does that satisfy your nosy doctor mind?"

I pulled in under the portico and parked. "Not especially," I answered honestly. "You're starting a book club with only two people and you're reading Harry Potter?"

He nodded his head. His brown hair bobbed, and his one crooked tooth smiled at me. I climbed out of the car and unlocked the clinic door, where he joined me. He laid his hand on my back and I moaned a little bit when I rested my head on the door for a second.

"Are you okay?" he asked.

"Yeah, I just realized who's in your book club." I groaned, stepped into the clinic, and flipped on the lights.

"Took you long enough." He laughed while he locked the door behind him.

"Gray's been bugging me about reading Harry Potter. I'm just not sure he's ready for all of that. I don't want him to have nightmares," I explained while I walked backward toward the casting room.

"That's why I bought two. In case you would like to read it first. I've read the whole series, and I'm not concerned. He reads 39 Clues and Percy Jackson. He can handle Harry Potter. I figured if I read it with him, and we talked about the book together, then he wouldn't have any reason to be afraid of it."

He was walking toward me as I walked backward, and it felt like he was a wolf and I was a deer. I turned on my heel and flicked the lights on in the casting room then motioned toward the table for him to sit. I set up the saw and new casting supplies while he waited. "Well, you've thought of everything then."

He shrugged, but didn't look smug or superior. He just looked like he cared. "I did intend to talk to you about it before

I gave him the book, Autumn. I wasn't expecting to see you this morning."

I picked up the saw and laid the cast on a pillow on his lap. "I appreciate your interest in spending time with Gray, and I know he really, really likes you. I think he'll be super excited to be in a book club with you. It's okay by me as long as he doesn't get scared."

I held the saw to the cast and flipped the button. I started to cut through the fiberglass up to the palm of his hand. "It will feel warm, but it won't burn you," I told him as I worked, and he studied me the whole time.

"I really, really like Gray, too. I also really, really like you," he said when I flicked the saw off and set it on the table. I picked up the cast cutter scissors and cut through the padding. I forced my eyes to remain downcast to avoid eye contact.

"I like you too, Kade. I appreciate your friendship," I stuttered, thankful when the scissors cut through the rest of the material, and I set them down. "Okay, I'm going to pull this off, and I want you to slip your arm out, but don't bend or twist it," I instructed him. He did as he was told, laying it back down carefully on the pillow. I inspected it for skin breakdown or change in the alignment of the bones. The bruising was nearly gone, so I warmed a disposable washcloth and cleaned his arm, rubbing it between his fingers and over his palm. "Would you like some lotion?" I asked and pulled the bottle down from the cabinet.

"Anything to make it stop itching," he laughed, and I smiled.

"You aren't the first to say that." I pumped the lotion into my hand and smoothed it over his arm, then rubbed it in carefully. I wanted to avoid the broken area so I didn't hurt him. Then I worked it into his fingers and the back of his hand.

"I didn't know you gave massages." He groaned and closed his eyes. I pulled my hands back and his eyes opened and held mine.

"I—I learned when Gray was a baby. I still have to massage his leg muscles. Um, so it's been five days. Let's take a couple of quick pictures of the arm since the cast is off. We need to make sure it doesn't need surgical repair."

I took two steps backward to the door and then turned away. I couldn't stare into the depths of his eyes any longer. I busied myself by getting everything organized and ready for the x-rays. He strolled into the room and sat on the table with his arm cradled in front of him.

"How's the pain?" I asked in order to fill the silence.

"It's more like an ache," he answered and the tone of his voice made me turn. It only took one look at his face to know he wasn't talking about his arm.

Flustered, I stepped behind the shield and did the pictures in quick succession, then led him back to the casting room. He wiggled his sexy butt onto the table and I wondered what it would feel like under my hands.

Autumn, you're losing your mind.

I closed my eyes and breathed deep. Not enough coffee, not enough sleep, and not enough male contact in the last few years was catching up to me, apparently.

"I love how your cheeks get red when a thought crosses your mind that embarrasses you. I just wish I could figure out what those thoughts are," he mused.

I opened my eyes and his brow was raised. I waved my hand in front of me like a fan. "Nope, I'm just warm. Is it warm in here? It feels warm to me." I opened my computer and flipped up the screen so he could see it. "See this?" I pointed, and he nodded. "That's your arm right after the accident. See this?" He nodded again. "That's your arm today. Your arm is halfway healed already, in five days. I've never seen this before."

He smiled, smugly this time. "They don't call me Man of Steel for nothing."

As though he knew that's what I called him in my mind.

"Who calls you Man of Steel?" I asked the question while I filled a bowl with water. If I didn't make eye contact it would sound like the question was nothing more than making conversation.

"When I was in high school, I would break an arm, and in three weeks I'd be back out on the field. My bones heal fast."

"Must run in the family," I said, picking up the padding to wrap his arm. My hands stopped, and I hung my head. "I'm sorry. I didn't mean it like that."

He lifted my chin with his finger. "I know what you meant."

I nodded quickly and started wrapping his arm. "If you're the Man of Steel, is kryptonite your weakness?"

"Right now, I only have one weakness, and that's the beautiful woman standing in front of me."

My hands stilled on his wrist, and I took a step back to put distance between us.

"Like when I found out she was alone last night and didn't call me."

I rubbed my forehead. "I thought about it," I started, and he gave me his *I doubt it* look. "I did, but I figured you were probably at a game for work."

He held his arm up. "I'm not working, remember? You told my boss I had to take a few weeks off? Come here." He crooked his finger and I gave up trying to keep my distance. Get the cast on and get out.

I walked back to the table and got the first roll of fiberglass, blue, for the first layer of the cast. His left hand encircled my wrist and stopped me from dipping the roll in the water.

"Have I told you how beautiful you are today?" he asked, his voice husky and low.

I averted my eyes from his. "A couple times, but thank you. I wasn't planning to see patients when I got dressed this morning." I motioned at my shirt with my hand and rolled my eyes a little.

Shut up Autumn, you're rambling again.

His good hand traced the lace along the collar of the sheer shirt that tied at my waist, where it met my favorite pair of capris. His finger then traced back up the edge of my jawline to my lips. I instinctively flicked my tongue out to wet them and he groaned. "I'm going to kiss you right now. Your lips fill my dreams and I wake needing more."

He held me tightly between his legs, the table the only thing separating us. He brought his lips to mine, and his hand slid up my back to grasp my neck. He worked his lips over mine until they softened and parted on a sigh. His tongue hesitated at the edge of my lips and I whimpered a little, my way of begging him to let me taste him. Our tongues finally touched and he moaned low in his throat. The vibrations ricocheted to my toes, and I wrapped my hands in his hair, curling it into my fists and holding him to my lips. By the time he pulled his lips from mine I was dizzy from not enough air, but lost with the connection broken.

He leaned his forehead against mine, and his breathing was ragged and heavy. "You have no idea what you do to me, Autumn."

"It's not ethical to kiss patients," I said aloud, to remind myself as much as anyone.

"I'm not going to tell," he promised, his head still resting against mine. "Are you?"

I opened my eyes and looked into his, my mind racing with all the reasons this was, and always would be, a bad idea. "I need to cast that before—before." I couldn't even form a sentence.

"Before you let yourself explore this further?" he asked, holding me to him at the back of my neck.

"This?" I stammered, and he nodded against my head again.

"You and me. Us. This."

"There isn't any us. There's you and there's me. There's a connection I can't explain, but at the same time I also can't explore it."

"I won't give up, Autumn," he insisted, raising his brow high enough I could feel it against my hair.

I leaned back and he finally relented and released my neck. I set my jaw and laid the first roll of fiberglass around his arm. He said nothing, but I could feel the passion radiating off him as I worked. I wrapped a layer of blue followed by a layer of yellow and red. While I worked, his left hand rubbed my upper arm in a rhythm that relaxed me and keyed me up at the same time. I finished and laid his arm down on the pillow. I still couldn't speak. He was too close. Too perfectly imperfect. Too much like what I had always been looking for before Gray came into my life.

I stood at the sink and cleaned up the supplies but sensed him behind me. His cast-free arm came around my waist and rested on my belly and his mouth rested against my ear. His breath was warm and caused goosebumps up my spine. "Thanks for taking such good care of me."

He touched his lips to my neck, and I instinctively tilted my head so his lips could make their way up to my jaw. I turned in his arms then, determined to tell him this had to stop, that this couldn't go anywhere. Then he captured my lips and the spark when his lips touched mine wiped away my determination. When his hand cupped my bottom, I felt things in the one place I didn't know still had feelings. It turned out my heart wasn't dead after all.

∞∞∞

There was a knock on the front door and I dried my hands on the dishtowel. I had left Kade at his truck in the Walmart parking lot and told him I would see him soon. After picking up Grayson, we had chicken wrap and chips for lunch and he was resting on the couch.

I reached the door and saw him through the glass. He was waving the Harry Potter book in his hand like a lunatic. I passed the mirror in the hallway on the way to the door and stole a glance. Yup, I looked petrified. I pushed the screen door open. "Hi, Kade."

He was already smiling. "Hi, babe. Is Grayson home yet?"

Babe?

That sounded far more intimate than it should. Too bad I

liked the way it rolled off his tongue. "He's here. Come in."

I found myself holding the door for him without even thinking about it. He stepped through and followed me down the hallway to the living room.

"Grayson, you have company." I stepped aside, and Kade walked into the room.

"Kade!" Grayson exclaimed, clapping from the couch.

"Hi, buddy. Did you have fun at your friend's house?" he asked and sat down on the couch next to him. He reached out with his newly casted arm to pet Ace on the head.

Gray gasped. "What happened to your arm?"

I noticed he was near tears and Kade did, too. "You didn't tell him?"

I came around the couch and rubbed Gray's shoulder. "No, I couldn't tell him. That patient-doctor thing again."

The light came on in his eyes. "That's true, didn't think about that." He held his cast out to show Gray. "My arm got in the way of a truck door, but no biggie. I went to see your momma, and she fixed it right up." He put his hand to his mouth like he was telling a secret. "She tells me it's almost healed already. She even put this new cast on this morning. Isn't it a beauty?"

Gray nodded his head excitedly. "It looks like a Superman cast. Mom made that?"

"She sure did. You know, they do call me the Man of Steel around here." He puffed his chest out and winked at Gray. I tried not to snort.

"Silly, if you were the Man of Steel, you wouldn't have broken your arm." Gray shook his head like any idiot should know this. I, on the other hand, was still fixated on the cast. While I was busy thinking about how great a kisser he was, I had made him a Superman cast. Fantastic.

"Would you like to be the first to sign the cast?" He pulled a pen from his pocket and Gray signed the name of every superhero he could think of on the cast.

Kade inspected it closely. "Wow, that's the whole Avenger's team. Wait until I show Aunt Kat. She's going to love this."

He looked up at me and I smiled, thankful he cared about my son enough to make him feel special.

"So, guess what I brought ya?" Kade asked, and Gray rubbed his hands together.

"Whatcha bring? Something fun?"

Kade held out the Harry Potter book and Gray took it in his tiny hands. The book was so big he had to use both hands just to lift it to his lap. He laid it there as though it was a bar of gold and his mouth dropped open. "The Sorcerer's Stone," he said on a breath. "You brought me Harry Potter. I've wanted to read this book for a long time. Thank you." He threw his arms around Kade's neck and squeezed as hard as his little body could muster.

I noticed Kade's smile was even brighter as he hugged him, then he set Gray back up against the couch, and pulled out his other copy. "I thought we could do a book club. We'll read it together and talk about all the best parts."

"Can we start now?" he asked happily and I laughed.

"I'm sure Kade probably has a ton of stuff to do, sweetheart." At least I was praying he had a ton of stuff to do.

"Your mom is right. I have something I have to do." Kade shook his head and Gray's face fell a little. "See a friend called me, and he has all these pumpkins he doesn't know what to do with. He asked me if I would come out to his house in Duluth and take some home."

"That sounds like fun," Grayson said politely, but I could hear the disappointment in his voice.

"I guess. I think it's going to be sort of boring if I go by myself. I don't know, maybe you, your mom, and Ace want to go with me?" Kade asked. He glanced up at me and winked. I had one hand on my hip in frustration. He was playing my son against me just to spend time with us.

"Momma, can we go?" Gray asked excitedly. I rubbed my forehead rather than answer. There was no way I could say no when he had already planted the idea in his head. Gray was already tired from his overnight stay and I debated the intelligence of spending the entire afternoon outside.

I sighed and prayed he wouldn't fight the only solution I had. "We can go if you agree to ride in the stroller. There may be a lot of walking over uneven ground, and I don't want any arguments when we get there. That has to be agreed upon first."

Kade stood and held up his finger. "Hang on. I picked something up the other day that might make this a little bit easier for him."

He strode from the room, and I told Gray I would be right back then followed Kade out. I grabbed his shirt by the sleeve and pulled him up short. "What in the hell do you think you're doing?" I demanded.

He stopped, but he didn't turn. He stood stock still and my anger rose with every passing moment of silence. "Dammit, Kade! He's my son. I'm his mother. Don't plant ideas in his head without asking me first. He's already tired and now I have to fight with him about the stroller." My hand sensed the rise and fall of his breath and I let go of his shirt. "I'm sorry," I apologized. "I'm sorry. Everything is coming apart at the seams inside me and I can't hold it all together anymore." I even surprised myself with that admission.

I took a step back and then sank to the front step, my hands going through my hair. He sat next to me and put his arm around me. "You're a great mom and you're doing a great job. I can't imagine how hard it is to be a single mom, but to be a single mom to a special needs child has to be even harder most days. Especially when you don't have anyone else to help shoulder the burdens."

I shrugged and tried to answer, but couldn't. I just couldn't. He held me for a moment and then stood and went to the back of his truck and pulled the tailgate down. He lifted something out, and I had to look twice as he rolled the chair toward me. He parked it in front of me, and then sat back down. The wheelchair was tiny with larger all-terrain wheels for Gray to push. It was black with Batman symbols everywhere, including a huge one on the footplate of the chair, so it would be right side up when he sat in it. It was so adorably cute I started crying. Right there as I sat on my steps, I started crying.

"It's so cute, Kade. He's going to love it. I'm such a bad mother making him ride in the stroller. I should have gotten him a chair a long time ago. He's just so little. I don't want him riding in a chair all the time. That will weaken his legs and I'm trying to make him stronger. It's not an excuse, though. I shouldn't make him ride in a stroller." I swiped at my nose as tiny arms went around my neck.

"I'm okay, Momma. Please stop crying. I'll ride in the stroller without complaining, I promise. Please stop crying." His little voice pleaded in my ear and I held his arms around my neck. Ace licked my face and then lay down next to me with a whine.

"Come here, buddy," Kade's deep voice boomed, and he pulled Gray around and sat him on my lap, so he could hug me tightly. Then Kade wrapped his arms around both of us.

I held my son and stuffed all those emotions that had escaped back into the too small a place I kept them, unless I was alone in the shower or bed. How they escaped I didn't know, but I needed to do a far better job of keeping them in check. Kade's warm arms around me made me feel safe, and that was making it even harder to pretend as if I could keep doing this on my own.

"God, what was I thinking when I thought I could do this?" I whispered against Gray's hair. Kade loosened his arms and tried to take Gray off my lap.

"You don't have to ride in the stroller anymore, bud. I gotcha something else." He pointed to the small wheelchair and Gray's eyes got huge, but he refused to let me go.

"It's a Batman wheelchair," he whispered in little boy wonder.

"It's your wheelchair. There's even a place to hook up Ace, so you can wheel the chair while Bat-Dog walks beside you."

Kade tried to pull him away from me, but he refused to let go, so Kade eased off a little. "It's a very cool chair, but Momma wants me to ride in the stroller, so thank you anyway," my son said politely, then grasped my shirt again in his tiny fists.

I hugged him tightly for just a second and then picked him

up and sat him in the chair, buckling the belt and brushing the hair from his eyes. "I don't think we should let this really cool chair just sit here. Ace, come," I called and Ace was next to me in one second. I handed the leash to Kade, and he showed Gray how to connect him to the special swing arm on the chair.

"Take it up and down the block and see what you think, bud," Kade encouraged him.

Gray gave me a look that said he didn't know if he should, so I smiled. "Go ahead."

He grinned and commanded Ace to walk. They rolled down the sidewalk slowly and Kade sat next to me, his arm clasped between his knees and his head turned to keep an eye on them.

"I overstepped. I can't apologize enough for that. You're his mother, and I shouldn't have stuck my nose in your business. I don't know what I was thinking. Forgive me?"

I shook my head slightly at the situation. "You were thinking you wanted to help. There's nothing to forgive, except maybe my outburst. Look at him. He loves it." I motioned at Gray as he rolled back toward us, a huge smile on his face. He sat proudly and looked so grown up. It made another tear fall from my eye.

"He looks pretty sharp in that chair." He smiled and waved as Gray went by us, still talking excitedly to Ace.

"Where did you get it?" I asked suddenly. "Wheelchairs are a couple grand …"

He laid his hand on my leg. "I put some feelers out and it turned out there were several chairs in the district that needed to be replaced. This was one of them. I bought it from the school."

I'm sure I looked confused. "But it looks brand new."

"It needed some work, I'll admit. When I got it the tires were gone, and the paint was missing in some places. It wasn't safe for the special education room, but with a little elbow grease it turned out pretty nice."

I held up his arm. "I think doctor's orders were to rest."

He laughed then, a deep head back, heartwarming laugh. "This was not in the equation when I got the chair." He shook his cast. "I called up my buddy with a body shop, and for the price of a twelve pack, some new tires, and a great time with Lax, we still got the same end result. It's a chair that will fit him for a long time and one you can get in and out of your car easily. Hopefully the chair takes a little strain off these strong shoulders."

He put his arm around me again, and I couldn't even stop myself from laying my head on his shoulder. "Thank you. I would like to pay you for what you have in the chair, if you'll let me."

He kissed my forehead and I didn't even freak out. "I didn't pay much for it, but if you insist then I would rather you write a check to the service dog organization so other kids can have a dog like Ace."

I watched Ace pulling Gray up and down the sidewalk and I swear the dog was smiling as big as Gray was. "Nothing would make me happier."

Chapter 12

I glanced in the rearview mirror at Gray asleep, his head resting against Batman's ear. Ace licked his hand and whined a little, then lay down next to the chair. We were on our way back into Duluth from the pumpkin patch where we had spent the afternoon picking pumpkins and taking hayrides on the big farm wagon.

"I had no idea your friend was *thee* Maxwell Leonard," I said again, surprised when I came face-to-face with one of the best suspense writers in the nation.

He shrugged. "We went to college together. I've known him so long I don't even think of him as *thee* Maxwell Leonard, but I'm glad it made your day."

I turned left and found myself driving past my old house. "Was I totally fangirling to embarrassment?"

"It was totally the correct amount of fangirling," he assured me.

Not only did I get every book of his signed, but we had the back of my Equinox full of pumpkins and fresh apple cider. His pumpkin patch was on a secluded farm of fifty acres just on the outskirts of Duluth. Gray had a chance to try out his chair, and after all that excitement had fallen asleep immediately once the car started moving. Ace whined again and my eyes darted to the rearview mirror. He was sitting up now and licking Gray's face. I pulled the car to the side of the road in front of the old house.

"Ace, hush, Gray's sleeping. Settle," I commanded and he quieted, but continued to bounce back and forth between his front paws.

Kade pointed at the house in front of us. "Is this a friend's house?"

I shook my head. "No, it's our old house. The one we sold when we moved to Cloquet. I haven't been back since we left." I fell silent, and the memories from the house flooded back through my mind. He took my hand and rubbed his fingers over the top knuckles in support. Ace barked loudly from the backseat and I jumped. I whirled around to scold him but he was licking Gray's face. Then he stood up and licked mine with a whine in his throat.

"What's wrong with him?" I asked Kade. "Does he have to go out?"

I found it unusual since we had just been outside all afternoon. He barked again, several barks in succession that raised the hair on the back of my neck. Kade unbuckled his seatbelt and climbed out, then opened the back door. "Come Ace. Break," he commanded, but Ace just barked at him again then growled. He licked Gray's face and pawed at him, but Gray didn't move.

"Something's wrong. I've only seen a dog do this one other time. Something's wrong with Gray," Kade said frantically and climbed into the backseat.

I jumped out of the car and pulled the door open on the side where Gray sat. Ace immediately jumped across the seat and licked his face.

I shook my son. "Gray, wake up, buddy." His head rolled the other direction, but he didn't wake. I noticed his shirt was wet, and I felt his forehead. He was burning up and his cheeks were flushed. "Gray!" My voice was desperate when I shook him. "Gray, wake up!"

I gazed up into Kade's eyes. They were searching mine and filled with worry. His hand was on Gray's forehead, and his face was set in a grim frown.

I climbed into the backseat and slammed the door. "He's sick. Something is very, very wrong. We need to go to the hospital." I aimed for my calm doctor's voice, but the frantic mother voice slipped out instead. Kade climbed over the console to the driver's seat and squealed the tires away from the curb. I was never happier that we were only minutes from the hospital. I prayed then, long and hard, that He wouldn't take my son from me, too.

∞∞∞

"Dr. Hanson?" I turned from Gray's bed and saw a young man in scrubs with a chart in his hand.

"Yes, I'm Dr. Hanson," I answered quickly. He came forward and set the chart at the foot of Gray's stretcher in the ER cubicle. The one we had been in for the last hour.

"We have the results of his blood work and urine test. He has a raging urinary tract infection. Has he been complaining of any pain?" he asked, and I shook my head.

"No, up until a couple hours ago he was his usual self," I said surprised.

"When was the last time his catheter was changed?" he asked, checking Gray's blood pressure and temperature.

"I changed it Thursday, no wait it was Wednesday night. It didn't want to go back in easily, though. It was like the stoma wanted to close almost instantly, but I finally got it."

"That would be about right then if you changed it Wednesday and today is Saturday. He has an extremely high number of white cells in his urine, so we need to treat him for the infection." He was hanging a bag on the I.V. pole next to Gray's fluid bag. "We'll treat him with ampicillin since it's a catheter infection, and the I.V. fluid bolus will help."

An arm slipped around my waist and Kade's body pressed up against my back. A catheter infection was not uncommon, but he hadn't had one since we switched to an external catheter. I was about to ask more questions when Dr. Collins walked into the cubicle.

"Hi, Autumn," he said, immediately moving to the bed to assess Gray.

"Dr. Collins. He shouldn't be this sick just from an infection. What else is going on?" I demanded. Dr. Collins was Gray's pediatric urologist, and I trusted him completely.

They had to sedate Gray as soon as we arrived and Gray's eyes told me how scared he was. They had too many tests to do, and he was moaning, crying, and holding his stomach. I didn't know if he was really in pain or if he was just anxious about being in the hospital.

"Kids can get really sick from urinary tract infections, but you're right, something else is going on." He opened his computer and I stumbled backward a little bit right into Kade, who held me up and kept a firm hand on my stomach.

"I ran a CT scan on him. Do you see this?" he asked, pointing to a dark white streak across his abdomen. I nodded. "That's scar tissue. I think what we have going is a tense peritoneum from scar tissue around the ventriculoperitoneal shunt."

"The shunt isn't functioning anymore. We just didn't see the point of removing it or ligating it since it wasn't causing any problems," I shared, holding Gray's little hand.

"That's the news I was hoping to hear. The shunt is causing problems now. As long as it isn't being used, then I don't need to call the neurosurgeon to scrub in."

I shook my head. "It hasn't functioned for years."

"Okay, then I'm going to ligate it and take out that portion. I'll clean out the scar tissue after that. If we don't do this we could end up with a big mess on our hands as far as his bladder is concerned. Look here." He pointed at the end of the white streak. "The scar tissue is nearly encasing his stoma for his catheter site. If we don't do this surgery, we're running the risk of the catheter perforating the bowel."

I put my hand over my mouth. "I had trouble replacing his catheter Wednesday night. I was going to make an appointment with you. He's starting to use the catheter less and less as he gets older, but I didn't want to get rid of it just yet."

Dr. Collins nodded and laid his hand on Gray's leg. "I can see why it might be hard to insert the catheter at this point. It's probably the reason he has the infection."

I brushed the hair off Gray's face. He looked so peaceful sleeping, but the truth was he was drugged and probably scared to death. "Do we have to take out the ventricle portion of the shunt?" I asked, tracing the scar on his head, and trying to keep my voice from cracking.

"No, I don't want to mess with that. If we leave that portion in place, and he ever becomes shunt-dependent again, we can put a catheter into the other side of his abdomen. For now, I'm going to ligate the one he has now, and clean out the scar tissue that surrounds it. I'll widen his stoma for his catheter as well. I don't want to remove that just yet, either. He's young and we don't know how well his bladder is going to come back from his brain injury."

I nodded in agreement and caught my lower lip between my teeth. "Okay, I'll consent to that surgery. When can you do it? Tomorrow?" I asked, and he shook his head.

"No, we need to do it tonight. I can't risk that shunt catheter migrating any further. If we don't move on this, he could get even sicker," Dr. Collins said, trying to ease the news gently.

"But he has an infection. We shouldn't do it with an active infection without antibiotics."

He laid his hand on my shoulder after coming around the bed. "Autumn, we don't have a choice. He's very sick. Waiting until morning could mean the difference between him walking out of here or not. I'm not willing to risk that, are you?" he asked. I shook my head no and one tear fell over my lash. Kade used his thumb to wipe it away. "He's had a heavy dose of antibiotics already. We'll give him one more right before the surgery. I'm not concerned that the urinary tract infection will cause any problems. I do surgery on patients with these types of infections all the time. Some have chronic infections and come out of surgery with no problem. I'll use every precaution. I'm confident that by morning Gray will feel like a million bucks."

"Okay, I trust you Dr. Collins. Let me go find some surgical scrubs, and I'll scrub in," I said, starting for the door, but Kade held me by my waist.

"Not tonight, Autumn. You're a mother tonight, not a physician," he said firmly.

I shook my head over and over. "No, I'm a trauma surgeon. I can do this. Let me scrub in," I pleaded, but he shook his head again. His eyes drifted to Kade's and a look passed between them. I didn't like it, and I whirled around on him.

"Let me go, dammit! I'm going to scrub in, and you can't stop me. I'm his mother, and you're not his father," I hissed. The look in his eye told me I hit him right where I wanted to, but he didn't release me. His lips were a thin line, and he kept his arm around my waist, with his hand wrapped around my belly.

Dr. Collins took me by the shoulders. "Autumn, listen to me. You don't have surgical rights at the hospital anymore and you're an orthopedic surgeon, not a urologist. You aren't a physician tonight. You're a mother. I'm not going to have this boy's mother in the operating suite while I'm trying to do everything in my power to make him better. I can't handle that kind of stress and neither can you. I'll make sure you get updates every half an hour. That's the best I can do."

My shoulders fell, and I gazed at my son again. "He's the only thing I have in the whole world," I whispered. "If I let him go into surgery alone, he may never forgive me."

Dr. Collins grasped my shoulder not as a colleague but as a friend. "If you don't let him go into surgery, he may not be alive to forgive you. Kids are resilient, Autumn. He's already off in dreamland and won't even be aware we're going to do surgery. By the time he wakes up you'll be with him again and there will be nothing to forgive. Time is of the essence here."

I finally nodded and bit my lower lip to keep it from trembling. "I want to stay with him as long as I can," I whispered, and he let out a breath.

"He'll stay right here until anesthesia is ready. The nurse will be in with the release forms for you to sign. I'm going to go gather my team and we should be ready in twenty minutes or less. Stay calm, Autumn. I'm going to take care of him, and in a few hours, he'll be back on track. You've been through this so many times with him I know it's hard, but it's imperative we do this now. If I thought I could treat this successfully any other way, I would. You know that."

I nodded and wrapped my arms around my chest. "I know."

He patted my arm one more time, shook Kade's hand, and patted Gray's leg. "I'll be back in a few hours to give you the specifics on how the surgery went, but I'm confident when the sun comes up, we'll have our fun-loving Grayson back. Stay strong, Autumn."

I nodded my head quickly, and he left the room. In a breath the nurse was in, and the room became a bustle of activity. I signed the paperwork and Kade pulled me back away from the stretcher where they were unhooking Gray from the wall mount units, and connecting his I.V. and monitors to portable units. Kade had his arms wrapped around me and held me up, so I didn't collapse to the ground.

"I'll be taking him for surgery now, Dr. Hanson," the nurse from earlier said.

I went to the side of the bed and picked up Gray's hand. It was warm, but not burning up like he had been when we first got here. I held it to my lips and kissed it. It still smelled like cinnamon and apples from the cider he had at the pumpkin patch. My eyes were filled with tears and I leaned down and kissed his forehead.

"I love you baby boy," I said, half sobbing. "I'm doing this to make you better. I'll be right here in a few hours when you're all done, and then I'll never leave you. I'm sorry I have to leave you right now," I sobbed.

Kade pulled me back and I wrapped my arms around his neck and sobbed into his shoulder while they wheeled my life away.

Chapter 13

I paced from one end of the room to the other, the last update having come in thirty minutes ago that he would be in surgery at least another hour. The room was too small and I could barely breathe. I was trapped and there was no way out of this hell.

Kade took my shoulders and led me to the small loveseat against the wall. The wall was covered in some kind of flower, the name escaped me, but the happiness of the design mocked me. The loveseat was soft, and when my bottom hit the seat my legs sighed in relief, thankful for the rest, if only for a minute. A cool glass was put in my hand and he instructed me to drink, so I did. The cold water slid down my throat until it hit my stomach like a cold snowball to the face.

I glanced down at the floor where Ace slept. He had his head on his paws and whimpered every few minutes. I climbed onto the floor and hugged his big head to me. "We won't lose him, Ace. We can't lose him. He's our boy. We need our boy," I whispered into his ear while I kissed his furry head, and he licked my face.

Strong arms pulled me up and settled me onto his lap. He held me tightly and rubbed my arm until I stopped shaking. "It's okay to be scared, Autumn," he murmured against my ear. "I'm scared, too."

"This is my fault," I cried. "He has this infection because I didn't keep everything sterile. I got frustrated and just wanted to get it back in before it closed over. Now he's in surgery, because I was careless. God, what am I doing acting like I can be a mother?"

Suddenly, I couldn't breathe. Everything was collapsing around me and I couldn't breathe. It was like I was in that operating room again all those years ago. Everything was going dim and I fought against it. I couldn't wake up and find my child gone again. I couldn't. I thrashed at the straps holding me and sobbed, screaming her name over and over. Darkness was coming. I stilled and waited for it to wash over me, so I could let this world go.

"Autumn! Oh no you don't, come on baby." Hands shook me and his fingers squeezed my cheeks. I whimpered and reached out. He could save me from the darkness if I let him, but I couldn't let him.

"Autumn, you have to stay strong for that little boy." His words were softer now as he cradled me. The roughness from the cast on his arm drew me back to reality when it rubbed against my belly. His soft lips were on mine, and I finally opened my eyes. His were open too, and his lips didn't move on mine, they just laid there while he stared into my eyes. It was as though his lips were made to be on mine, and mine were made for his. They fit perfectly and I wanted so much more of him than I could ever have. He kissed me once. It was short and not more than a peck, but it filled me in places I didn't know were empty.

He held a tissue in his hand and wiped my eyes. I was certain the mascara I had put on before we left for Duluth was now running down my face in streams of black. With each swipe of the tissue it went from stark white to a murky grey.

"I should go wash," I said and swung my legs off his lap. He stood too and steadied me on my feet. There was an attached bathroom in the room and I closed the heavy wooden door behind me. I had to get away from him. I could feel the burning in my stomach and the clammy cold feeling that started in my chest and moved upward. I leaned against the toilet and gulped air, doing anything to ward off the impending revolt of my stomach. I moaned far louder than I intended to and leaned over the bowl while my stomach churned the acid and apple cider. Then the wave hit me and I retched. I had to grip the edge of the toilet to keep from falling, but my legs were too weak and I fell to my knees.

"I'm here, Autumn," he said soothingly, holding my hair

back while I retched in agony for my son, and pure horror that he was witnessing it. "It's okay, sweetheart, let it pass. It won't last forever," he murmured. His strong hand was splayed across my belly, and the other was holding my hair. I tried to breathe normally, but couldn't. I started to pant, which was bad, but I was helpless to stop it. He pulled me back from the toilet and tucked my head between my legs. "You can't do that, honey. You have to breathe normally or I'm going to call for a doctor. There's a string right over there. I'm going to pull it if you don't listen to me and start breathing slow and even," he demanded.

I listened to his voice, the position he had forced me into left me no choice but to slow my breathing from the compression of my ribcage. I locked my hand onto his forearm and slowly he let up and I raised my head.

"I'm okay now," I said without looking at him. "You can go."

He knelt down in front of me and tucked the hair behind my ears. "That might not be a good idea. I don't want you to fall."

I shook my head, and my hair fell over my face again. I left it there so I didn't have to see the look in his eyes. "I'll call you if I need you."

He sighed and stood then walked to the door. I didn't look up until I heard it latch and then I hauled myself up to stand at the mirror. I gave myself a hard stare. "Get it together, Autumn. You can't fall apart now. You can't fall apart, ever."

I kept talking to myself, trying to reason with the woman hiding in that little spot in my heart. She was determined to make me listen, but I couldn't. I couldn't let my feelings for him cloud my judgment. I scrubbed at my face and washed the makeup away with the institutional soap and rough paper towels. Every swipe left a red mark on my skin and I accepted it as punishment for not taking the right steps to keep my son safe.

When I finished, I splashed cold water on my face and then pulled down more paper towels, absently drying my hands. The running water and the spiced cider I'd had at the farm were colliding, and I was grateful there was a toilet in the small bathroom. I sat there, my shoulders slumped, and hated that I could do something as simple as empty my bladder, but my son was in surgery because he couldn't. When I finally pulled the door open, Kade wheeled around and met me at the door. He took hold of my elbow and helped me to the loveseat again.

"Any updates?" I asked, my voice a little hoarse, but he shook his head and sat next to me.

He traced a finger down the red marks on my face. "You're so beautiful. I would fix this and take all the pain away if I could."

"I'm scared," I whispered. I couldn't speak in normal tones or I'd start crying again.

"Me too, Momma." He held my hand and patted it twice.

"I knew he was tired, and I shouldn't have agreed to go into town this afternoon. My instincts said something was off," I fretted, my other hand grasping his like a lifeline.

"It's my fault for even suggesting it. The only comfort I have right now is that if we had stayed in Cloquet it would have delayed his care."

"We have a hospital there," I started to say, and he nodded.

"Yes, but you know they don't deal with pediatric patients any more than they have to. You know they would have transported him to Duluth anyway, and that would have scared him even more."

He made sense and I knew it. "It's always hard to accept the right place, right time scenario for me. I've seen too much."

He reached up and tucked a piece of hair behind my ear. "I know. That's why I'm sorry for not mentioning it out of earshot first. It will never happen again. I'm praying, hard."

I watched his jaw lock down and wondered what else he was going to say. "I'm not sure it was anyone's fault," I mused. He stared into my eyes and I saw the pain there he had for me. "The doctor in me knows if I had waited any longer to get that catheter in, he would be here anyway getting it reinserted. I also know I can't control the events of the past."

"No, you can't, but you can cut yourself a little slack. You're the woman who was meant to be Gray's momma, whether you gave birth to him or not. Don't second guess your decisions about his care. He's a happy boy, and for the most part he's pretty darn healthy. You've given him so much love in the last seven years. Never discount that. We don't always get things exactly right as parents, but our kids surprisingly grow up to be good and decent human beings. Or at least so I'm told by my aunt. She didn't ask to be my mother, but the Lord trusted her with that job, just like He did with you for Gray."

I leaned my head on his shoulder and nodded against it. He was right, but it didn't take the sting away from all those years ago. "I'm sorry about earlier. I wasn't thinking clearly. No, that's a lie. I was angry, and I took it out on you."

He stared down at the floor with his hands grasped together. "It's already forgotten."

But I knew it wasn't. I'd hurt him. "Why do you keep coming around, Kade? Haven't I made it clear enough that we can be nothing more than friends?"

"You've made that crystal clear, Autumn. I keep coming around because I love you and I love your son. If friends are all we can be, then friends we will be. But in those brief moments of weakness when you kiss me, I feel like someday you might let me into your heart. It's like someone else takes over your body, and for those few seconds you get to feel again, before the other you shutters everything down."

"You—you love us?" I asked shocked. "No one loves us."

He rubbed my face and shook his head. "For a doctor, you really have a lot to learn."

The phone rang at that moment. I jumped up and pulled it from the cradle and listened to the woman on the other end of the line. The tears started again and I thanked her through wobbly lips. The phone slid to my lap and I started to laugh through my tears. He hung up the phone and took my face in his hands.

"Autumn, what did they say, honey?" It was in that moment, as he waited to hear the news, that I saw in his eyes what he probably meant when he said he loved us.

"She said he's in recovery and awake. He asked for his

momma, his dog Ace, and his best friend, Kade."

Chapter 14

"And Spiderman, the Silver Surfer, and Hulk lived happily ever after," I read and closed the book with a resounding clap.

Gray shook his head. "Momma, it doesn't say that. I know it doesn't say that."

I smirked at him, so happy he was feeling better. "You're right, it doesn't say that. I was checking to see if you were paying attention."

"Let me read it to you." He held his hand out for the book and I gave it to him. He was resting upright in bed, and for the second day out of surgery, he looked pretty darn good. Hopefully, after lunch they would let him go home. I had spent the last few nights here, and Kade came and went with Ace. He made sure Ace went on walks and was fed. He made sure I had everything I needed to stay here and he called my office to ask Phoenix to change my appointments.

I listened to Gray's little voice reading the words on the page as I rubbed his thigh. He never complained, but I could tell his tummy hurt when he moved wrong. He was going to be okay though, and I hoped a week out of school and the antibiotics would take care of his infection

My eye caught movement from the door and a bounding ball of fur came barreling at us. I held out my hands to catch him but then remembered it was Ace. He stopped on a dime in front of my chair and laid his paw on my lap.

"Good morning, Ace. We missed you last night," I sang, and he licked my hand as I pet his downy head.

"Good morning, Ace," Gray sang from his bed, and I lifted the dog up to rest at his feet. He sensed he couldn't get any nearer, but never wanted to be any further away than that. He laid his snout across Gray's thigh and was rewarded with the love he had come to need.

My eyes strayed to the door and I wondered where the love I had come to need was. I couldn't deny it any longer. He loved me. He loved us, but that didn't mean I had to love him back. I could just accept his love, and let it get us through this time. When he came through the door, there was a flutter in my belly that I didn't focus on too long or too hard.

"Good morning." I stood and hugged him, the way a friend would hug a friend. I didn't want Gray to get the wrong idea.

"Good morning. How is everyone today?" he asked, patting Gray's leg and rubbing a hand across Ace's head.

"I'm feeling better. I even had some lumberjack pancakes this morning," Gray informed him happily.

"You ate lumberjack pancakes without me?" Kade frowned, and Gray slipped his hand inside Kade's giant one.

"Don't worry, they weren't very good. They were from the freezer I think." He stuck his tongue out and pointed his thumb down, which made Kade crack a smile.

"As soon as you have room in that tummy for good pancakes, I'll take you for the kind not from the freezer," he promised. He reached out with his hand to pat his tummy, but pulled it back.

"You can touch it, see?" Gray said, patting the thick bandages over the incision, and Kade laid his hand on it gently. I saw him look to the ceiling before he could make eye contact with Gray again. I discreetly moved away from the bed to fuss with my purse while he settled in.

"You're my superhero, you know that?" Kade pulled the chair I was in up to the bed before he ruffled Gray's hair. He picked up the book and turned it over reading the title. "This is Iron Man, level one." He held it in his hand and looked at Gray dubiously. "Isn't this a little bit too easy for you?"

Gray's head bobbed up and down. "It's all they had, so we've been making up stories using the pictures. I can't wait to get out of here."

Kade patted his leg and smiled. "I bet you can't, but you know what?" he asked and Gray shook his head. "I'm super proud of you. I know it's not easy to be in the hospital. It's scary. You don't feel well and you want to go home. Thank you for being so cool about this. You sure made it easier on me, because I was awfully worried about you. I think your momma was, too." He winked and Gray glanced up at me. I gave him the palms up, and he giggled.

"You're welcome. I was scared, but Ace helps me stay calm. He's so smart. He even knew I was sick." His little hand was rubbing the dog's ears, and Ace was happily thumping his tail on the bed.

"He is smart, just like you are. I think when we get home, he deserves an extra special treat."

"Knock, knock," came another familiar voice from the door.

I turned and relief washed over me. "Hey, Trey! Look Gray, Trey came to say hi," I said to Gray, who had stopped smiling.

Trey gave me a quick hug. "I got a note to come see my favorite superhero. Looks like you had some problems with your equipment, huh?"

"You could say that." I laughed and Trey went to the bed to see Gray. Ace stood up on guard, and Trey stepped back automatically.

"Friend, Ace. Rest," Kade instructed him firmly, and the dog settled down again, and his tail thumped. I went to the bed and stood next to Kade.

"Trey, meet Ace. He's Gray's service dog," I explained and Trey reached his hand out for the dog to sniff. He passed muster, and Ace gave his hand a nudge with his snout until he rubbed his ears.

"He's incredible, Gray. How lucky are you?" Trey asked and finally Gray gave him a small smile.

"I'm really lucky. He takes care of me really good. I mean well." He nodded his head, proud he remembered to use proper English.

"Trey, this is Kade Franco. He's a friend from Cloquet," I

introduced them, and they shook hands.

"Nice to meet you, Kade. I'm glad Autumn has a friend in town. We miss her here, but this little guy is so much happier in Cloquet."

"He's doing really well in school, and with Ace helping him, his legs are stronger than ever. I'm a little worried though, his braces have been getting shorter and shorter, and I think he needs a new pair." I noticed my voice definitely sounded discouraged and defeated.

He nodded. "That was the script I got from Dr. Collins. He feels the braces are causing compression of the bag and he's worried the infection will linger if we don't get them fixed fast."

Gray shook his head and crossed his arms in front of him. "No, I'm not making new braces. These braces are my favorite."

Trey glanced to me and then to Gray. "Hey, we can make the new ones look just like those. They'll just be bigger because you're growing, and that's good stuff."

Gray wasn't having any of it. "No thank you," he said politely, but crabbily, and he wouldn't make eye contact with any of us.

Kade leaned on the bed. "Why not, little dude? We want you to get better, and it sounds like the braces are causing the problem. We can't have that."

Gray gazed up from under his bangs at Kade. "I don't like getting them made. It hurts and takes forever. I'm not doing it and you can't make me."

Kade glanced at me and I shrugged. "It does take a while to do the casting and get them made, but it doesn't hurt, Gray," I admonished.

Kade laid his hand on Gray's tummy protectively and looked between me and Trey. "Maybe he's scared it will this time? His belly is probably really sore."

Trey knelt down, so he could look my son in the eye. "Is that the problem, Gray?"

Gray nodded a little, but wouldn't look up.

"I might have a solution for that. Do you want to hear what it is?" Trey asked, but Gray still didn't make eye contact.

"I do," Kade said, and I agreed enthusiastically.

Trey held up a finger and jogged from the room. He was gone just long enough to go to the nurse's station and then returned with a bag that had Iron Man on the front. Gray's face perked up a little, even though he tried to keep his eyes downcast.

"Here's my solution. Who wants to open it?" Trey asked, holding the bag out between the three of us. The bag was about two feet high and swung on a black cord. It swung near Gray, and he finally reached out and pulled it to him. Curiosity was shining in his eyes as he inspected the bag.

We waited while he opened the drawstring and peered inside. He pulled out a brace that looked nothing like the one he was wearing and turned it over in his hands. It was metal on each side, and the straps had the logos of each superhero including Spiderman, Superman, and Batman.

"Whoa ..." Gray breathed out, laying it on his lap and pulling out the matching one. "Are these for me?" he asked on cloud nine.

"Do you like them? I had them specially made just for my favorite Iron Man." Trey smiled, and Gray gave him the finger wave, until he leaned down so he could hug him.

"I love them! Look, Momma, they're different and so cool!" He handed one to Kade to check out.

Trey came around the bed and Kade handed it to him. "This is a new design going on the market. It's adjustable for up to six inches of growth at a time, just by changing the length of the sidebars." He showed me the adjustments, and how to apply the brace. "This is the first adjustable, non-custom KAFO on the market for kids. It's very much needed in my opinion."

"What's a KAFO?" Kade asked confused, and Trey turned to him.

"It means knee, ankle, and foot orthosis. It supports all of the joints of the leg for patients with limited mobility. It'll work the same as his old ones, but won't require the constant refitting. They're basically off the shelf, and we add the custom orthotic to the bottom. All I have to do is use the press kit on his feet, and I can have these ready in a couple of days."

I took the brace in my hand and turned it over. "This is a great new product. I'm sure it won't work for all kids, but the population it will support is going to benefit greatly. Are they comparable in price to the custom-made ones?" I asked and he gave me the so-so hands.

"Upfront, they're more expensive, but because they grow with the child, you're buying two or three fewer pairs. So, for their life span they are going to be considerably less expensive."

"How much are we talking?" I asked.

"I'm not really sure. They aren't on the market officially, yet. My guess is they will cost around three thousand a piece."

"If they aren't on the market, how did you get them?" Kade asked and Trey smiled.

"I'm glad you asked." He turned back to Gray and laid his hand on his head. "I was at a convention, and they had these out as their up and coming product. I got to talking with the guy and found out they were looking to get it on patients to test them out. I told him I knew the perfect kiddo who would put these to the test. Before I left, I gave him my info, and he called me a few weeks ago that they were ready. This is a one of a kind set, Gray. No one else in the whole world has a pair like this." Trey grinned and so did Gray.

"Holy coolness, Robin!" Gray squealed and then grabbed his belly, remembering his limitations.

"Right? Do you think you can do me a favor and wear these for a few months?" Trey asked and Gray nodded eagerly.

I laid my hand on Trey's arm. "Trey, thank you. I can't tell you how much I appreciate that you thought of Gray."

"It's no problem, Autumn. I was actually going to call you today. When I got to the office and saw the note, I was worried. I was also relieved that I already had the braces in hand."

"Are you sure they don't want me to pay for them?"

He shook his head. "Nope, but there will be some paperwork to fill out at certain time intervals. I figured you wouldn't mind that part since you do paperwork a lot, and I can trust you will get the information back to the company. They really need to know how these perform in the real world before they launch them to the masses. They've spent years developing them and they know they work in the lab. Now they need to know if they can stand up to kids like Gray. The kind of kids who won't take no for an answer."

I let out the breath I'd been holding since he mentioned new braces. "I can do paperwork. This takes a big burden off my back right now as I get the clinic up and going. You're right, the price upfront is more, but not by much. If they work like you say they will, that will save me a lot of money." I did the math in my head, and it would save me a lot of money, like a lot.

"Won't your insurance pay for them?" Kade asked, and I grimaced a little.

"No, they don't pay a dime for them. We already reached his lifetime limit on orthotics. Now I pay for his medical devices out of pocket," I explained and his face was set in total bewilderment.

"He's seven. How can he reach the lifetime limit by seven?"

Trey shook his head in frustration. "Lifetime limit just means however much the insurance company decides they are going to pay for durable medical equipment. Some pay eighty percent, and you pay twenty, no matter what you need, and some will only pay for twenty-five thousand dollars worth of equipment. After that you've hit the cap. If you need anything more, then you pay one hundred percent."

"But he needs those braces to walk," Kade said logically and Trey nodded.

"Yup, and my patients who need legs and arms are in the same boat. It's a battle we've fought for years, and we're slowly gaining ground, but you know how long it takes to pass legislation," Trey said frustrated. "Anyway, if you're cool with this, Momma Hanson, I'll take the molds of his feet, and then you can pick the braces up when you come in for his follow-up at the end of the week."

"I'm more than cool with it, except he can't stand up." I

motioned at his belly, and he jogged around the bed and picked up a box.

"Not a problem. With these new molds he can just push his foot down into it while he's in bed." He flipped the box open, and in just a few minutes he had both feet molded and was packing up the braces.

"Thank you, Trey. I can't wait to wear them next week when I go to school again. Can I tell you the truth?" Gray asked. Trey stopped what he was doing and sat next to him on the bed.

"Of course, buddy," Trey answered.

"My old braces are too small, but I know they cost lots of money and so I didn't want Momma to buy new ones yet. It doesn't really hurt when you make them. I was just making that up, but then I felt bad 'cause you're always nice to me."

Trey chuckled a little, and Kade slipped his arm around my shoulder and kissed my temple. "You're too smart for only seven, Gray. I appreciate your honesty, and I know these new ones will make you, and your momma, feel much better." Trey patted Ace on the head, and then shook Kade's hand again before leaving.

When he was gone, I let out a breath. "Well, I think all that's left is getting Dr. Collins to cut you loose, so we can go home and watch some Spiderman."

Kade smiled, but it didn't reach his eyes. I wondered if that little informational session was going to bring on the beginning of the end of his love for us.

Chapter 15

Who was whimpering? I opened my eye and Ace stood by the bed long enough to get my attention, then went to the door again. I sat up, and Gray was still asleep next to me in the bed. I slipped out of the room and followed Ace down the hall to let him out the back door. While I waited, I checked the clock and noted it was almost eight already. We'd had a rough first night home from the hospital and by the time I had finally fallen asleep, it was almost four in the morning. I had no intention of staying up, so when Ace came back to the door, I let him in, filled his food bowl, and went back to my room. I climbed back under the comforter and laid my head on the pillow.

Yesterday was Gray's last day in the hospital. His infection had cleared to the point he could take oral antibiotics, and his stoma and catheter were pain-free and working well. His incision on his abdomen still hurt him, and he had a hard time getting comfortable if his medication wore off, but I hoped today would be a much better day for him. Nothing was worse than watching your child in pain and not being able to make them feel better.

I closed my eyes and tried to keep my mind on relaxing and falling asleep, but it wanted to wander everywhere but there. It wanted to think about how I was going to be a doctor and take care of Gray. It also wanted to think about Kade Franco, a lot. He had hardly left the hospital from the time we got Gray into a room until he drove us home yesterday. He took over Ace's care, and I was never more grateful. Ace was a nervous wreck the whole time. When he wasn't being walked by Kade, he was laying at the bottom of Gray's bed in the hospital room.

Funny how the dog knew exactly how I felt. He didn't want to let Gray out of his sight either, and I knew he was the reason Gray was home already. Getting up and walking was painful and scary, but Ace was there to nudge him along, and be his little furry walker. We'd been in the hospital more times than I could count in his early life, and he was never so agreeable for the nurses or free of anxiety. Ace was a lifesaver. I literally owed him my son's life. If he hadn't alerted us to his fever, we might have kept driving and lost precious time.

Ace was here because Kade was here, and that was the part I tried to keep my mind from investigating further. His words *I love you and I love your son* kept echoing in my ears the past few days. Gray was easy to love. I could completely understand why he was in love with my son, but me? I had a much harder time with that. We lived on opposite ends of the spectrum of life, and he had no reason to love me. I'd done nothing but keep him at arm's length. I'd fought how I felt about him since the day we met.

How do you feel about him, Autumn? my mind asked.

I moaned and rolled over. My hand fell off the edge of the bed to pet Ace, who had come right back to the room after his breakfast. Honestly, Kade Franco was probably my meant-to-be, if I actually deserved a meant-to-be. That was the part I hadn't quite accepted yet.

∞∞∞

My phone chirped, and I lifted my head off the pillow to glance at the clock. It was almost ten, and I had fallen asleep thinking of Kade. I dreamt about us walking hand-in-hand down by the river, alone.

"Who is it, Momma?" Gray asked, and I laid my head back down on the bed to shake off my dream.

"You're awake, baby. How come you didn't wake me up?" I

asked. I rubbed my eyes and rolled over to look at him. He was leaning up against the makeshift pillow ramp I had made him, and had his Harry Potter book in his hand. Kade had shown up with two more at the hospital the day after surgery. They had spent the whole day reading and napping. It had been a welcome few moments for me to shower and check in with Phoenix about the state of my clinic.

"You were sleeping, and I didn't want to wake you up. I am kind of hungry though," he said, putting his book down on the bed.

I smiled and sat up in the bed then swung my legs over the side. "You are? Then we better get some food in that belly."

My phone chirped again, and I grabbed it while I slipped my bathrobe on. "You better answer that first," he said very grown up.

I already knew who it was. It was Kade's ringtone. I opened the bar on the phone and saw his message. *I'm outside in my truck. When you're up, come let me in.*

I groaned a little, and Gray stared at me, one brow furrowed. I forced a smile back on my face, tapped out a quick message, and then slipped the phone in my robe pocket. I slid my hands under his legs and cradled his back while I swung him into the wheelchair by the side of the bed. His braces weren't an option right now, so we had no choice but to carry him or use the wheelchair. The wheelchair at least forced him to use his core muscles to sit up straight. I pushed the chair through the hallway and Ace padded behind me to the kitchen. Gray's face broke into a huge smile when he saw Kade at the fridge waiting for him.

"Kade, how did you get here?" Gray asked excitedly, holding his belly.

Kade glanced around secretly, and then bent down near the chair. "Your mom told me where the spare key is, so I let myself in. I heard someone was hungry." He raised a brow and Gray nodded his head with enthusiasm.

"I am hungry. That hospital food isn't fit for a human. Even

Ace wouldn't eat it."

I started to snort and so did Kade, pretty soon we were laughing so hard Gray had to beg us to stop, because it hurt his stomach to laugh.

Kade took a couple of deep breaths before he spoke. "Okay, how about a lumberjack breakfast then? Eggs, sausage, and flapjacks with a side of juice." He turned and winked at me. "And coffee."

I felt the heat of his gaze as he looked me over. My bathrobe came just above my knees, and the V in the front was cut low. I turned quickly to the cupboard. "I'll make the coffee," I sputtered, but he came over, took me by the shoulders, and walked me to the door of my bedroom.

"I'll make the coffee. I want you to take a nice hot shower. You look like you need it."

"Do I smell?" I asked horrified, lifting my nightie to sniff.

He moaned and laid his hand over my chest. "You smell like heaven, and if you don't put that shirt down all my good intentions are going to go out the window. We may just be friends, but I'm still a man, and I still want you."

I sucked in a breath at the heat of his hand over my breasts and the feel of his hardness against the back of my thigh. I turned my head toward his voice and closed my eyes. Almost as though he knew what I wanted without saying a word, he kissed me. It wasn't a gentle, soul searching kiss, either. It was a barely contained explosion that had our lips melting together and his tongue forcing his way into my space.

His hand cupped my breast, and my knees started to shake at the overwhelming surge of desire. It was a feeling I hadn't felt in over seven years and didn't think I would ever feel again. He moaned low in his throat and then he broke the kiss abruptly and stepped back. "Go now before I do something I can't take back."

∞∞∞

"Hi, Phoenix. How are things?" I asked as I swept into the office the next afternoon. I had been planning to bring Gray to work with me for the afternoon, but instead he was happily ensconced on the couch with his homework and a tutor. It was the tutor who forced me out to the office with the promise of dinner when I got home.

"Hi, Autumn. Better question is, where's Gray?" She stood and I leaned on the reception desk.

"He's at home being tutored on subtraction skills." I smiled, even though I knew it was a dead giveaway.

"They don't make them like Kade Franco anymore. Just in case you were wondering," she said slyly, and I laughed.

"I wasn't, but thanks for the tip. So how bad off are we here? I'm sorry to dump all of this on you in the middle of your Saturday."

I had apologized profusely, and she had refused to accept it profusely. I was awfully glad she knew the people in this town so well.

"We aren't bad off at all. You only had three surgeries scheduled for this week, and they were happy to push it back. The two emergencies that called in I sent to the ER for the on-call doc. I was able to reschedule Monday and Tuesday's appointments into the rest of this week, by opening you up Friday morning. So, as long as you can work the rest of this week, and make-up those three surgeries next week or Saturday, we'll be back on track." She clicked around her computer, and showed me the schedule. There was only one conflicting appointment she had to change, since I had to take Gray back into Duluth for a post-op appointment.

"I owe you, girl. I can't thank you enough for keeping the ball rolling here. I don't know what I was thinking trying to start a business as a mom. It can all fall apart in a moment."

Phoenix stared at me with her head tilted. "You started this business so you could spend more time with your son. I say that's the absolute right reason. Any job can fall apart in a moment, but you just do the best you can, and rely on your friends to cover your back. In a few weeks, Gray will be back to school, and everything will be back to normal again," she assured me, but I shook my head and rested my hand in my chin.

"No, nothing will ever be normal again. At least not my normal."

"Is Gray not going to get better?" she asked. Her voice wavered and I took her hand.

"Oh, I'm sorry, no, Gray is already better. He wants to go back to school, but he can't until next Monday."

"Oh good, you scared me there. That little pipsqueak has stolen my heart."

"You aren't the only one," I muttered, and her ears perked up.

"What's that? Did you say Kade has lost his heart, too?" She smirked, and I rolled my eyes toward the ceiling.

"He told me he loved both me and Grayson, but we were stressed, and he probably wasn't thinking clearly."

She took my hand and led me to the office where a bouquet of red roses sat on my desk. "Those were delivered an hour ago. Better check the card to see who sent them." She rolled her eyes, and I bit the inside of my lip to keep from smiling. I opened the card, and it said, *Take time to stop and smell the roses.* Where his signature should have been it simply said, *I won't give up.*

I slipped the card into my pocket and inhaled deeply. The deep red flowers were fragrant and reminded me of a summer day.

"That doesn't look like a stressed-out man to me. Looks like a man in love," Phoenix laughed softly and I cringed. I didn't need love. Love hurts.

"How long has it been, Autumn?" she asked with her hand on my back.

"How long?" I asked confused, and she pointed at the roses.

"How long has it been since you believed in love?"

"I don't think I ever really believed in love, but seven years ago I knew for sure there was no such thing," I said, my voice harsh and sardonic. I took a rose from the vase and noticed the thorns had been removed from the stems.

"See, love doesn't have to hurt. Kade made sure of it," Phoenix teased, patted my back, and left my office.

If only I could believe her.

Chapter 16

"Thank you, Dr. Hanson. I don't know what we would have done if you hadn't been here." A worried woman sat wringing her hands on the couch in the family waiting room. She was flanked by her husband who was patting her shoulder, and appeared a little green around the gills.

"I'm glad I was here to help Carter. He'll be just fine after a few months of rehabilitation. They do a great job here at the hospital with pediatric rehab. I bring my own son to them every week. I'll put a referral in before I leave today, and they'll see him before he leaves. They'll show him how to use crutches, and how to get in and out of the car. Once we advance his activities, they'll help him strengthen his muscles and tendons. I'll have you bring him in to see me in a week, so I can replace the splint with a hard cast. I'll be by in the morning to check on him, and most likely release him then, okay? Kids bounce back fast, and I'm confident Carter will, too."

I stood and shook hands with Carter's parents again, and then made my way to the locker room to change out of my scrubs. Carter was a nine-year-old boy who had been helping his dad fix an ATV when it came crashing down on them. His leg took the brunt of the weight and he fractured his femur, but he would be okay after a relatively easy surgery to insert a rod. It was one of those cases of me being in the right place at the right time or he would have been sent to Duluth, which would have delayed treatment. I was just finishing a make-up knee repair from earlier this week, when they had paged me.

I tapped out a text on my phone to Kade, who had agreed to spend the morning with Gray. Now, it was almost three and I still wasn't home.

Just have to change, and I'll be home. Sorry again, it took longer than I thought.

I hit send and opened my locker for my clothes. I could just wear the scrubs home, I guess. I sat down on the bench, and rubbed my face between my hands. The weeks were catching up to me, and next week was already Halloween. "One thing at a time, Autumn," I mumbled just as my phone lit up. I read the incoming message.

We're in the middle of Harry Potter. Come home and relax in the tub. You deserve it.

I laughed a little into the empty room. They had finished the first book in the series and Kade had promised they would watch the movie, which he had obviously come through on. I grabbed my bag and decided a relaxing bath sounded pretty darn good, even if he was in the house while I did it.

I stood in front of the mirror and turned right and then left. Looking at yourself naked is never a relaxing experience, but something held me there instead of getting the clothes from the drawer. I was blessed with good genes and at forty I still had a sporty body. Is that what the kids call it now? Sporty? I ran my hands down my flat stomach to the small scar. It was the only thing to mar my skin, but also the most painful. Over the years, I often cursed my 34DD chest, wishing if I had to look like Dolly Parton that at least I could sing.

I shook my head and opened the drawer looking for underwear and a bra. Soft lace caught my eye, and I pulled it out. I forgot I had even bought the bra but I slipped it on and put my arms through the straps. The lace was soft against my skin, and the velvet of the cups was cool, causing a chill to run up my spine. *What am I doing?* My hands went for the snaps of the bra, but hesitated. It's just a bra. I sighed, and slipped into a pair of pink bikinis. Then I stood in front of my closet, and rubbed my forehead.

What should I wear and why am I not putting on the first thing I can find? Probably because of that guy sitting out there on my couch, drinking soda with my son, and looking at me like a finely cut steak every time I walk into the room. I went to the window and pulled back the curtain. At four-thirty, it was almost dark already. Our pumpkins were on the deck and waited for next Saturday when we would carve them into jack o' lanterns for Halloween. Of course, if Gray had anything to say about it, we'd be turning them into Iron Man or the Man of Steel.

I grimaced at the thought of the Man of Steel. The roses sat on the nightstand by my bed, so I could stop and smell them every night as I lay down. I was ashamed to say the card was always in my pocket, and sometimes, when things were hard, I reread it to remind myself someone loves me. Even if that someone and I can never be anything more than friends. The stars in the sky twinkled back at me and I thought about the star-crossed lovers' idea. I wondered if that's what William and I had been. Destined to never be together. His name rolled around in my mind, but the anger I used to feel toward him was gone. I no longer felt anything when I thought about him. He was just a name now and the last seven years had washed away the hurt he caused. Maybe that meant I'd forgiven him, or maybe it just meant being angry was wearing thin, and he didn't deserve to control my life. Truthfully, it was probably a little bit of both. I would never forgive him for the way he left, but I could forgive him for knowing we could never share a life.

I let the curtain drop and lifted a flower from the vase. It was starting to look a little wilted, but the deep fragrance still emanated from the petals. I couldn't resist the old childhood game, as the petals looked ready to fall. "He loves me, he loves me not," I whispered, pulling the petals off the flower, and laying them in a pile on the stand. Around and around the flower I went. "He loves me, he loves me not. He loves me, he loves me not."

"He loves me," came a voice from the door. I jumped back using the flower to cover myself, which was just plain dumb.

"Kade, you scared me." I laid the flower down and picked up my robe, holding it in front of me.

He strode into the room and his body filled the space around me and forced me to focus on him. His thin t-shirt did nothing to hide the cords of muscle underneath and I swallowed hard around the dryness in my throat. He took the robe from my hands and threw it on the bed, but he never took his eyes off me.

"You're so beautiful. Please don't hide from me," he whispered, his hand on my face and his eyes locked with mine. I waited for them to drift lower, to leer at my breasts and my pink covered triangle, but they never wavered.

"I'm always hiding," I whispered, and then closed my eyes at my admission. *Why did I say that? Why do I even talk to him?*

I was in his arms, and he was holding me against his chest. My breasts were crushed into his abdomen and my head was on his chest. "Someday I'll figure out from what. When that day comes, and it will come, I'm not going to let you hide anymore. I'm giving you fair warning." His voice was firm and I nodded against my will.

His hands ran up and down my bare back, leaving goosebumps over my arms. He caressed my bottom and went instantly hard against my belly. "See what you do to me, Autumn?" he ground out, and I nodded against his chest.

"It just can't be," I whimpered, and he stroked the tender flesh under my arm, stopping at the edge of my breast. I shivered and sighed at the same time.

"If your son wasn't sitting out there on the couch, I would work a lot harder to show you why it can be." He released me a little, and I stepped back, noticing my nipples were bursting for his touch. I tried to cross my arms, but he held them out to the side, and this time his eyes wandered my body. It wasn't a leer. It was a sensual, nipple tingling, foray of hunger that made me squirm a little out of pent up sexual need.

His eyes met mine again and he kissed my knuckles. "Get dressed. We're going out to dinner."

He dropped my hands, and I let them fall to my side. "We are? I'm not sure Gray will feel up to that."

"Tina's on her way here. She called and wanted some time with Gray. I was happy to oblige." He grinned, but his eyes were filled with lust.

I stood there watching him as he closed the door, listening to his footsteps headed down the hall. I turned back to the flower, and there was one petal left. "He loves me," I whispered as it fluttered to the floor.

∞∞∞

"It's beautiful out here," I sighed, hugging my knees to my chest and listening to the river flow down its path. "It's been a long time since I've been this relaxed."

Kade was leaning back on his elbows, his chest covered in a sweatshirt, and his ankles crossed. The air was cool, but the stars were bright, and other than the occasional car going over the bridge, it was quiet. He had insisted we come out to Dunlap Park and have a picnic. He even packed a cooler full of food while I was in surgery, and brought me back to the same spot we had been a few Sunday's earlier. That day felt like a lifetime ago.

"I heard what you did for Carter," he said as he stared out over the river.

"I was just doing my job, Kade. It saved him a trip to Duluth, so I was happy to do it. I can't talk about my cases," I added, just so he wouldn't ask more questions.

"I'm not talking about the surgery."

I hugged my legs tighter and rested my chin on my knees. "Wow, word travels fast around this town, or do you have my shoes bugged?"

"I don't need to bug your shoes. I know everyone in this

town. Carter's dad is the little brother of a guy I went to school with. Joe and I graduated together and still play league basketball."

"I see," I answered, hoping he would let it drop. "Again, I was just doing my job."

"Your job would have been fixing his leg, and going home. What you did was fix his leg, and waive your fee, as well as promise all follow-up appointments would be pro bono. Doing your job doesn't include making sure the hospital takes his case pro bono either."

I shrugged. "His family was already struggling and now they won't have Carter to help on the farm. It was a small thing to do to try to ease their worries."

He laughed and shook his head a little. "Yeah, a small thing. Right."

I whipped around and stared him down hard, "Let it be, Kade. If I want to work for free that's my prerogative. What's the good of having a skill that can help someone if the only thing you get out of it is money? Look at what this community did for us when Gray got sick. He got new braces to fix the problem, free of charge. I came home to my lawn mowed and my house cleaned. My office grounds were cleaned and raked of leaves by the high school agriculture class. I've had a hot meal delivered to my door every day for the last week from the churches in the city, most of which I've never even attended. One of the vets in town offered free vet care for Ace for the rest of his life, just to take a little bit more off my plate."

He was smiling. "I told you. We take care of our own here."

"So that's what I'm doing. I'm taking care of the community. I'm giving back, because of my appreciation for what they've given me. I didn't decide to be a doctor for the money or the glory. I decided to be a doctor to help people. When Gray came into my life, I dealt with a lot of doctors who felt the same way I do, and I learned from them. Just by watching how they lived I got a better education about medicine than I ever did in med school."

He sat up and rubbed my shoulders through my thin sweater. "I wasn't trying to antagonize you. I was trying to engage you. That's the most heartfelt thing you've said since we met. I want to know more about you than what's on the surface. You try to hide the fact that you're a woman, and focus on being a mom and a doctor. I want to get to know the woman. I feel like over the last few weeks I'm finally seeing glimpses of her. It was the woman I held in my arms earlier in your bedroom. It was the woman who put this shirt on tonight, because she knew it would make me want to kiss along the swell of her breast. It was the woman who pulled petals from a flower and wondered somewhere deep in a heart full of iron if what that card she'd been carrying around all week said was true."

I hung my head and stared at my shoes. I tried for the life of me to figure out what to say, but I couldn't. Out of the corner of my eye, he stood and took my hand.

Once I was standing, I held back a little bit. "Where are we going?" He didn't answer, but started walking in silence down the bank of the river. "I had a dream that we did this," I blurted out, and he turned one eye toward me. I saw the slight curl of his lips, but it was the only indication that he had heard me. "It was the first morning we were home from the hospital. I had been up with Ace and when I laid back down all my mind wanted me to do was think about you. I must have dozed off, and I dreamt we were walking down here hand-in-hand. Like we are now."

He squeezed the hand he held. "I like spending time with you, even if it's in your dreams."

I glanced down at the shirt I had on, his words playing in my ears. I remembered the way he held me in his arms and the way his eyes had ripped the bra off and made love to my breasts in the span of a few short seconds. The linen blouse left the swell of my breasts bare, and I wondered what it would feel like to have his lips there. I noticed the cold was having an effect and once again my nipples were hard and arched toward the sky.

"Do you dream about me?" I asked suddenly. The question burst from my lips before I could use my good judgment and hold it back.

"Every.Single.Night," he said, his lips pressed together.

"Oh." That was all I had.

Don't ask questions if you don't want to hear the answers, Autumn.

"There are times I dream I'm watching you from behind a camera as you play with Gray. I'm not taking pictures. I'm just watching through the lens, because it's the only way I can be part of your life. I'm there, but I'm not allowed in to be part of it. There are times I dream I am part of your life, and we're all laughing, playing a game, or reading quietly together on the couch. Those are the dreams where I wake up and wish I hadn't, because I liked being in those dreams with you that way."

I nodded and stayed mute. I didn't want to say the wrong thing, or dash his dreams of being a family. It could never happen, but I can't stop him from dreaming.

We approached a fort-like structure, and he walked along the side, then pressed me up against the old grooved wood. "Then there are the times I dream I'm holding you in my arms in my bed. I'm making love to you painfully slow, drawing out every last bit of pleasure from your moans, and leaving my mark on your neck when you toss your head back and let go. Those are the dreams where I wake up like this."

He took my hand and held it to his zipper. The bulge was hard and throbbed against my palm.

I sucked in a breath before I answered. "I have those dreams, too."

His lips crashed down on mine and I kissed him back with the same kind of passion he offered me. I wrapped one leg around his back and wrapped my arms around his neck. I didn't have a choice. I had to give in to the desire that coursed through me. He held me to the fort with his body, and my belly pressed against his need. I moaned low in my throat as his tongue battled its way past my lips and entangled mine. He tasted of the wine we had shared and my stomach dropped. I was lost in his scent, and his touch, and didn't want to think about how dangerous this was. His lips drifted away from mine, and his head dipped, to run his tongue along the ridge of my breasts. I tangled my hands in his hair when his tongue dipped between them, and the warmth of his caress lit me on fire.

"Oh, Kade, please make me feel again," I begged, and his tongue stilled. He kissed his way back up to my mouth, and tortured me with precision slowness. He carried me to the highest peak, and then pulled back and left soft kisses against my lips.

"How do you feel?" he asked against my cheek where his tongue flicked out against my earlobe.

I whimpered with desire. "I feel so good. I want to feel better. Please," I cried, but his tongue stopped moving across my ear, and he wrapped his arms around me, holding me to him while he rested his head against the wood of the shelter.

"I won't make love to you, Autumn. No matter how much it's killing me not to, and it's killing me." He ground his hips into my thigh and groaned. I stayed stock still in his arms until he loosened them enough for me to step out of them.

"We should go. We have church in the morning, and I'm sure Tina wants to get home," I stuttered, smoothing my shirt with my hands and running from the building. The picnic blanket was still on the ground and the indentations from our bodies were still visible. They taunted me, and I threw the dirty glasses and the empty wine bottle back in the cooler. I picked up the blanket, wadded it up in a ball, and forced the tears back from my eyes. I felt stupid and ashamed of my behavior. I acted like a hormone driven teenager without half a brain. I reached for the cooler when he spun me around and grabbed my upper arm.

"You didn't let me finish," he said, his voice a little angry.

"There's nothing left to finish, Kade. I'm sorry for throwing myself at you like that. It won't happen again," I promised. My voice, however, didn't want to say the words it was being forced to say, and it broke on the final word.

"That's where you're wrong. There's so much left to finish here, Autumn. Believe me when I tell you every fiber of my being wanted to lay you down back there and relieve the pressure building in both of us, but I can't. I can't make love to you until you stop being afraid of love." I gazed up at the heavens and shook my head back and forth, until he started to recite a poem. *"There is no fear in love. But perfect love drives out fear, because fear has to do with punishment. The one who fears is not made perfect in love."* He spouted the words as if they were part of his soul.

"That's poetic," I said, trying not to think about the implications of the words.

"It's not poetry. It's scripture, *1 John 4*, and after that he says we love because He first loved us. Whoever claims to love God yet hates a brother or sister is a liar."

"You're calling me a liar," I stated, and he shook my shoulders a little.

"No, I'm saying that I can't make love to you because you're afraid. You fear, and so our love is not perfect. Fear means you're afraid of the punishment afterward. Our love is so far from perfect, because you still fear me."

"Our love?" I questioned, almost to myself as to him.

He blew out a breath and let me go, took the cooler from my hand, and stalked to the truck. He lowered the tailgate and stashed the cooler inside. I forced my feet to take the necessary steps to the truck and climbed in, then cuddled the blanket in front of me. He drove in silence, the kind of uncomfortable silence that makes you want to fill it with endless chatter about nothing important, but I couldn't force the words past the knot in my throat. He pulled up in front of my house, and kept his foot on the brake.

"I have a journalism convention to attend this week. I'll be gone most of the week, but if you need me you have my number. I promised Gray I would be Robin for Halloween and I won't let him down."

I nodded and opened the door of the truck. The tears that sat behind my lids the whole way home were threatening to spill over. The light in the truck threw shadows into the cab, and I saw the pain and fear in his eyes as I climbed out. The first tear fell when my feet hit the grass. I turned back, so he could see them. I wanted him to see the fear I had, and just what a liar I really was.

"You have an appointment for x-rays and to have your cast removed on Friday. Should I cancel that?"

He shook his head. "No. I'll be back."

I nodded my head. "Be safe, Kade."

I shut the truck door and climbed the steps, certain he could see my shoulders shaking as he drove away.

Chapter 17

I hung up the phone and leaned back in my desk chair. Gray's teacher had called to give me a report on his first week back. He insisted on returning for the whole day so I could work, but I was concerned he would tire too quickly. We compromised by me agreeing to him using his wheelchair for the first week, and by him agreeing to call me if he needed to come home. He never called, but every night he barely made it through dinner before he crashed for the night in my bed.

His teacher had just reported he spent time every day on the couch in the office, but each day those rests were shorter. Today he had rested only while the other kids were at recess and was now back in his classroom. I thanked her for taking good care of him and for understanding that he was the kind of kid I couldn't keep home if he didn't want to be there.

I glanced at the new clock on my desk. It was delivered on Wednesday, exactly at noon. It was silver, and the clock was the top of an open doctor's bag. Around it sat silver instruments, and the doctor's shield. Engraved on the front it said *Love does not boast, it is not proud.*

When I got up Monday morning to let Ace outside, my cooler sat on the back deck. I picked it up and carried it inside to empty it. My heart was still heavy from Saturday night, and the sight of the cooler made me want to cry all over again, if only I'd had any tears left. I opened the cooler expecting to clean it out, but instead I found an old Bible and a pot of flowers. The Bible had a sticky note on it, and in his handwriting it said, *Love is patient.* The flowers were indeed impatiens, and I had to laugh at the irony of his gift.

The old Bible had passages highlighted, and the pages were dog-eared from years of reading. I knew without hesitation it was his Bible. I held it to me, inhaling the slight scent of the Old Spice on it mixed with the smell of old paper. Monday night I sat curled up in the chair and went through the book reading the many passages he had highlighted. It was then I began to understand him in ways I hadn't before.

Tuesday, when I got home from work at five, Gray and Tina were smiling when I walked in the door. On the table was a pizza from Sammy's, and scrawled on the top of the box was the message *Love is kind*. Tina stayed for supper, and we laughed together over pizza and ice cream. When she came back in and asked for a ride because her car wouldn't start, Gray and I took her home. That night I called the only mechanic in town I knew, and he fixed her car by morning. Because Love is kind.

Yesterday I received an envelope. It was delivered by the paper to my office while I was in surgery. I found it on my desk and the front of the envelope said, *Love keeps no record of wrongs*. When I opened the envelope, I sat in shock. I was holding the newspaper clipping of my mother's death notice from Hudson where she had lived when she died. The second newspaper clipping was fresh and dated yesterday. It was an obituary and I read it with tears clouding my eyes.

It had her name and date of death then said, *a mother's love cannot be measured, because it is never-ending. It will be part of you forever, whether you're alone and afraid, or filled with joy and happiness. Sydney is survived by her daughter, Autumn Hanson and her grandson, Grayson. Love does not delight in evil but rejoices with the truth. Private services were held at the time of her death.*

He had written an obituary for my mother. It was simple, but it was important. More important than I had even realized. With those simple words, I had closure I hadn't about her death before. I may not have agreed with her lifestyle, but she had been dealt a hard hand to play.

The obituary was now at home in my scrapbook, with several rose petals that I had dried. I showed Grayson and explained to him about his grandma. He was too young for me to explain all of the adult things to him, but the image of his family tree still haunted me. Introducing him to his grandma made me feel a little bit better about the secrets I still keep from him.

The clock on the desk was nearing one, and I stood, putting on the best face I had for what I was going to go through next. I was going to have to face the man who over the last week had tried to release my fear. It had nearly worked too, until I had gotten the letter last night at home. It had been forwarded from my old address and the return address made me want to vomit before I even opened it. The letter was hidden in my desk drawer now, and I had already made my appointment with the devil.

Phoenix stuck her head in the door of my office and snapped me out of my reverie. "Kade is waiting in room two."

Her face was void of emotion when I nodded. Her usual bubbly teasing was gone, and I knew it was because she sensed what I was dealing with wasn't something to joke about, but to be respected. I picked up my computer and took the six steps to the door of room two. It was slightly ajar, but I knocked anyway. His voice told me to come in, and I took a deep breath before I pushed open the door and then closed it with a click. He sat in a chair near the desk with his legs covered in a pair of dress slacks and a long sleeve blue dress shirt adorning his muscles. The sleeves were rolled to the elbow, in light of his cast, and his tie was loosened with the top button open. His hair was styled, and his suit coat was hung over the back of the chair. He looked like he belonged here and I took a deep breath.

"Hi." I walked to the desk and set the computer down.

"Hi, Autumn." He smiled, but I saw the uncertainty in his eyes. "Sorry for the formality, I just got back in from the conference, and didn't have time to change."

I smiled at his nervousness. "You look nice. I've never seen you all spiffy before. It suits you."

"Thanks, so," he held up his cast, "is this coming off today?"

Okay, if he wanted to play it that way, I would play it that way. "Yeppers. We'll cut it off and then have Nick x-ray it. If it all looks good, we'll just brace it with a removable brace for a few weeks, and have you start some therapy." I motioned to the table and he climbed up on it. I noticed the way his shirt pulled tight across his chest, and it was all I could do to keep from running my hand over it.

He sat silently while I cut away the cast material, and then cut through the padding that was now matted and hard. It took me a long time to get through it, and I couldn't make eye contact for fear of losing my composure. *Fear.* That was his point. I had too much fear to let any other emotion into my heart. I got it, but I still didn't know what to do with it.

The material finally released and I pulled the cast open so he could pull his hand out. I noticed writing inside the cast and held it up to my face. He had slipped a piece of paper inside, and it said, *Love always protects, always trusts, always hopes, always perseveres.*

I set the cast down on the table and picked up the disposable washcloth, running it over his arm and through his fingers again, the way I had done just a few weeks before. The verse from *1 Corinthians 13* kept running through my mind. *Love is patient, love is kind, love is not boastful.* My hand stopped moving over his arm, and he laid his other hand over mine. My composure was gone, wiped away by the words I was trying to wipe from his arm. They were backward, but they were a reminder to me that I don't deserve someone like him. Love always fails for us Hansons', always.

"I'm sorry for Saturday night, Autumn. I just wanted to show you love is patient and love is kind. Did I do that?" I nodded my head, unable to speak. "I'm not too proud to say that this past week was one of the longest weeks of my life. Every time I closed my eyes, I saw your tears as I drove away. Every morning, when I woke up, I saw Grayson's smile the way it sits crooked on his face when I come in the door. I wanted to leave there, come home, and walk in the door and see that smile. I wanted to see you and wipe away the vision of you crying." He lifted my chin up with his finger, and I couldn't hide the tears on my face.

"But I come home and you're still crying. I wonder if everything I did this week just made things worse. Did I just make you more fearful? Are you crying because I scared you instead of comforted you?" His questions were pleading, and I wrapped my arms around his neck tightly. His came around my back naturally and held me to him. I let his heat seep into my body and prayed in a way I'd never prayed before. My mind was a big jumbled mess of pain and I didn't know what to do about any of it.

"I don't know why I'm crying. Maybe I'm crying as a way to heal. I smiled when I got your Bible, and I read all the passages you had marked. I learned more about you curled up in a chair reading that book than I ever could have in any other way. I laughed when I got the pizza on Tuesday, and Gray, Tina and I had a fun night together, but I wished you had been there, too. I wished with all my might you would walk in the door and hold me. I had a sense of satisfaction and accomplishment with the clock that sits on my desk in my office. It reminds me that as a physician, and as a woman, I shouldn't be boastful, but I should be humble. Yesterday, when I opened the envelope and saw the obituary, I cried. I haven't stopped crying, at least on the inside. I never had closure about my mother, but I never took the time to find it either. Maybe I just didn't know how. In the few lines of that obituary you wrote, you gave me the closure I didn't know I wanted."

He rubbed my back slowly. "I didn't write it with my eyes closed either."

I laughed when he threw my words back at me. "I'm trying to say I don't know how to not be fearful, but if you don't want to give up, I won't make you."

"I told you, I won't give up. Love is not self-seeking and it always hopes," he recited.

"Love never fails," I finished.

He kissed my neck gently. "Never."

Chapter 18

I sat on the bed in the hotel room and ran my hands through my hair. It was already six and the remains of my half-eaten sub sandwich were still on the TV stand. All I wanted was more Southern Comfort, but I had finished the sample sized bottle when I got here, and now I was out. I picked up my phone to Google local bars when it started to sing in my hand. I hit the answer button and smiled, anxious to hear the sound of his voice.

"Hi, Momma," Gray greeted me, and I sighed.

"Hi, baby. Are you having fun with Tina?"

"We just finished giving Ace a bath. He didn't really like it, but he was a good boy and didn't get water everywhere."

I laughed at the image of a very sad dog in my bathtub. "Sounds like he earned a treat. There are some of those special ones in the freezer if you want to give him one."

"He would love that! He's snuggled under the Batman blanket with me right now watching TV." He giggled at something I couldn't see.

The image of the two of them buddied up on the couch made me smile. My heart ached a little bit that I couldn't be there with them, but this was important. I was here to ensure his future. I was willing to give up one night with him to make sure I didn't lose him forever.

"Bedtime by seven. You have school tomorrow," I reminded him and he sighed.

"I know, momma. I'm all ready for bed, so I called early. I didn't want to fall asleep and not talk to you. I didn't want to interrupt if you got busy either."

"I'm never too busy for you, Gray. Besides, I'm just sitting here. My meeting isn't until tomorrow, but I promise I'll pick you up from school." There was silence on the other end of the line for a long few seconds. "Grayson? You still there?"

"Yes, Momma. I love you so much," he cried, and my hand gripped the phone.

"Gray, baby, what's the matter?" I asked him gently.

"I just miss you, but I'll be okay. I have Ace and Tina to keep me company until you get home," he promised in his wobbly voice.

"I miss you too, and I love you bunches and bunches, like the grapes that grow on the vines."

"I love you bunches and bunches, like the bananas that grow on the trees," he answered.

I smiled when I remembered the games we used to play when he was struggling to learn the simple things.

"Good night, Batman. I'll see you tomorrow afternoon. Call me if you need anything. I love you."

"Good night, Batgirl. I'll see you tomorrow afternoon. I love you," he sang and then the line was dead. I dropped my hand to the bed and set the phone down.

He was such a funny kid. If you close your eyes and picture him, what comes to mind the most is his smile. He's always smiling. Yesterday afternoon we had carved two of the pumpkins from the pumpkin patch, and thanks to Kade's designs, and my trusty scalpel, we had a perfect Batman symbol glowing from the front porch, and a traditional jack o' lantern with the mouth sporting holes where the teeth should be, just like Gray's happy smile.

Friday night, Kade came over at exactly six o'clock and Gray was a happy ball of excitement to see him again. Then, he did the most unusual thing. He invited us to his house for dinner. He drove us to Sunnyside, and I was anxious about being in his space and surrounded by his things. It was so far outside my comfort zone that I was shaking at the thought of seeing where he lived and slept. When he ushered us in the door though, it felt safe. It was a small house on the hill overlooking the elementary school. It was masculine, and smelled like him. His leather sofa and chair should have felt cold, but instead they enveloped you, warming you. He cooked lasagna and garlic bread, with ice cream from Dairy Queen for dessert.

While he cleaned up dinner, I walked through the house looking at the pictures he had sitting around and hung on the walls. I watched him grow up in the pictures. From being a boy about Gray's age with his Aunt Kat, all the way up to last year when he accepted his master's degree in journalism from Saint Scholastica. His degrees hung on the wall, and I picked Gray up and showed him an award that hung next to them. It was the Livingston Award for excellence in journalism. I asked him about it, and he shrugged, telling me he won it when he was twenty-nine for a story he did about our nation's Korean War vets. About how they are the forgotten war heroes of our century. He didn't boast about winning a prestige award the way so many others would. Even though I had asked him about his award, he answered with a rundown of the story and about the people he had interviewed.

I was thankful then that he brought us there, and thankful that I didn't let fear keep me from going. I got a glimpse into his world and what made him tick. Gray fell asleep watching Friday Night Lights, and he offered to let us stay the night. Unlike mine, his guest room actually had a bed in it, and Gray snuggled in for the night with Ace at his feet. Kade and I had sipped wine and talked about our early careers, and shared stories about our childhoods.

When I couldn't keep my eyes open any longer, he took me to his bedroom and laid me down. He'd stripped off my shoes and pants, and put a pair of sleep pants over my bikinis. I'd slipped under the covers and laid my head on his pillow. It smelled like him, and my heart pounded in my chest. The room was masculine with heavy wood furniture surrounding the king-sized bed. My eyes lit on the picture that adorned his nightstand, and I'd picked it up with a shaking hand. It was the silly selfie we had taken at the pumpkin farm on the big hay wagon. We were grinning, and even Ace popped his head into the picture at the last minute. I'd held the frame to my chest and asked him for a copy of it. Now the same picture sits on my nightstand by my own bed.

I had watched as he stripped down to his t-shirt and jeans, and then went into the bathroom and returned in a pair of sleep pants and nothing else. He picked up the pillow from the other side of the bed and leaned in to kiss me without touching anything but my lips. He had wished me a good night saying he was going to sleep on the couch, so I could have the bed. It didn't take much for me to convince him to stay with me, but he still wouldn't be with me. He lay on top of the covers while I was underneath. Eventually I fell asleep on his chest, to the rhythm of his hand on my arm.

I sighed and checked my phone for messages. I hated that I was disappointed there wasn't one from him. After the pumpkins were carved, we put on our costumes for the party last night. Gray was Batman, Ace got a cape and was instantly Bat-Dog, I was Batgirl, and Kade was Robin. He was decked out in the full costume, and he and Gray had spent the night saying, *Holy candy Batman* and *Holy Long John Silver Robin.*

I laughed most of the evening, which was a great distraction from how hot he looked in tights and a silky leotard. It was all I could do to keep my hands off him. His well-placed hiss through his teeth about his self-control being pushed to his limits when I did rub my hand over his chest, kept me in check. I wasn't ready for him to lose his self-control. I didn't think so anyway, maybe. No. Definitely not.

I blew out a breath and shifted uncomfortably. He wasn't the only one whose self-control was barely hanging on by a thread. Thankfully, once we got to the school party my mind was distracted with other things like making a sock puppet of the Joker and the Penguin, and battling good against evil. There was bobbing for apples, face painting, and way too much candy. We listened to Dracula read *The Spider and the Fly,* and ate caramel apples and popcorn balls. At the end of the night, the party organizers voted on best costumes, and we won the grand prize.

It was a basket of goodies from all the businesses in the area, including one free movie a month for the next six months for the whole family. Gray was over the moon excited naming all the movies he wanted to see. I promised him we would go to the first one next weekend, and he wouldn't let it go until I promised him Kade could come, too.

Kade.

I closed my eyes and pictured the smug look on his face when the x-rays showed his arm was completely healed. He begrudgingly took the brace I strapped onto his arm, but it was mysteriously missing already by the time he showed up at my door Friday night. After our fun weekend together, not telling him about the meeting tomorrow made me feel guilty. It was deceptive, but he would want to come with me, and I couldn't be locked up in a hotel room by myself with him for a whole night. I would implode from being that near to him. Apparently, not having sex in seven years is an unusually long time, and I was starting to feel the effects of the lack of male companionship over those years. Unfortunately, or fortunately, I'm not a woman who believes in sleeping around, or in one-night stands. I did that once and I paid the ultimate price.

The reality is I'm raising a child, and I also have a career to protect. I can't risk the complications that could come from hooking up. Besides, physical needs can be satisfied in other ways. This clearly had more to do with the emotional lack of companionship. I'd tried to tell myself that once life had settled in, and we had been in Cloquet for a while, everything would even out. The problem was myself just didn't want to listen to that kind of logic when it knew Kade already loved me.

I banged my head on the pillow and hoped eventually my brain would unscramble, but it didn't. I still loved him too and that scared the hell out of me, frankly. How could I not love him? He was perfect in every way. He loves me, and he loves my son. He has a stable job and a solid head on his shoulders. He doesn't sleep around, from what information I could gather, and he was pretty much an upstanding community member. Why was he still single? Why hadn't some woman snatched him up over the ensuing years? Why wasn't he at home with his wife and two kids with a white picket fence?

Because, he was meant for you, Autumn.

My eyes popped open, and I shook my head. "Whoa, either I'm drunker than I thought I was, or I haven't had enough."

I climbed off the bed and grabbed my purse and car keys from the TV stand. I was going to find a few glasses of Southern Comfort and then I would fall asleep and deal with the rest of my life in the morning.

Chapter 19

Kade

"She must really be something for you to be chasing her halfway across the state. I hope she's worth it."

I stared at Lax who was in the driver's seat of my pickup truck. "She's more than worth it, so just shut up and drive," I ordered, and he held his hands up off the wheel and mimicked me like an idiot.

"I'm just saying. I've never seen you running around like your ass is on fire the way I saw you in my shop. Are you afraid she's leaving for good?" he asked, and I rubbed my forehead to keep from calling him stupid.

"She has a son and he's at home. No, I don't think she's leaving for good. I just don't believe she has a meeting for work tomorrow. I think she's there for another reason. If it's what I think it is, she won't do this alone." I tapped my fingers on my knee and checked my phone for messages. There weren't any, and that just made me more agitated. She'd lied to me, and I wanted to be angry with her. I guess it wasn't a lie, it was more an omission, but my gut was still twisted in knots. When I went to see them this afternoon, Gray was there with Tina, and he told me she was gone for a meeting. The investigative reporter in me didn't buy it. With a few well-placed phone calls, I had a pretty good guess as to the real reason she was residing at the AmericInn in Stillwater for the night.

"She's gonna be ticked when you just show up at her door. Maybe she wanted a night of peace and quiet. No kid and no nosy reporter." Lax laughed, and I wanted to punch him. I'm not a violent man, but he was seriously getting on my last nerve.

Maybe asking him to drive me down here was not the smartest idea, in hindsight.

He steered the truck down the street where the annoying GPS woman directed him. He shook his head and laughed a little. "All right, buddy, I'll stop now. I've been hassling you for one reason, and one reason only. Lydia. I didn't want you to make another Lydia sized mistake. The fact that you're ready to beat me, tells me Autumn is anything but a mistake."

I laughed against my will at his assessment. A Lydia-sized mistake. "Dude, Lydia wasn't a mistake. Lydia was a lesson."

"Leave it to you to say something like that. I sorta get it, though. There have been some women in my life that were lessons," Lax joked, and I smacked my forehead.

"Lax, you're gay." I laughed, and he nodded, and pointed at me.

"And those women are the reason." He snickered as the hotel came into view. Her Equinox was parked in the lot and I let out a breath. I was happy she was here, but hurt that she didn't want me to know why.

Lax pulled up and dropped me off at the door. "Are you sure you don't want me to hang around town? What if she doesn't want you here or she's here with another dude?"

That thought hadn't even crossed my mind, because it was as ridiculous of an idea as Lax dating Elton John. I leaned back in the door and pulled my duffel bag off the floor. "Go home, Lax. Thanks for the ride. I'll let you know how it went tomorrow when we get back."

He smiled and gave me a jaunty salute as I closed the door. I slung my bag over my shoulder and pulled open the heavy glass entry doors. *Time to bring your A game, Kade.* I stopped in the vestibule of the hotel and closed my eyes. I said a prayer I would know the right things to say and the right way to show her I'm not like all the guys who came before me.

∞∞∞

Autumn

I flipped the lock off the door and pulled it open. It was time to find a bar. I took one step and walked directly into a wall. "What the hell?" I sputtered and then caught a hint of Old Spice. My nose was pressed against a shirt filled with muscles that were far too familiar. I stepped back a hair and gazed upward. "Kade?" I asked, my eyes traveling from his blue flannel shirt, all the way to his brown shuttered eyes.

"Autumn," he answered, stepping forward until I was back in the room and he closed the door behind him. He dropped a duffle bag on the floor and set a bottle of Southern Comfort next to the ice bucket.

"Ho—how, did you find me?" I stuttered like a scared four-year-old. I put distance between us and hovered by the window. The back of the hotel had a berm of trees between it and the next building, but the lights from their parking lot shone faintly through the branches. There was probably no way I could get out the window and away from him. I was probably going to have to talk to him.

"You mean how did I find you, since you didn't mention you were leaving?" he asked, walking toward me. He thought better of it and sat on the foot of the bed. "I asked Tina. She apparently wasn't told it was a secret."

I walked past him without making eye contact. "I need a drink."

I opened the top of my Subway cup that was half full of warm Coke, and dumped in the amber liquid. I added a few ice cubes from the bucket, and fastened the lid. I sucked hard through the straw.

"Don't you know you shouldn't drink alcohol with a straw?" he asked, and I set the cup down and tore the plastic off a cheap plastic glass. Dropping in two more ice cubes, I poured a finger of comfort in and slammed it back.

"Happy?" I asked, and he leaned back on the bed.

His face told me no and guilt filled me. I didn't owe him any explanations. We weren't dating. We were just in love. I choked on the swallow I had just taken, and he jumped up and rubbed my back until I could breathe again. I stepped away quickly and went back to my perch by the window. I heard him opening a cup, and he added ice cubes then a long pour of the south. From my peripheral vision, I saw him go to the left side of the bed and set his glass on the nightstand. He walked back to the door and shut off the lights, leaving only the light next to his glass burning. He kicked his shoes off and climbed up on the bed to lean against the headboard. He took a long swallow of the booze and grimaced as it went down.

I sighed. "Why are you here, Kade? I didn't ask you to come."

"Clearly you didn't, but I'm not here for you. I'm here because of Gray," he answered, and I spun around on him.

"What's wrong with Gray? I just talked to him a few minutes ago and he was fine. Well, not fine, he seemed tired, but he said he was going to bed." I replayed the conversation in my mind and remembered the part about not wanting to bother me. Suddenly, I sensed a set-up.

"Nothing's wrong with Gray, except that he's worried about you. I stopped by there this morning after church, and you were gone. I asked him if he wanted to go to McDonald's for lunch, and he said he wasn't hungry. Then I got really worried because he loves McDonald's and with his," he rubbed his hand around his belly, "but then he told me you went to a meeting and he was scared."

"Scared?" I asked with my arms wrapped around myself. "I go to meetings a lot. He never gets scared. He loves Tina."

"As it turns out, he wasn't scared about being there with Tina. He was scared for you." He took another drink from his glass, and raised one brow above it.

"I'm confused. Oh, you mean because I was driving alone?" I questioned, and he shook his head, and set his glass down on the table.

"No, he was scared you would start crying in your sleep

tonight, and he wouldn't be here to rub your arm and wipe your face."

His words ripped through my heart, and I sat down on the floor of the hotel room. It was more like I fell to the floor of the hotel room. He was off the bed and next to me in a flash. He pulled my face up and I saw the concern in his eyes. It was there, it was real, and I wanted him to hold me in a way I'd never wanted anything before in my life. "I told him I would come and make sure you didn't get scared and cry."

I hung my head again and he let my chin go. He picked me up off the floor and set me on the bed, then knelt in front of me. "Is Gray sleeping with you at night?"

I gazed over his shoulder at the ugly picture of ducks on the wall. "He couldn't get comfortable the first night home from the hospital, so he slept in my bed. He just hasn't left."

"Are you crying in your sleep?"

"I told you, I dream about us. I try to wake myself up before the end, but sometimes I can't."

"Why do you cry?" he asked, but I shook my head and wouldn't make eye contact. "Autumn, I'm not going away. I'll sit right here all night until you tell me."

I sighed with frustration. "The end of the dream, whether you've just made love to me for hours, or we've been together with Gray, you leave." My breath caught and I stopped the sob that threatened to erupt.

He rubbed my thighs and gave me a moment to get myself under control. "But I always come back. I've never left and not come back."

I nodded. "I know, but the psyche is a weird thing. I guess it takes your deepest fears and lets them play out in your dreams." I rubbed my forehead and tried to put my thoughts together. "I think it's just what I expect, so no matter how much fun we have, or how hot the kisses are, I know it will come to an end."

"You just expect I'm going to leave?" he asked perplexed.

"Yes, that's how it works," I explained. "I've been living it my whole life."

"Your father?"

"He was the start, yes." I rubbed my forehead, and he pulled my hand down again. "I need a drink."

I tried to stand, but he held me there with his hands. "Alcohol won't make this go away, and it won't make me go away. We're going to talk about this now. For the last three hours I sat in a car and tried to figure out what I did that made you so afraid of me."

"You haven't done anything," I whispered.

"So why are you punishing me?"

I stood and went back to the window. "I'm sorry. I don't deserve you. I don't deserve the way you care for me and Gray. I won't hate you if you're done."

"If I were done with you, I wouldn't be here, Autumn. I'm begging you to be honest with me. Tell me what you're really afraid of."

I wrapped my arms around myself. "Do you want kids, Kade?"

I watched him from the corner of my eye and read the emotions that washed over his face. "I've always wanted kids. When I got married, I thought she wanted kids, but it never happened."

I whipped around. "You're married?" I was stunned silent, and he stood.

He held my arms and my eyes. "No, not anymore. It was a long time ago. I met her in college and we got married shortly after graduation. We had the big wedding and the long white dress. I wanted kids, but she didn't. We eventually divorced."

"Where is she now?" I asked surprised.

"In Cloquet. Her name is Lydia. She lives with her husband and three kids. I see her all the time, and we still exchange Christmas cards. Her son is a year older than Gray."

I waved my hand. "Wait, you said she didn't want kids."

"I realize now she didn't want kids with me. I wasn't her meant-to-be, and she was smart enough to sense it before we brought kids into the world that would be innocent bystanders to us falling out of love. Hindsight tells me it never was love. It was too easy to give her up."

"And you're still friends with her?"

He shrugged and gave me the palms. "It's not in my nature to hate anyone. I don't know how. I only know how to respect the choices people make, even if I don't agree with them. She did me a favor by leaving, and I'm happy she found the person she was meant to be with."

"How long ago did you divorce?"

"Almost a dozen years, I think."

"I can't figure out why you haven't remarried. You're the most eligible bachelor in Cloquet," I joked, and he rubbed my shoulders lovingly, which took the punch out of the words I had hoped would rile him.

"After I broke up with Lydia, I promised myself I wouldn't get married again until I found my meant-to-be. I focused on my career and waited. I had no doubt when the right woman came along, I would know."

He tried to lead me back to the bed, but I refused to move. "And now you know?"

He nodded. "I walked into this little office building to do a story about a new community doctor, and I walked out completely enamored by the woman I had met. There was no doubt in my mind she would be the mother of my child."

I shook my head and walked over to the TV stand and took another long pull off the straw. The alcohol was bitter, and the Coke was flat, but I didn't care. His hands were on my shoulders again, and he leaned in, only his chest touching me.

I shrugged out from under his hands and went to the corner of the room. I leaned my back into the small space and crossed my arms. I wanted to scream and cry, but I didn't, instead my voice held no emotion when I spoke. "I can't be the mother of your child, Kade. I can't have children."

His shoulders sank, and he came to me. He filled up the little bit of space left in the corner when he stood in front of me. "I'm not going to make you tell me why, Autumn. As far as I'm concerned, you are a mother. Gray is your son, and he's all I'll ever need."

He hugged me but I remained stiff in his arms. I couldn't let myself believe what he was saying. I had to make him understand. "I had another child," I started and then stopped.

He led me to the bed, and this time I let him. I sat down and put my head in my hands. "I was a resident at the Children's Hospital. I was almost six months pregnant and was working a trauma in the ER. It was a teenager who had been in a bicycle accident. I was coming around the stretcher, and he kicked out. He barely glanced my stomach and I didn't think too much of it. He went to the OR and I went to bed to sleep between patients. When I didn't respond to the next page, they found me in the bunk covered in blood. The placenta had ruptured, and my baby had died. It was only because they found me so quickly that they were able to save my life. They rushed me to surgery and delivered my daughter. Then they had to do an emergency hysterectomy. When I woke up, I had no baby and no chance to ever have another."

"Autumn, sweetheart, I had no idea," he whispered, and wrapped his arm around me.

"I held my daughter for an hour after I woke up. She was gone, but I memorized every part of her. She was so little, but so perfectly formed. I named her Eden, because it means paradise. She would be fourteen on Tuesday." I choked on the words, and he turned me into him and laid his chin on my head.

"It must be a hard day to get through."

"Some years are worse than others. I always make it a special day. Gray doesn't know why, but someday I'll tell him."

"What about her father?"

"Her father was a mistake. He was gone as soon as he found out I was pregnant. We had been together for a year, and his parents were very influential in the town. They paid me to keep quiet about the whole thing and not sue him for child support. I took the money for the child I thought I would have to raise alone. After she died, I tried to return it since it felt dirty to keep it."

"He was an idiot," he said, kissing my head. "I would have never left your side. We would have grieved the loss of our child together, and celebrated when a child like Gray came into our lives."

I laughed loudly, and it shocked him. He sat up and held me by my shoulders. There was hurt in his eyes and I grimaced. "I'm sorry, I wasn't laughing at you. I was just laughing at how opposite our lives have been. So opposite I'm not sure we can ever be anything but."

"Something happened when you got Gray, tell me what it was," he said, and I gazed at him surprised.

"How did you know?"

He caressed my face patiently. "I didn't."

I flopped back on the bed dizzy and exhausted. "I'm tired. I can't talk about this right now."

He stood and went to the bathroom. I heard the water come on and when he came back, he took my hand and led me to the bathroom. "Take a hot shower and I'll order some food. We have all night."

He tried to let go of my hand, but I wouldn't drop his. "Shower with me," I begged. He sucked in a breath, and I noticed the war waging in his eyes. "Please."

I let go of his hand and lifted my shirt over my head. His eyes were glued to my face, and I unbuttoned his shirt. I pulled it down and off his body, and ran my hand over the hard muscles of his chest and through the dark hair that tapered to his belt.

"Autumn, I—" He tried to speak, but I put my finger to his lips and unzipped my jeans, stepping out of them, then unbuckled his belt and his jeans. He let them fall, and I sucked in a breath at his lack of underclothes. He was gorgeous, and I wondered what the hell I was doing. He pulled me to him and kissed me with complete loss of control while he unhooked my bra and let it fall to the floor. He pulled my bikinis off and threw them in the corner, too.

He held out his hand, and I took it to step over the edge of the old cracked white tub to stand under the spray. He stepped in behind me and pushed my wet hair out of my face, running his fingers through it until it was wet all the way through. The shampoo lathered in his hands, and he massaged it into my hair. My eyes closed and my head fell backward, as he rinsed it clean.

"God, you're so incredible, Autumn." He kissed my neck and down my chest, but stopped at the swell of my breast. He used the soap to wash each breast meticulously. The trail of his fingers made me weak with need, and when he ran the soap around each nipple, I arched and cried his name. The soap moved to my belly, and the water washed the soap from my breasts, leaving my tender nipples tingling. His lips came down over one, and I grabbed his hair to hold him to me.

He dropped the soap and continued to rub me. His tongue flicked across my breast and at the same time his warm hand slipped between my legs. I couldn't speak. I moaned instead and the walls of the shower echoed the sound. My legs shook from the pleasure of his touch and he stood, kissing my lips gently without breaking the rhythm of his hand.

"Ride the wave, baby," he whispered against my lips.

"Not without you," I cried, gripping his shoulders.

"No, ride it and let go," he whispered, and then claimed my mouth. He kissed me hot and hard and his fingers moved to a rhythm I couldn't stay on top of. The first wave hit me and I tensed with fear.

"Fall, sweetheart, I'm going to catch you. I love you," he whispered in my ear, his lips catching my earlobe. He bit down gently, and at that moment, I fell. The wave took me down under the water and I floated there, the pleasure wiping away everything but his promise to catch me with those three little words.

Chapter 20

Kade

I stood in the produce section of Kowalski's Market, and my mind was racing. The look on her face, when she told me she had lost a baby in the most horrific of ways, was like reliving it with her. Suddenly, so many things made sense. Her fierce love for Gray, adopting him as a single woman, and her brick wall of distance she kept between us. At least until tonight when I brought that wall crumbling down.

I picked up some strawberries, grapes, precut apples, and pineapple and set them in the basket. I left her to get dressed while I went to get something to eat. She needed something to wash the alcohol from her system, but I also needed to get away from her. I needed to put my head back in the right place after sharing that shower with her. My lower half still ached from the willpower it took not to make her mine right there, but I couldn't. She needed to see I was going to be here in the morning, and not just because I had spent the night making love to her.

My gut twisted at the image of how beautiful she was giving herself over to me. Watching her go from scared to trusting was more powerful for me than any physical relief I would have gotten from her. I set the basket of fruit and bread on the conveyor belt and paid the bill. I walked from the store lost in the story she told me and knew I was getting closer to the end of her past hurts. I also knew the most important chapters were still missing. The chapters that would tell me why she protected her heart so fiercely. It didn't take me more than a few phone calls to find out why she was here, but I wanted to hear it from her. I wanted her to share the most evil, scariest part of her life with me, so I could tell her it didn't matter to me. I stepped across the grass with the bag hanging down at my side. It dawned on me as I walked back that I didn't take the car, and that made it easy for her to escape. I was without a vehicle, and I would never be able to find her in time if she ran away. I would never be able to protect her from that monster if she left me stranded here. I started running, my heart afraid she couldn't handle what was happening between us, and she would build that wall back up and be gone from my life. I ran in the side door and ran full bore to the room, the bag of groceries swinging against my leg. I slid the key into the lock and then slammed the door open. "Autumn!"

She turned quickly with wide eyes. She wore a gauzy nightgown that made me instantly hard and I dropped the bag to gather her in my arms. "You're still here," I whispered and she rubbed my back with her tiny hands.

"Of course," she sighed. "You love me."

I let out a long breath and loosened my hold on her a bit. "I was at the store and got scared you would run. I want to be here for you tomorrow." I snuggled my face into her neck, and she stiffened a little at the word tomorrow. I released her and she sat on the bed, her hands clasped in her lap.

"Go home, Kade. This isn't your battle to fight. I'll say my piece, and the rest is up to them."

I picked up the bag of groceries and took the fruit out, thankful it was already cleaned and de-stemmed. I loaded it into a dish and brought it to the bed with plastic forks and napkins for the bread. I laid it out and climbed up, handing her a fork.

"I'm not going anywhere," I answered. "I'm not going to abandon you, now or ever. I'll tell you that every morning from now until eternity if that's what I have to do to get you to believe it."

Her eyes stared down at the fork in her hand, and she laid it on the bed. "You know why I'm here."

It wasn't a question. It was a statement and I gave her the so-so hands. "I suspect, but I would really like you to tell me."

She sighed heavily and rubbed her forehead. "Last week I got a letter from the parole board. Grayson's biological father is up for parole. Tomorrow is the hearing. He doesn't know who has Gray, and the records are sealed. They're letting me speak to the panel in private to protect my identity."

I took her hand from her head, and it was ice cold. She was shaking just talking about it, and I feared how hard tomorrow was going to be for her. I didn't doubt that she could handle it, but it was going to be torture on her soul. "Parole already? Gray's only seven."

She nodded quickly. "That's the legal system nowadays. Fifty years in prison means six or seven years. He was found guilty of second-degree murder of his girlfriend since it wasn't premeditated. He got aggravated battery on Gray. I think he should have been charged with attempted murder, but that's just my opinion."

"Mine too," I agreed. My lips pursed listening to the fear in her voice.

"I'm here to fight his parole. He's had problems in the jail with fights between inmates, and psychiatric issues. I don't think it's safe for him to be back out on the streets to hurt another child or kill another woman. I truly believe he'll do it again and more lives will be destroyed. As much as being here makes me want to throw up, I have to do this. I have to do it for all the other Grays in the world who suffer because of guys like him."

I held her hand and brought it to my lips, kissing the coolness of her skin and holding her eyes with mine. "You're a strong woman, Autumn Hanson."

"I don't feel that strong." She rubbed her forehead, and I reached up, taking that hand down to hold both. Her forehead rubbing in times of stress had endeared her to me, because it was a simple thing that not many would notice, but it calmed her and helped her deal. When some women would fall apart, she rubbed her forehead.

I pushed the food out of the way and moved both of us up

against the headboard. "I'm going to hold you tightly, and I want you to tell me the rest of the story about Gray."

She laid her hand on my chest and her head on my shoulder. "You know it all. I told you the truth before. I haven't told Grayson he's adopted because I'm not sure it matters right now. Part of me doesn't want to tell him. I know when I explain about his parents that will be hard for him to hear, no matter how old he is. Someday I know it will matter to him, and I'll tell him the truth, but for now it doesn't."

I kissed the top of her head and then her temple. "Gray is so lucky to have you. You've done so much, and given up so much, to keep him safe. Someday he'll know just how lucky he was that you came into his life."

She shrugged a little. "I feel like I'm the lucky one. I was at a point in my life where I was suddenly faced with wanting to be a mother and not being able to be one."

"I didn't believe you before when you said you had told me the whole truth about when Gray came into your life, now I know for sure. When you talk about those early days, your eyes are clouded, like there's some part of that time in your life you're trying to forget. If you were working in the Twin Cities when you got Gray, how did you end up in Duluth?"

She stiffened in my arms and tried to pull away, but I wouldn't let her. "Nope, you're going to tell me. You know the truth about Lydia, and I want to know the truth about whoever he is."

It was like someone popped a balloon, and she deflated in my arms. "We moved to Duluth for a couple of reasons. The first was I wanted to get Gray out of the Cities, so no one knew where he was. Out of sight out of mind, so to say. My fiancé, William, had gotten a job offer at a bank in Duluth, so we took the opportunity and left. Duluth was on the other side of the world at that moment in time and I held onto it as a new beginning for us. Little did I know it was just the beginning of the end. I stayed home with Gray for the first few months we lived there and we were happy. Then one day Gray got sick and ended up in the hospital for a few weeks. I went home after an especially long night and William was gone. He had moved out and left a note that he was never coming back."

I rubbed her shoulder and ground my teeth to keep from swearing aloud. She was serious when she said everyone leaves her. What a bastard, and a coward. "Was William in for adopting Gray with you at the time?"

She nodded her head. "He was all in when we brought him home from the hospital. He wanted children, and since I couldn't have any of our own, he understood we would have to adopt. He said it didn't matter to him that they weren't his own flesh and blood. He would love them as if they were because I was their mother. But after we moved to Duluth, when I would talk about setting a date to get married, he would change the subject. There was suddenly a distance there, but with a new job, new town, and new baby, I figured it would pass."

"What did the note say?" I asked, and she shuddered a little in my arms. She shook her head, and I held her eyes. She didn't have a choice but to see the love I had for her in mine.

"He said he couldn't handle having a retard for a kid, and be saddled with him for the rest of his life. He knew I would choose Gray over him anyway, so he was gone. Don't contact him, it was over."

I sucked in a breath. "He didn't use that word, did he?" I asked angrily, and she nodded.

"And so many more. He wasn't the man I thought he was. Gray was a baby. He had no idea what kind of child he would be. The truth is he just used it as an excuse to end the relationship. It would have ended anyway at some point, so I should probably thank him for doing it before we were married. I just can't find a way to thank him for leaving me like he did."

I held her to me and rocked her a little. "Then you got a job at St. Mary's and raised that little boy all on your own."

"And swore I would never look at another man, much less love one, ever again," she whispered.

"I understand. I'm sorry for pushing you, but if I'm going to lose you, then I have to know why. Sometimes there are parts of our hearts that just can't heal, and I get that. I see the pattern. First your father, then Eden's dad, and then William. Three strikes and you're out." I sighed, and loosened my grip on her, afraid I would never let her go otherwise.

"I see now in my more mature years that I didn't love David or William. I was in love with the idea of being in love, but when push came to shove, I didn't care about either of them enough to fight for them. It's really hard to learn how to love someone when you aren't given the tools early in life," she admitted and picked up a strawberry, chewing it thoughtfully.

"I don't think so. I think we're inherently born to love. Sometimes though, when bad things happen, we no longer trust that feeling of love because we aren't shown how to nurture it. Look at Gray. Because you love him so unconditionally, he's blossomed into an incredible little boy. He has his challenges, but because he's firm in the knowledge that you love him, he keeps trying. Imagine if you hadn't taken him and he was in a foster home all these years. He would have given up by now because he didn't have a stable rock of love to build on. It was the same way for me. I didn't have parents, but I had Aunt Kat who made sure I knew how much she loved me. That she wasn't raising me because she had to, but because she wanted to."

"You're really good at loving people." She sighed and leaned back into me which made me smile.

"You are, too. Look at all the people you take care of day after day. You have to love what you're doing to keep doing it. You love Gray enough to give your life for him. I know that. I also know in your own way that you probably love me," I added, caressing her face.

She gazed up at me, her eyes like saucers and rimmed with tears. "It scares me so much. I'm frozen in place every time you say it. There's one part of my heart that wants to say it back, but the other says, *don't believe it, it's a trick.*"

"*There is no fear in love. But perfect love drives out fear, because fear has to do with punishment.* If that scripture is true, why are you punishing yourself?" I asked, and she gripped my shirt in her fist tightly.

"I'm not punishing myself. I'm protecting myself. You say love never fails, but it has so many times for me."

"No, sweetheart, it hasn't. The times when you felt let down and abandoned, it wasn't love. You just said that."

She was silent, and I held her in my arms. Her grip eventually loosened on my shirt, and her hand splayed across my chest. "Why didn't you make love to me in the shower?" she finally asked quietly, and I wondered how we got here, but was willing to answer.

"Because that would have been self-seeking. The definition of self-seeking is to be concerned only about yourself and not caring about what happens to others."

"You put aside your own needs to take care of me. To make sure I felt good. To take the edge off and help me relax?"

"Yes, because love is kind and patient. If all I wanted was sex, I could have sex with any number of women, but I don't want just sex. I wanted love and now I've found it. I have to protect it, honor it, and hope that if I show you all the love I have for you, and Gray, you can learn to trust it."

"I haven't been intimate with a man in almost seven years. What you did tonight was tell me you cared more about me than you did about yourself, and that didn't go unnoticed. When I pulled you into the shower, I just wanted to release the pent-up feelings I'd been struggling with for months now. I knew if you climbed in with me, and we had sex, it would be a matter of time before this all ended. Instead, you made love to me. Maybe not in the true sense of the phrase, but you did, with your words, your hands, and your heart. I could only let go because you promised to catch me with those three words. Somehow, I trusted you would."

I set my glasses on the bedside table and leaned down, inches from her mouth. Her lips were like a magnet pulling me closer until I touched them, the heat and the taste of them making me moan. She reached up and cupped my cheek with her hand then kissed me with the same kind of pent up passion I was holding back. She tasted of strawberries and I ran my tongue along the edges of her lips, waiting for them to part and give me entrance to own her. She twisted up and pushed me down, but never broke contact with our lips. She settled every curve of hers into my body and I felt the moan before I heard it. It rumbled through her chest and all the way to my core. I tore my lips from hers and gazed into her beautiful hazel eyes.

"Your eyes are brilliant tonight. I've never seen them shine like this," I told her, kissing each lid. Her face was scrubbed clean of makeup, and she was never more beautiful.

"That's because they've never been in love before," she answered. Her voice was strong, and her words didn't falter.

I pulled her forehead to my lips and kissed it. I held her there for a long time, letting her words sink in. "Are just your eyes in love?" I finally asked, not sure what her answer would be.

She pulled her head back and ran her fingers through my hair. "Don't you know? The eyes are the window to the soul."

"I need to hear you say it," I begged, and she rested on top of me, her mouth near my ear.

"I love you, Kade Franco."

Autumn

I snuck from the bed and picked up my phone then headed to the bathroom, so I didn't disturb his sleep. I pushed the door almost closed and opened my phone to check the time. It was only five, which meant I had a few hours before I had to be up and ready for the meeting. There were two emails I responded to quickly, and then closed my phone, and sighed. Now, I would go back to bed, and snuggle in with him for another few hours. Being in his arms was far more comforting than I ever dreamed it could be. I tiptoed to the bed and stood there, watching him sleep.

Last night, after I told him I loved him, I begged him to make love to me, but he wouldn't. He said he wanted to show me he would be here in the morning, and not just because he had spent the night making love to me. He said love is patient and he could wait. Then he took me higher than I've ever been with his lips and his hands. He left me so relaxed I fell asleep in his arms, naked, and not even caring.

My chest was so much lighter than it was twelve hours ago. Twelve hours ago, I was trying to do everything by myself when I didn't have to. He might not be able to go to the meeting for me, but he would be waiting for me when I was done.

He had asked more about Eden last night and it mattered to me that it mattered to him. He wanted to go visit her grave on the way home, since we're not too far from the Cities. The look on his face when I told him she didn't have a grave was painful. I second guessed myself for a moment, until he told me it wasn't because I chose to better the world by donating her body to science, but that I had no place to go and be with her.

He asked me so many questions about Gray. Things he wanted to know about, so he would know how to help. Things that he would need to know, if he ever got the chance to be his daddy someday. I had broken down at that point and cried softly. He wanted to know why I was crying, and I told him he would make a great dad, and he deserved more kids. I couldn't give him more kids. He told me he didn't want more kids. He wanted me and he wanted Gray. If he had us, he'd be happy for the rest of his life. I decided to answer all of his questions with honesty then. It wasn't easy raising a child with special needs. It was expensive, and sometimes scary and heartbreaking. He had experienced firsthand how scary it can be. He told me he would do everything and anything to keep him out of the hospital, but if he goes back in, he would be there to hold our hands and love us.

I shared with him all the ways his special gifts last week touched me, and apologized for not telling him about the meeting today. It wasn't a matter of asking for forgiveness, as much as it was about him knowing it was how I was dealing with all the changes I was experiencing.

He shifted and his leg was bent under the sheet. The sheet fell away, and his boxers couldn't hide the proof that his selflessness was torturing him. I wanted to make him feel as good as he made me feel, but I also wanted to show him that love is kind. My heart was pounding when he called my name in his sleep, his hand rubbing himself. I slipped onto the bed and took him in my hand. I lowered my head to kiss the tip and his hips thrust up as he moaned and called my name. I let the motion of his hips carry him in and out of my mouth while I licked the tip and let my tongue leave a trail of wetness the length of him. His hand grabbed the back of my nightie and held me still.

"Autumn, what are you doing?" he hissed. I held him in my hand, stroking him while I answered.

"Loving you." I could see the uncertainty in his eyes and I rose up to kiss his lips. "You said you wanted to show me that you would be here in the morning. It's morning, and you're here. Love is kind, just trust me," I whispered, and he moaned, pushing up against my hand.

I explored him, tasted him, and then picked a rhythm to bring him up to that same kind of wave he put me on. He wound his hand in my hair and held me to him. His hips thrust and his moans filled the room before he stilled his hips and tried to pull me away. I kept the rhythm even until I heard him calling my name with love.

Chapter 21

Kade

I set my duffle bag on the floor of my kitchen and let out a breath as I ran my hand through my hair. I had left her early this morning before Gray was awake. I'd held her all night and thought about the rest of my life.

I took a long drink of the hot McDonald's coffee I had picked up on my way home to change clothes and go to work.

Yesterday, after the meeting, she wasn't a mess the way I expected her to be. She was confident, said they were receptive, and even if he got parole it wasn't because she hadn't tried.

We had only made it halfway home before she got a phone call from her lawyer. I pulled off the highway and listened to the one-sided conversation. Gray's father wouldn't be released. He would remain in prison for at least another ten years. When she hung up, she clung to me, so happy that for the first time she could quit worrying about Gray's safety. Even if the bastard got out in ten years, Gray would be an adult, and there was no chance he would ever find him. When we pulled up in front of the school, I spotted Gray and Ace standing by his teacher. I put the car in park, and Autumn jumped out and ran to him. She scooped him into her arms and I heard Gray tell her he was worried about her. I put my hand on his back and told him I never break a promise.

We were so happy to be home we ate pizza together, and I skipped my weekly basketball game with the guys. Nothing was going to drag me away from that house. Autumn was fretting about how much work I had missed, and I told her I had already sent my story to the paper while she was at the meeting. It was a lie, but at that moment it didn't matter.

I slid the bar open on my phone and opened the picture app. I stared at the picture she had no idea I snapped and closed my eyes, thinking back to last night.

"Whatcha doing?" I'd asked from the door to her bedroom. She had her back to me, and she froze.

"Nothing," she answered, but I noticed her swipe at her face with her hands.

"Gray fell asleep while we were reading, so I tucked him into bed. Ace is with him."

She nodded, but didn't turn. "Okay."

I noticed her voice was tight, and her hand went to her face again. "Sweetheart, what is it?"

"What were you two whispering about all night?" she asked me, and I laid my hand on her shoulder, startling her. I noticed the tears on her face immediately. "Boy stuff, no big deal. Why the tears?" I asked and turned her to look at me. She stared down at my shirt and I noticed a box and some papers, on the bed. There were tiny footprints on a card on top of it all.

"Eden," I whispered, and pulled her into me.

She sighed. "I'm sorry. I thought you would be reading longer."

I rubbed her back and laid my mouth to her ear. "Introduce me?"

She had finally relented and showed me the pictures she had of Eden, her precious little girl. The fetal death certificate was a terrible thing to see. It wasn't even a birth certificate, as though her child meant any less because she never took a breath. She told me everything she remembered about her, and how lost she felt those first few weeks afterward. She had no one to grieve with over her death. Eden's father, and his family, were thrilled they were in the clear.

The card with the tiny foot and hand prints read, *Eden loves Mommy*, and it brought me to tears. I told her she was the most amazing mommy, and she had a special angel that made sure she and Gray were safe. I hugged her and we grieved together, for Eden, but also for the lost opportunity to have more babies. I held her until she cried herself out and lay spent on my chest, drifting in and out of sleep. When she was deep in sleep, I packed the pictures and papers back in the box, and stowed them away on the shelf in her closet, but not before I took this picture.

I told her I loved her every time she woke up, and she told me she loved me. It was natural and I eventually dropped off to sleep for a few hours, but not before I spent a long time thinking about what I needed to do, and how I was going to do it.

I sat down at my desk, and pulled my computer from the black leather satchel at my feet. The clock on my laptop read five-thirty, and I was ready to write. I had two hours to get it to the paper, but I would be hand delivering it with a major explanation, and prayed my editor was in a forgiving mood.

The trip back from Duluth was especially long and I forced myself to keep from pushing the gas pedal down harder. I glanced at the clock knowing what it would say. It was only one o'clock. I had four more hours until I could see her, but my whole body hummed with anxiety I couldn't explain. Today was Eden's birthday, and when I left her this morning, she assured me she was fine and going to work.

Her eyes didn't agree with her though, and I suspected this would be the hardest birthday yet for her. My phone rang just as I took the exit off 35 into Cloquet. The ringtone sent a chill through my body.

I punched the button on my Bluetooth. "Autumn?" I answered without any other greeting, but got no response.

"Kade? Kade, can you hear me?" The little voice on the line asked.

"Gray? I can hear you. Why are you calling me? Why aren't you in school?" I was almost at Washington Avenue, and wrenched the wheel to the left. I slammed on the brakes and waited for the cars to pass.

"I didn't go to school today. Momma said she wanted to stay home and have a movie day." He was whispering his explanation, and I had to struggle to hear him.

"Why are you whispering, buddy?" I cursed the traffic that was holding me up.

"Momma's in the shower, and I don't want her to hear me. Ace got me the phone so I could call you."

"Tell me why you're upset, Gray," I begged him. He was crying, and I was scared.

"Momma won't stop crying. She wanted to watch movies, but she keeps leaving to cry in the bathroom. She thinks I can't hear her, but I can. I'm scared, Kade," he cried, and I gunned the pedal. The engine roared, and I bounced across the intersection. "Can you come over? You can make her stop crying. I know you can. Please?"

"I'm almost at your house, Gray. Is the water still running?" I asked, and there was silence then a quiet *yes*.

I pounded the wheel and knew she was in the shower crying so she could hide it from her son. "Today is a hard day for your momma, buddy. I want you to understand something, are you listening?" I asked, and he gave me another soft yes. "You haven't upset her, okay? She isn't crying because of anything you did."

"I don't know, Kade. Every time she looks at me, she starts crying. I was a bad boy this morning." His voice was reticent, and I turned onto their street.

"What happened?" I asked him softly, and he sniffed.

"I didn't want eggs for breakfast, and I talked back. I shouldn't have talked back to her, but I really wanted a smoothie. She cried the whole time she made it."

I reached into my back pocket and pulled out the old wallet Aunt Kat had given me at graduation.

"Gray, she's not crying because you didn't want eggs. I can promise you that. Look out the window, do you see my truck?" I put it in park and the curtain pulled back.

"I see you, but I can't open the door, I don't have my braces on." He was crying again. "The water is quiet now."

I pulled the key out of the wallet. The key she had given me this morning before I left. The key I had hoped was to her heart. "It's okay. Hang up the phone. I have a key. I'll be right there."

I punched the button off on my headset and threw it down on the seat. My hand searched for the bag I knew was sitting next to me, and when my fingers grasped it, I was on the ground running toward the steps. I took a breath at the door and inserted the key quietly, so she didn't hear me coming in. I closed it with a soft click and Gray sat on the couch. Ace sat by him licking his hand and they were both upset. I went to him and knelt down by the couch then pulled him into my shoulder.

"Thanks for calling me, Batman. You did good." I patted his back, and he clung to me.

"I just want Momma to stop crying."

I held him out away from me and wiped the tears away with my thumbs. "I know. I do, too. I don't like when she cries. It makes my heart hurt," I whispered, and he nodded very seriously.

"Do you love my momma?" he asked in a whisper. I nodded and gave him a little smile.

"I do love your momma. I love her a lot, and you know what that means?" He shook his head, and I kissed his forehead. "That means I love you, too. I'll do anything for either one of you. Is it okay if I love you?" I asked him, and he threw his arms around my neck.

"I love you, too, Kade. I want you to be my daddy."

I rubbed his back, and a little laugh escaped my tensed-up heart. "Do you know how proud it would make me to be your daddy?" I asked him, and he finally smiled a little. "I tell you what. I'm going to go talk to your momma, and then there's something I need to talk to you about. I'm going to need your help with it. Can you do that?" I asked, and he nodded. I ruffled his hair and gave him an encouraging smile. "Do you need anything before I go find your momma?"

He shook his head. "I'm okay, just take care of her. She's so sad."

I hugged him again and rubbed his back. "You got it, buddy."

I pulled back and my phone vibrated in my pocket. I pulled it out and her cell number was on the ID. I held my finger to my lips and answered it. "Hey, beautiful. How are you?"

Gray's eyes got big, and he covered his mouth with his hand, while I stood up.

"I just wanted to hear your voice," Autumn said, and I could hear how much she had been crying.

"I love you, sweetheart. Are you between patients?" I stood at the entry to the hallway and wondered if she could hear my voice from down the hall.

"I didn't go to work today. I wasn't feeling well," she said choked, and my heart ached. I walked the ten feet down the hall and stood at the door of her bedroom. She was sitting on her bed, her back to me, and her head hung low. She looked at the phone then put it back to her ear. "Kade? Are you still there?"

I hung up the phone and slid it into my pocket. "I'm always going to be here, Autumn," I said from the doorway. She jumped and turned toward me. Her face was red and blotchy, and her hands shook.

"Could you use a hug?" I asked and she fell into my arms.

"How did you know?" she cried.

I sat down on the bed with her. "Before I left on Sunday, I programmed my number into the home phone for Gray in case he ever needed me. I told him if he pushed that button it was like pushing the Batman light, and I would drop everything and come over. He pushed that button a few minutes ago. He was scared and asked me to come, so you would stop crying."

She struggled against me. "I have to check on him."

I held her tightly. "He's fine. I just talked to him. He's watching a movie and Ace is with him. Just relax for a few minutes."

She snuggled into my chest, and I rubbed her arm while she took deep breaths and nodded for several minutes. She was all cried out, but her emotions were still raw.

"It makes me a terrible mother that I'm crying over a child I never knew, when the child He gave me is scared and alone."

I held her away from me, so she was forced to make eye contact. "It makes you human, Autumn. You're human. You're not Wonder Woman. You've put that little boy first in every aspect of your life and that makes you a devoted mom. What you're feeling right now makes you human. It makes you a woman. Even if you never had the chance to raise Eden, you're still her momma. You loved her more than anyone else in this world."

"I've been trying to figure out why I'm so bothered by it this year. Normally I can get through the day just remembering her beautiful face, and knowing she's my angel now. This year I can't."

She ran her hand up and down my face, and I reached up, holding her hand to my cheek. "Do you think maybe it's because this year, you're in love?" I asked, and she grimaced a little.

"Maybe. I can't give you children, Kade." She rubbed her forehead and I kissed her. I kissed her hard, letting go of all the passion I had been holding in for the last two months. My tongue controlled her, owned her, and possessed her. She clung to me and whimpered against me until I tore my lips from hers.

"Listen to me right now. Are you listening?" I asked, and she nodded, her eyes still glassy from the kiss.

"I know you can't have children. I'm not in love with your uterus. I'm in love with you. The beautiful, caring woman who with one smart-aleck remark stole my heart. Do you understand? I'm in love with you, Autumn Hanson, not Doctor Hanson and not Momma Hanson. I'm in love with Autumn, and everything she is in here." I tapped her chest, and she nodded without tearing her eyes from mine. "I'm not going to leave you just because you can't have my child. I'm far more interested in you having my heart and sharing my life."

Her hand rubbed my cheek, and she twined her fingers with mine in the other. "I love you, Kade. You're an incredibly good man."

I laid my lips on her forehead and closed my eyes. "I love you, too. Now, let's go check on our boy."

Chapter 22

Autumn

I sat next to Gray on the couch and patted his leg. "Hi, baby. I'm sorry if I scared you today."

He shut the television off and slipped his little hand in mine.

"It's okay, Momma, but I'm sorry if I did something to upset you. I didn't mean to," he said sadly. I pulled him to me and hugged him tightly.

"Baby, I wasn't crying because you upset me. I'm sorry I made you feel scared, and worried. Momma is just having a hard time today. Thank you for calling Kade. That was smart. I needed him," I admitted, and his little head bobbed.

"Why were you crying?" he asked against my chest, and I sat back, my eyes drifting to Kade. He was kneeling by us, and he laid his hand on my knee. We had talked in my room, and decided I should tell him the truth. I guess it was probably time.

"I'm sad today about Eden," I started and stopped, looking to Kade. He nodded and sat down on the floor Indian style.

"Who's Eden?" Gray asked in his little boy voice, and my chin started to quiver.

"Eden is, was, your sister. Today is her birthday. If she had lived, she would be fourteen," I explained.

He picked up my hand and held it between his little ones. "I had a sister?"

I smiled weakly and fought against my need to protect him. "You did have a sister. She was born seven years before you were. I had an accident, and she was born too early."

"You had an accident like mine when I was a baby?" he asked very seriously.

I stared at him unsure how to answer that. Kade squeezed my knee and answered for me. "You know how when you see a pregnant lady and her belly is sticking way out?" Kade asked Gray, and he nodded. He giggled a little as Kade made big motions with his hands. "Well, your momma's tummy was big and she was helping a patient. The patient was hurt and in pain, and he accidentally hit her in the tummy. Sometimes when that happens, the baby is born earlier than it should be. That's what happened to Eden. The doctors had to deliver baby Eden early, because your momma was very sick after the accident. If they hadn't done that then your momma wouldn't be here either."

Gray looked up at me under his long lashes, and his chin quivered. "I'm sorry about Eden, Momma. I'm glad the doctors saved you. I need you to take care of me."

I hugged him, and Kade held my hand tightly. "I'm so glad they did too, honey."

Gray jumped back and clapped his hands. "Maybe you can have another baby and then I could be a big brother!"

My heart sank, and my throat closed over. I shook my head until Kade sat next to me and put his arm around me. "Gray, your momma can't have babies now. The doctors saved her, but she can't."

Oh Lord. I held my breath. Would he catch on that he was born after Eden? Would he realize he wasn't mine? I looked at Kade with my eyes wide, but he didn't blink. His confidence was far greater than mine was.

Gray picked up my hand and patted it gently. "It's okay, Momma. Maybe, if you want to, you can adopt me a brother or sister."

I sucked in a breath and Kade laid his hand on my back. I focused on that warm spot and smiled weakly. "You know about adoption?" I asked, my voice squeaky.

"You're silly, Momma. They teach us about that in school. My friend Samantha is adopted from China. Her name was Jing-Yang there, but now they call her Sam. My other friend, Jonathan, lived in a foster home because his mom couldn't take care of him, so a new family adopted him. He has a nice Momma now, and she comes to our room every Wednesday."

"That's nice that they teach you about that in school, buddy. I can tell you really paid attention." Kade smiled, and Gray nodded eagerly.

"They said there are lots of ways to make families, and it doesn't matter as long as you love each other," my son parroted.

I laughed then and released the tension I had been feeling about this. "They're right, buddy. As long as you love each other, nothing else really matters," Kade assured him, and Gray stared at me intently.

"Do you have a picture of my sister?" Gray asked quietly, and I froze.

Kade took my hand and then Gray's. "They didn't take pictures back then like they do now, buddy. But she has the cutest little picture of Eden's footprints if you would like to see those."

I looked up at him and laid my head on his shoulder. I couldn't show Gray the pictures of Eden, and I was never more grateful to him than at that moment.

"I would like to see those," Gray said excitedly, and Kade sat me up.

"Then now is the perfect time to give your momma her surprise," Kade said and walked to the table by the door where a bag lay. He pulled a box from it and brought it over.

"I was just getting back from Duluth when Gray called me. I was going to bring this over tonight for you. I hope it will make next year a little easier, and every year after that."

I gazed at him questioningly and took the ribbon off, lifting the lid on the box. Inside was a heart-shaped locket. The front was engraved with the words *Love Never Fails*. There were two roses and a small diamond in each flower.

"It's beautiful, Kade." I glanced up, and he had the best look on his face. It was pure love, and it felt great. My hands were shaking, and I couldn't get the locket open. He sat next to me and pulled Gray onto his lap, then took the locket and opened it.

There were two pictures. The first was a picture of me rocking Gray in the hospital, just our heads, but it was so powerful. I remembered those days, and the feelings it invoked to hold him. The picture opposite it made my breath catch. It was a picture of her footprints

"How did you get these?" I asked, staring up at him, and he hugged Gray a little tighter.

"I snapped a picture last night of both with my phone. I was able to size it down to fit in the locket. I wanted you to wear both of them against your heart, always."

Gray was gazing intently at the pictures and ran his little finger over the picture of Eden's feet. "They're so tiny, Momma."

I nodded and wiped away a tear. "She was tiny, but so perfect."

I picked the locket up in my hand and noticed another notch. I caught my nail in it and popped another section. I pushed it open, and there were spots for two more pictures, but only one was filled. It was the selfie we had snapped on Halloween, all of us smiling like a family. "It's missing one," I said, running my finger over the empty space.

"No, it's not missing. It just hasn't happened yet. That's the future. Someday you'll find the perfect picture to put in there." Kade smiled, and I nodded quickly, swiping another tear off my face. I took the locket off the pad it lay on and closed it. There was a roughness on the back and I flipped it over. It said, *There is no fear in love.*

"God, I love you," I whispered.

Gray clapped his hands excitedly and threw his arms around both of our necks. "She loves you, Kade! I love you too!"

Kade laughed his deep, happy laugh. "I love you both."

He took the locket and slipped it around my neck, fastening it in the back. I lay my hand on it and kissed him gently. "Thank you. I feel much better now."

"You're welcome," Kade said and pecked me gently on the lips.

Gray stared at his hands and twisted them around a little. He glanced between us and his eyes filled with tears.

"What's the matter, Gray?" Kade asked as his eyes bore into mine.

"I was thinking about Eden and how she would love to be part of our family, but if she had lived, I wouldn't be here to be part of it. That makes me think she was a really good big sister," he explained and wiped the tear that ran down his face. Ace whined and laid his paw on Gray's leg.

"What do you mean, Gray?" I asked confused.

"Kade said the doctors saved you, but you couldn't have more babies. I know what that means." He stared at his hands and wouldn't look at either of us.

"Oh, God," I whispered, and Kade rubbed my leg to keep me calm.

"It means I'm not your real son," he said quietly.

"Yes, you are. You are my son," I said fiercely, and hugged him to me.

My eyes met Kade's and he reached for me, but pulled back. "I'm sorry, I didn't even think."

Even in my anguish I couldn't hate him. I may not be ready to tell Gray the truth, but he would have found out at some point. I reached out and ran my hand across the scruff on his face and down his arm to grasp his hand. "Love never fails. There is no fear in love," I whispered. He leaned in and kissed my lips, and then Gray's temple. He pulled Gray back onto his lap, so I could talk to him.

"The truth is, Grayson, I didn't carry you in my tummy like most mommas do. I met you after your accident when you came to the hospital where I was working. You were so tiny and barely a few weeks old. You didn't have anyone to love you." I stopped and tried to get my voice back under control.

"Where were my parents?" he asked, and I hesitated. There were some things I couldn't tell him yet. He was too young, and wouldn't understand.

"They were both in the accident with you."

He looked up at me. "They died, right?"

I nodded. "They did, but they made sure you got to my hospital. I took care of you every day after that. I held your little hand in the special bed you were in until you were well enough for me to hold you. Then I held you to my chest and kept you warm, singing songs and telling you stories about all the things we were going to do together. Soon you were strong enough to learn how to drink from a bottle, and I was so proud of you that day. You were fighting to get better, and I was fighting to take you home."

He opened the locket and looked at the picture of us, his little head covered with a hat and tucked under my chin. "He picked you."

"Who picked me?" I asked confused, and he closed the locket again.

"God. God picked you to be my momma. That's what He does. You're a doctor, and He said, *my baby Grayson is going to need a special momma to take care of him*, so He gave me to you."

I didn't try to stop the tears that sprang to my eyes at his words. "Yes, that's exactly right. You're such a smart boy." I grinned and held his face in my hands. "I love you, Grayson Hanson," I whispered, kissing his cheek.

"I love you, Momma Hanson," he answered, kissing my cheek.

"And I love you both, so very, very much," Kade whispered, hugging us tightly.

Chapter 23

I pulled the car into a spot at Washington Elementary, killed the engine, and checked my phone for a message from Phoenix. Winter had missed her appointment this morning, and I was worried something had happened to her. I had Gray's *About Me Day* at school this afternoon, so I sent Phoenix over to check on Winter while I went to the school. There were no messages, so I switched the ringer off and climbed out of the car.

After Gray had found out he was adopted he went to school and told everyone how he came to be my son. After getting a frantic call from his teacher, I assured her it was true and agreed to come in for a question and answer time.

I held my coat together over my scrubs and hurried to the door. Next week was Thanksgiving already, and the weather was getting colder, with that *take your breath away* wind. I was looking forward to a long weekend with my new family. Aunt Kat was making Thanksgiving dinner at her house. Then she and I were going shopping on Friday, while Kade and Gray do *guy stuff*. I had coffee with Kat this past weekend, and she showed me old pictures of her and Kade when he was little. She told me she likes how happy he is since he met me, and I told her I like how happy I am since I met him.

I tucked Gray's baby book under my arm and pulled the door open. I pushed the button to be buzzed into the building and waved at the secretary. I stopped at the classroom door and caught his teacher's attention before stepping into the room. Gray saw me and waved excitedly from his seat.

"Hi, Gray," I said, setting the book on his desk. "How's your day?" I asked and rubbed Ace's head.

"It's a good day, Momma. I'm glad you're here. We've been waiting. I'm so excited!" He smiled so brightly I couldn't help but tweak his cheek. He might have been a bit overly exuberant about me coming to school, but I wasn't going to complain. He loved school and I was happy he was happy here.

His teacher, Ms. Roberts, stood in front of the classroom. "Class, we have a special guest in our room today. Grayson's mom has come to talk about families. She's going to explain how she adopted Grayson, and answer any questions you might have. Okay, everyone, let's have eyes to the front and use our manners."

She motioned to us, and Gray wiggled from his chair holding onto Ace, who walked him to the front of the room. I joined them, and Gray introduced me as the momma God chose for him. Hearing his little voice so willingly accept the adoption took away all the anxiety I had about him knowing. He knew, and he didn't care. Just like Kade knew I couldn't have more kids and didn't care.

I spent the next fifteen minutes answering questions from his friends about how I adopted Gray. We shared the pictures in his baby book, and they asked about the tubes and braces he had on in various pictures. We heard stories they shared about their families, and when the topic changed to how families are created, Gray whispered in Ms. Roberts' ear. She went to her desk and brought him two pieces of paper, and he held one up.

"When I first came to school here, Ms. Roberts asked us to make our family tree," Gray said, and held up the picture he made of me and him on the swings. "This was my family tree. See, it's just me and Momma." I took the picture from him and held it up so he could hold the other piece up. "Then we met Kade, and he brought us to Aunt Kat's house, and she had Ace," he said, his voice going up with the mention of each new name. He looked at me and grinned. "I asked Ms. Roberts if I could make a new family tree, because I didn't make the first one right." He handed me the second piece of paper, and I took it from him.

He had made the same tree of yellows, reds, and oranges, but this time there was a branch that said *Grandma Sydney*, and her branch was high up in the tree, looking down over us. On a cloud in the sky lay a baby stick figure, and it said *Baby Eden*. I tried to keep my face neutral as my eyes traveled down the page. On this drawing there was only one swing, and the stick figure on it said *Grayson*, and next to the swing sat a stick figure dog that said *Ace*. Standing next to the swing were two stick figures holding hands. I swallowed hard when I saw the words *Momma Autumn* and *Daddy Kade*, and *Aunt Kat* stood to the side with her many puppies in amongst the leaves.

I put my hand over my mouth and knelt down to Gray's level. "Grayson this is a great family tree. I really like it, but you know this part isn't real. Kade isn't your daddy," I whispered, and my head snapped up when I heard *yet* in a deep, Mr. Puddlemaker voice.

I glanced up, and all the kids were focused on the back of the room where Kade stood dressed in a suit and tie. He patted Ms. Roberts on the shoulder and walked to where Gray and I stood at the front of the room. He knelt and gave Gray a great big daddy hug and then set him down on the ground.

"That's the best family tree ever, Gray," he told him, taking his little hand. "Thanks for all your help in getting your momma here today."

"You're welcome," Gray giggled and I groaned.

"I feel a set-up," I laughed, and Gray nodded his head enthusiastically.

"We wanted you to come today, Momma. Didn't we, Kade?"

"Yes, we did, because today you're talking about families, and I want to be part of your family." Kade smiled, ruffling Gray's hair. "But first, I have to ask you a very serious question." He held both of Gray's hands in his. "Grayson Hanson, nothing would make me prouder, or happier, than to be your daddy. Do I have your permission to marry your momma, and be your daddy?"

Gray threw his arms around Kade's neck and wrapped his legs around his waist. "Yes! Yes, I want to be your little boy!" he squealed, and I gazed at Kade, tears in his eyes as he held my son.

With Gray holding him like a spider monkey, he turned to me and took my hand. I was already shaking from the question he asked Gray.

"Do you remember a few months ago when I asked you if there was a Mr. Hanson?" he asked, and I nodded, laughing a little while trying not to cry. "Your answer was no, but I already knew that. I already knew it because when I stepped in your office that day, I knew you were my meant-to-be. I've searched for you for so many years, and as each year passed, I wondered if I would ever find you. Then one day my editor said, *Kade, there's a new doc in town. Put on your neighbor hat and go introduce yourself*." He winked at me, and I nodded but my chin quivered. "Since that day I've tried to show you that you don't have to be afraid of love. Have I done a good job of that?"

I nodded with my hand over my heart. "A very good job," I admitted through my tears.

He set Gray down on the floor and pulled a ring from his pocket, holding it up. The light caught the diamond in the middle, which was surrounded by orange and yellow sapphires. "I've already spent so many years without you. I don't want to spend a minute more. I love you Autumn Hanson, and I want you and Gray to be my family. I want to hold you every night and kiss you awake every morning. I want to raise Grayson with you, and teach him all the things a father teaches a son. Say you'll give me the honor of being Mr. Autumn Hanson, now and forever."

I got down on my knees and took his face in my hands. I kissed his lips and my tears were salty as they ran down my face. I whispered yes over and over against his mouth. He wiped my eyes with his thumb and slipped the ring on my finger then gathered Gray off the floor. He held us in a tight embrace, as the room erupted in little kid laughter, and lots of clapping.

My heart was so full it was painful and I buried my face in his chest. Gray's little hand held mine and the room was a cacophony of sounds. It didn't matter. All I heard was him whisper in my ear, "I told you I wouldn't give up."

Epilogue

I sat on the couch in my jammies while Ace chewed on his new reindeer antler, and Gray snuggled next to me with his box set of Harry Potter. He had gotten us up at the crack of dawn to open presents, and soon we would have to get ready and head to Aunt Kat's for another round of Christmas. Kade checked out his new camera and my lips curled into a smile. It was morning and he was still here. It had been two weeks' worth of mornings since our wedding day. I hugged Gray closer to me, and closed my eyes, my mind wandering back to that day.

"I can't believe you're finally my wife," Kade had grinned.

"Finally? You only proposed three weeks ago," I had laughed and shook my head.

He really meant it when he said he didn't want to spend another minute apart. We spent Thanksgiving making wedding plans, and decided on a simple ceremony at my church. With a few embellishments, the dress I wore the first night I danced with him, had become my wedding gown. All those years ago, I had bought the dress for Gray's adoption, and the party we had planned for after, but I didn't get to wear it that night. Standing in the church with him, I understood why. Kade and Gray were so handsome in their matching suits. He had taken Gray shopping, and they teased me mercilessly that I wouldn't like their ties, but when I saw them that day, I loved them. Gray's had tiny Batman symbols all over it, and Kade's, well, Kade's had Superman.

We invited only a few work friends, and planned for a small ceremony at the church, with refreshments afterward. When I stepped into the narthex on Gray's arm, the church was full.

The community was once again supporting the *underdog*, and I saw faces from the hospital, church, and school, as well as so many faces I didn't know. What I did see was love. Gray and Ace proudly walked me up the aisle to where Kade stood, and we said our vows to each other, and to Gray. A small group of high school band and choir kids had taken it upon themselves to come and serenade us, and I was in tears through the whole ceremony.

We signed our marriage certificate and then went to the church basement for cake and coffee. That too had been transformed into a lacy land of love. The church women were in the kitchen cooking dinner for everyone and there was even a tiered wedding cake with a bride, groom, little boy, and a dog. The picture of all three of us cutting the cake was now on the nightstand next to our bed.

It turned into a day of great joy and memories because of the community's kindness. Aunt Kat took Gray and Ace home, and Kade spirited me away to stay my first, and last, night in his house. We had pulled up to the house, and the street light illuminated the for sale sign with SOLD slapped across the front. Kade was moving into my house since it was handicapped accessible. I was going to miss his little place though and I knew he would, too.

I still heard his words in my ear as he swept me up to him and pushed the door open. "I'm going to carry you across this threshold and tomorrow I'm carrying you across yours. Don't argue."

I didn't argue. Instead, I grabbed his face and kissed him, giggling as he kicked the door closed and locked it. He carried me to his bedroom that was bare of furniture, except for the king size bed. There were flower petals strewn across it, and a champagne bucket on the floor. I picked up a few petals, blowing them at him.

"He loves me," I'd said, my voice filled with nervous energy.

"He does, and he can't wait a moment longer to make you his wife."

I scooted away from him, and shook my finger. "Oh, but love

is patient," I reminded him and he put one knee on the bed.

"Love is also kind," he growled and captured my lips, kissing me and working his tongue into the mix. He'd pulled my lip through his teeth until I was whimpering.

"I'm nervous," I admitted, and then his kiss turned gentle.

"Me too, but only because this will be the only first time we'll have together."

His honesty was all I needed. He knelt in front of me and untied the sash of the dress. I pulled his tie loose and unbuttoned his shirt while he stole kisses across my neck and covertly pulled the straps down off my shoulder. When he stripped his t-shirt off and knelt before me, his muscles corded across his chest and his pants bulged at the zipper. I had begged him to make love to me then.

He laid me back and kissed me, his teeth leaving gentle kisses across my bottom lip while he worked me out of my dress, until I lay before him in the special panty set I had bought for him. "So beautiful." He had whispered, his hand running the length of my ribcage. He lowered his head and laid kisses across the full length of the scar on my lower belly, and I wanted to cry from his tenderness and from the love I had for him.

Before I could finish that thought though, his hands moved up to slip under my back and unhook the bra. I moaned as his lips encircled my breast, and the speed in which our need for each other took over made me dizzy.

He was naked, and his need pressed against my leg. I had gripped him in my hand and he moaned long and low. He kissed my lips and begged me to let him go so he could finally make me his wife. He pulled me sideways and linked his hand in mine, then took his time torturing me until my hand was taut, and my back was arched, begging him to let me feel him. He held my eyes for a long time, and then slipped inside me. I'd moved no more than a hair, and his eyes rolled back in his head. The room echoed the sound of our cries of love for each other and when we were spent, he gathered me to him and held me. "He made you perfect for me."

"Perfect love knows no fear," I answered. We'd spent the rest of the night, and every night since, exploring our perfect love.

Last weekend we had a mini-honeymoon in Minneapolis for a night. He was accepting the nomination for Excellence in Journalism from Bethel College, for his three-part series on obtainability of orthotics and prosthetics. Standing in the hospital that day and listening to Trey explain to him how little insurance companies cover for medical equipment had stirred fierce anger within him.

He took his frustration out on paper, and had written the first article about prosthetics and the absurdity that they were considered a luxury item. The second was about orthotics, where he interviewed me and several other moms who dealt with the astronomical cost of braces and wheelchairs as their children grew. The final segment was about the legislation currently being considered around the country to require orthotics and prosthetics to be paid the same way general and surgical care is.

When he got up and spoke to the room about the ways Gray had changed his life, I was happy I was sitting in the dark shadows of the room. I couldn't hide the emotions that rolled down my face from his words. He told them how joyful Gray is in life, and how he fights so hard to do the same things we do with ease. He told the story of raising service dogs all his life, and he never really knew why until he met a little blond-haired boy one Friday night, and he changed his life. As he received a standing ovation for a full three minutes, the award didn't matter. What mattered was sharing that night with him, and it was forever etched in my mind.

"Momma, I got you something," Gray said, rousing me from my thoughts. I opened my eyes to see his sweet face. He was holding a flat package and handed it to me excitedly.

"Merry Christmas, Momma." He grinned, and I laid the package on my lap, and kissed his tiny head.

"Merry Christmas, baby. I wonder what this could be," I said, shaking it a little.

He giggled. "Don't shake it, it might break. Just open it!"

Kade was standing over my shoulder, and I tore the paper open, my hand slowing when I saw what was underneath. It was our family tree. The new one he had made the day Kade proposed.

"Oh, Gray, this is so wonderful," I whispered, pulling the rest of the paper off, so I could see the whole thing. Surrounding the tree were color photos of everyone in our family. Kade must have found a picture of my mother, as she was smiling at me from under the glass. There was a picture of Eden's tiny hand holding my finger, and one of the three of us dressed for Halloween. Kat was in the corner with Kipper, and Gray in the other with Ace. The little plaque below the paper said, *My Family Tree*.

I rubbed my hand over the glass and Kade wiped away a tear from my face. "I love it so much, Gray."

"I love you, Momma Franco," he said, kissing my cheek.

"I love you, Grayson Hanson," I said kissing his cheek.

"And I love you both so very much," Kade whispered.

I patted his cheek and laid the framed picture on the coffee table and picked up the final gift under the tree. I motioned Kade around and made space on the couch for him between us. "I have one gift left for you."

He sighed and kissed my lips. "The camera was more than I could ask for, sweetheart."

I nodded and tried to keep control of my trembling lower lip. "This gift doesn't have a monetary value, Kade. Its value lies in what you do with it," I explained. Gray was wiggling excitedly on the couch.

Kade took the flat box and set it on his lap while he unwrapped it. He winked at Gray. "Do you know what this is, Batman?"

Gray nodded in exaggerated secrecy and zipped his lips. Kade ruffled his hair and then pulled the lid off the box. He eyed the clipped pack of papers, and lifted them out with a shaking hand. "Petition for Stepparent Adoption," he read aloud the title on the top page. His hands continued to shake as he paged through the forms. He stopped on a page and took a deep breath as he read through it. "What is this form?" he asked, his arm coming around Grayson protectively. My son gazed up at him with such adoration on his face it was hard to answer him with a steady voice.

"It's the form I fill out as his legal guardian. I had to tell the court I want you, his step-father, to adopt him. We fill the petition for stepparent adoption out together," I explained. "If you want to, that is."

He pointed to question seven on the form. "This says your consent is irrevocable ten days after the date of signature." His voice was strangely choked and garbled. "You signed it two days after we got married."

I nodded and wiped a tear off his face. "I did," I agreed as Gray patted his cheek, understanding how emotional this was for the man he already loved like a daddy.

"Why? It's too late now, it's been more than ten days. You can't take it back," he whispered.

I shook my head. "No, I can't, and I don't want to, even if you decide you don't want to adopt him yet."

He laughed, but the sound was a strangled sob as he kissed Gray's head and then my lips. "I want to, sweetheart. God, you don't know how badly I want you all to have my last name." He rested his cheek on Gray's head as I rubbed his back, his shoulders overcome with the emotions he had to let out. Gray, in his wisdom, didn't say a word, just patted Kade's back with his tiny hand. I brushed a tear off his cheek when he sat up and motioned at the paperwork. "I'm blown away. I wanted to bring it up after the first of the year, but this—" He patted his chest and took a deep breath. "It means everything to me that you trust me to be Gray's daddy."

I brushed his hair behind his ear. "Love always protects, always trusts, always hopes," I whispered, "and the most important thing you've taught me is, love never fails."

About The Author

Katie Mettner

Katie Mettner wears the title of 'the only person to lose her leg after falling down the bunny hill' and loves decorating her prosthetic leg to fit the season. She lives in Northern Wisconsin with her own happily-ever-after and spends the day writing romantic stories with her sweet puppy by her side. Katie has an addiction to coffee and dachshunds and a lessening aversion to Pinterest — now that she's quit trying to make the things she pins.

Books In This Series

The Northern Light Seires

Granted Redemption

When Grant Harris walks through the doors of Carla's Kinky Café, his cold dead heart thumps against his ribcage for the first time in a lifetime.

When Carla Coffer's gaze meets the man's standing across the counter of her small coffee shop in Duluth, Minnesota, her heart wonders if he'll bring her the one thing she's always wanted- unconditional love.

A cup of coffee, a car, and a confession will bring them together, but it will be up to them to decide if their pasts will tear them apart or be their catalyst for redemption.

Autumn Reflections

Autumn Hanson's busy life as a doctor and single mom leaves her with no time for love. At least that's what she tells the unrelenting loneliness.

As the city's most eligible bachelor, Kade Franco could have any woman he wants, but he's waiting for his Lois Lane. He doesn't expect to find her while interviewing the newest doctor in town.

A surprise visit, a service dog, and a seven-year-old will bring them together, but it will be up to Kade to break through Autumn's heart of steel to create their happily ever after.

Winter's Rain

Winter Cheyne is on the run from the man who tried to break her. Her betrayal set this cat and mouse game in motion, but if she doesn't win, she'll have signed her own death warrant.

Doctor Jedidiah Raintree has never forgotten his friend Winter. He just doesn't expect to find her huddling in his cabin, injured and afraid.

Hidden inside Winter are the secrets she's being hunted for. Hidden inside Rain is the strength she'll need to be free. If they want a future together, they must survive the next three days.

Forever, Phoenix

When Phoenix Korby makes a desperate call to 911 for help, she doesn't expect the man who betrayed her years ago to be the one to answer it.

Adam Erwin is ready to start over in his hometown, but he isn't prepared when a call about a missing woman brings him face-to-face with the sad brown eyes of the woman he'd run from years ago.

Thrown together by circumstance, they must work together to find Winter before she disappears forever. Only then can they resurrect a forgotten love from the ashes of their past.

A Note To My Readers

People with disabilities are just that—people. We are not 'differently abled' because of our disability. We all have different abilities and interests, and the fact that we may or may not have a physical or intellectual disability doesn't change that. The disabled community may have different needs, but we are productive members of society who also happen to be husbands, wives, moms, dads, sons, daughters, sisters, brothers, friends, and co-workers. People with disabilities are often disrespected and portrayed two different ways; as helpless or as heroically inspirational for doing simple, basic activities.

As a disabled author who writes disabled characters, my focus is to help people without disabilities understand the real-life disability issues we face like discrimination, limited accessibility, housing, employment opportunities, and lack of people first language. I want to change the way others see our community by writing strong characters who go after their dreams, and find their true love, without shying away from what it is like to be a person with a disability. Another way I can educate people without disabilities is to help them understand our terminology. We, as the disabled community, have worked to establish what we call People First Language. This isn't a case of being politically correct. Rather, it is a way to acknowledge and communicate with a person with a disability in a respectful way by eliminating generalizations, assumptions, and stereotypes.

As a person with disabilities, I appreciate when readers take the time to ask me what my preferred language is. Since so many have asked, I thought I would include a small sample of the people-first language we use in the disabled community. This language also applies when leaving reviews and talking about books that feature characters with disabilities. The most important thing to remember when you're talking to people with disabilities is that we are people first! If you ask us what our preferred terminology is regarding our disability, we will not only tell you, but be glad you asked! If you would like more information about people first language, you will find a disability resource guide on my website.

Instead of: He is handicapped.

Use: He is a person with a disability.

Instead of: She is differently abled.

Use: She is a person with a disability.

Instead of: He is mentally retarded.

Use: He has a developmental or intellectual disability.

Instead of: She is wheelchair-bound.

Use: She uses a wheelchair.

Instead of: He is a cripple.

Use: He has a physical disability.

Instead of: She is a midget or dwarf.

Use: She is a person of short stature or a little person.

Instead of: He is deaf and mute.

Use: He is deaf or he has a hearing disability.

Instead of: She is a normal or healthy person.

Use: She is a person without a disability.

Instead of: That is handicapped parking.

Use: That is accessible parking.

Instead of: He has overcome his disability.

Use: He is successful and productive.

Instead of: She is suffering from vision loss.

Use: She is a person who is blind or visually disabled.

Instead of: He is brain damaged.

Use: He is a person with a traumatic brain injury

Printed in Great Britain
by Amazon